THE TAYLORS VERSION

Cruel Summer

Also by Elizabeth Eulberg

Young Adult

The Lonely Hearts Club

Prom and Prejudice

Take a Bow

Revenge of the Girl with the Great Personality

Better Off Friends

Just Another Girl

Past Perfect Life

Take a Chance On Me

Love Stories (The Taylors Version #1)

Middle Grade

The Best Worst Summer

The Scared Silly Series

Curses Are the Worst

Zombie Wedding Crashers

Vampires Ruin Everything

The Great Shelby Holmes Series

The Great Shelby Holmes

The Great Shelby Holmes Meets Her Match

The Great Shelby Holmes and the Coldest Case

The Great Shelby Holmes and the Haunted Hound

THE TAYLORS VERSION
Cruel Summer

ELIZABETH EULBERG

SCHOLASTIC INC.

ISBN 978-1-5461-7675-6

10 9 8 7 6 5 4 3 2 1 26 27 28 29 30

Printed in the U.S.A. 40

First printing 2026

Book design by Stephanie Yang

For Ginny—who took me to the Eras Tour, a night that will Long Live in my heart. We sang. We danced. We cried. I don't know about you, fellow Swifties, but that joyous hat moment during "22" gets me every time. 🫶

THE TAYLORS

Teffy

Taylor

Tay

TS

Our Chat (The Taylors Version)

TAY🎉: SO LONG, FRESHMAN YEAR!

TAYLOR🐝: And what a year it was

TS ⚽: You got that right, Madame President

TAYLOR🐝: You know it, District Soccer MVP and State Champ

TEFFY📚: Yeah, my friends are kind of big deals.

TAY🎉: THE BIGGEST!!! And let's not forget YOUR songs, Teffy!

TAY🎉: AND YOUR . . .

TEFFY📚: NOT IN WRITING.

TAY🎉: 🙊

TAYLOR🐝: And YOU being the frontWOMAN of a band, TAY!!!!

TAY🎉: I CANNOT WAIT to see how this summer goes!!!!

TS ⚽: Taylors, let the summer begin

ONE
. . . Ready For It?

"We did it! Goodbye, freshman year, and hello, first day of summer vacation!" Tay opens the front door to TS with her signature high kick. Even though cheerleading season is over, Tay is perpetually in cheer mode. While TS has to do a lot of cardio and strength training to keep her stamina up on the soccer field, she's pretty sure Tay exists on rainbows and sunshine. "And please tell me today is one of your fun days. I can't believe you're going to be on your way to *London* tomorrow and then Taylor is off to summer camp. We need to make today *extra* epic, so Dad and I made cupcakes *and* brownies."

Tay also exists on sugar. Lots and lots of sugar.

"Um, I'm *always* fun," TS replies with the intense glare she'll give an opponent on the soccer field, before breaking into a laugh.

"You know what I mean!" Tay bumps TS's hip as she leads TS into her house, which over the last five years has sort of become the official meeting place for the Taylors.

TS does know. Getting the varsity girls' soccer team to state *and winning* takes a lot of discipline. At the beginning of freshman year, she maybe was a bit too strict with her regimen. Okay, there's no maybe about it. It was all protein shakes and running and not having a life outside of soccer and the Taylors. Then TS met Gemma and realized that she can have fun *and* still rock at soccer. Oddly enough, taking it easy two days a week and focusing on life outside of soccer has made her an even better player.

And not to brag, but she's a pretty awesome girlfriend, too.

Tay links arms with TS as they head into the living room, but TS stops in her tracks as she takes in the scene. She hardly notices Teffy amid the chaos. "Tay, what did you do?"

"I told you that would be her response!" Teffy gets up from the couch but then sits back down, which is probably best for her safety, given the circumstances.

"What?" Tay looks around the living room, her big brown eyes blinking in that innocent way Tay has about her.

"It looks like your closet exploded!" TS tries to take in all the pastel-colored dresses that have been laid out on every surface of the living room, and it's *every* surface. The sectional sofa. The armchairs. The floor. The coffee table. Everywhere TS looks there are dresses, dresses, and even more dresses.

Tay's bottom lip juts out in a playful pout. "You said you wanted to borrow a couple dresses."

"Yeah, *a couple*, not your *entire closet*."

"Please." Tay scrunches her tight brown curls. "This is only my summer dress section, category chic, playful, and somewhat fancy."

"What do you call the dress you have on, then?" TS gestures toward Tay's light pink empire-waist sundress.

"This?" Tay spins around. "Cute and casual."

For TS, casual is shorts and T-shirts. She basically exists in sportswear, like the INDIANA STATE CHAMPIONS T-shirt with light gray mesh shorts she's wearing now. Which is exactly why she asked Tay for help, since this summer will require TS to dress up. Her friends have always been into fashion more than TS. Tay is usually in pastel colors, which is so *Lover*. Teffy, who is currently wearing a burnt-orange oversized T-shirt with jean shorts, is the boho-*folklore* of the group. She makes casual look cozy and stylish—she even has her blond hair up in a braided crown—while TS usually throws her long red hair in a ponytail.

But casual (TS's Version) probably isn't going to cut it this summer.

Tay runs over and holds up a pink-and-blue sundress. "And I think this would look soooo good on you!"

"Are you sure it won't wash me out?" TS gestures at her pale white skin, which always looks extra pasty next to Tay's brown complexion.

"Try it on! Try it on!" Tay says with a clap. "Come on, Teffy, join me! Try it on! Try it on!"

"Please, Teffy." TS holds out her hands in hope that the quietest of the Taylors will be able to contain the energy bomb that is Tay Johnson.

"You're on your own, kid." Teffy bites her lip to stop from laughing.

"How *dare you* use a Taylor Swift song against me!" TS opens her mouth in mock horror.

Teffy replies by taking a bite of a cupcake.

"I still can't believe you're going to England!" Tay sings with another excited clap. Although, *excited* and *Tay* are synonymous.

To be honest, TS can't believe she's going, either. Gemma invited her to spend part of the summer in London and the English countryside with her family. TS has never left the country before and doing it with her girlfriend seems like a big deal, especially since Gemma's family seems sort of fancy. Like, there's this huge house—oh, wait, *estate*—that's been in Gemma's family for centuries. *Centuries!* Gemma has been excitedly talking about these formal dinners and charity balls, and . . . it's *a lot*.

Ergo (TS feels like she has to start using words like *ergo*), the need to borrow some of Tay's clothes.

"Are you nervous? Excited? Are you going to come back with an accent? Are you going to Camden Market in the afternoon? Nights in Brixton? Oh! And the Black Dog!" Tay plops down in the middle of the floor and starts rifling through a collection of accessories. "I also think you need to wear more headbands and get those little hats like the royals wear at weddings. We won't recognize you when you come back! And you better come back, we're going to hold on to *the hat* for ransom."

TS ignores Tay's barrage of questions and picks out a few dresses that hopefully won't clash with her bright red hair. "I'm going to go try these on. Now who's on their own, *Teffy*?" TS shakes her head as she goes into the bathroom to change.

TS has no idea what England has in store for her, but she's excited to spend more time with Gemma. To be in her world. To be welcomed into her extended family. Because being with Gemma makes TS's heart sing. Like, she's starting to become a walking sappy love song and she's not mad about it. And she knows that this summer is when she's finally going to be brave enough to tell Gemma exactly how she feels.

It's just three little words, but for some reason, they get caught in her throat when she looks into Gemma's big green eyes. TS has promised herself that she's going to tell her in England.

And when TS sets her mind to something, it's going to get done.

She *is* ready for it.

Tay looks at the empty hallway and her shoulders slump. "I can't believe both TS and Taylor are going to be gone this summer."

"It's only for a few weeks," Teffy reminds her.

"Yeah, but we're the Taylors!" They've been practically inseparable since fifth grade, save for some boy drama early in the school year.

"We're still the Taylors . . . just a bit more spread out." Teffy crosses her legs and takes out her guitar and starts strumming. "We're going *international*."

"And how's . . ." Tay looks into the kitchen, where she sees her dad cleaning up from their earlier baking session. He loves being in on all the Taylors gossip—aka eavesdropping. Tay drops her voice. "How's the *songwriting* going?" Tay gives a playful wink, but it takes everything in her to not jump up and down.

Teffy's cheeks redden. "It's going really well. I mean, besides the obvious." Teffy plays around with a melody. "Are you excited about your gigs this summer?"

"Yes!" Tay shouts, because *that* she cannot keep in. Tay sort of can't believe it, but she's now the lead singer of the Archers, the band she used to watch rehearse. Reece, their former frontman, decided that Tay is a much more energetic and engaging lead singer. Which is true. Tay loves the spotlight: cheering, gymnastics, singing . . . It had been her dream at the start of freshman year to start a band with Teffy, but Teffy has made it very clear she's happy just writing her music and having Tay sing the songs for their close friends. Luckily for Tay, it turned out her vocals match really well with the Archers'. They started playing a few parties after the holidays and now they've got some proper gigs coming up.

And by proper, she means a couple of county fairs.

Still, a gig's a gig! Everybody has to start somewhere!

"And Reece?" Teffy mouths, her eyebrows going up and down playfully.

Tay holds her hands to her heart and swoons.

If it isn't obvious, *a lot* has happened to Tay in the last few months. And all good! Amazing! The BEST!

It's true. Tay and Reece are officially together. Again. It took Reece a couple months to earn Tay's trust after he got all weird and stood her up the first time they "officially" dated. But it's been so worth it. He's been a dream: kind, supportive, and so sweet. Leaving notes for her around school and his house. Looking at her with such pride when she takes the stage.

And Tay has done her best to help Reece with his confidence, even though she still has to do most of the talking.

Fortunately, talking is something Tay excels at.

But . . . and of course there has to be a *but* . . . while everything is great between Tay and Reece, Tay's dad does not forgive—or forget—so easily. Even though he allows Tay to go out with Reece and perform with his band, she tries not to talk about it much in front of him.

It's not like she's holding on to some big secret, like Teffy.

Teffy stops playing the guitar. "Where's Taylor?"

"You mean Madame President!" Taylor comes into the living room on her usual cloud of controlled chaos. "Y'all, I am so ready for the summer, and I know that we're gonna rule just like we did freshman year. Can I get a one . . . two . . . three . . ."

"Let's go, Taylors!" Tay screams out. Then does a backflip.

She can't help it. With a summer full of performing in front of her, Tay knows she's going to be a star.

Taylor practically collapses on the couch in the living room. She takes one of the cupcakes from the table and goes to put her feet up on the ottoman until she realizes it's covered in dresses. Instead, she puts her head on Teffy's shoulder. "Let me tell you, Teffy, it's exhausting being a woman in power. I need more of whatever Tay is on." Taylor takes a huge bite of the cupcake.

"But look at all you accomplished." Teffy leans her head against Taylor's.

This is true, of course it is. Taylor fought to become freshman class president. She wasn't going to let her classmates down. It all started with the glory that was beating Hannah Reed as a write-in candidate. Taylor vowed to make changes for the better. Starting next year, the cheerleading squad will be supporting the girls' teams as well as the boys'. If there's a challenge to a book in the school library, she fought—along with the school librarian—to pass a provision that the person challenging has to be quizzed on the contents of the book. She couldn't believe the number of people who don't read books they ignorantly label as "dangerous." Adults can be so closed-minded. What Taylor's most proud of is that she started a mentor program for underclassmen. So next year, when the new freshman class comes in, there will be upperclassmen assigned to help them adjust. She thinks about how much heartache she could have been saved if she was warned about . . . *him*.

Not like she listened when Teffy tried to talk to her, but that was months ago. Taylor has more than learned her lesson.

"And now I go from keeping students and administrators in line to doing it at summer camp." Taylor closes her eyes. She got a job as a camp counselor after being recommended by her boss at the city's parks and rec program last summer. "I can't believe the list of items I need to pack. I'm bringing my bracelet kit, since I'm going to want to do a bonding exercise with my bunk the first day."

"Listen, if anybody can wrangle a bunch of ten-year-olds, it's you, Taylor," Tay says, a playful smile spreading on her face. "And the butler."

"There isn't a butler!"

Whispering Pines is a sleepaway camp nestled on the outskirts of Potato Creek State Park, and it's not your average camp. It has air-conditioned lodges, water sports, a theatre and arts program, and really good food. Taylor always wanted to go there as a kid, but it's also ridiculously expensive.

"Okay, there may be staff to clean the bunks," Taylor admits.

"You poor thing, thank goodness you're being paid for this!" Teffy jokes.

"I'm looking forward to the peace and quiet, for real. I forgot how loud it is with my siblings home. Anthony is so disgusting, it's like he went away to college and forgot how to clean up after himself." Taylor is the youngest of five kids. She got used to being an only child this past school year and then they all started coming home for the summer. "I think sharing a lodge with ten little kids will be quieter."

"Are you nervous?" Teffy asks.

"Of course not!" Taylor flips her wavy brown hair, even though it's three weeks away from her family and the Taylors. Okay, she's a bit nervous, just like back in fifth grade during their school trip to Nashville, but she had the Taylors with her then. Although, if there's one thing you can count on when it comes to Taylor Perez, she never lets anyone see her sweat.

She's so got this.

Taylor holds up her empty plate. "Can one of you peasants get me another cupcake?"

♥♥♥♥

"Oh, I see how it's going to be," Teffy says with a shake of her head as she grabs Taylor's plate and goes into the kitchen, where Mr. Johnson is frosting another batch of cupcakes.

No surprise, Teffy is a bit nervous about how the summer will go without Taylor and TS. She's not the biggest fan of change. She also can't help but wonder how she'll handle Tay spending most of the summer performing with Reece and his band. And singing Reece's songs.

But you don't want *to get onstage*, Teffy reminds herself. There's a part of her that wishes she could be as confident as Tay, then there's the much louder part that reminds her what happened last time she got on a stage. Besides, she's going to be juggling a lot this summer.

"Back for more?" Mr. Johnson holds out a carrot cake cupcake, which Teffy happily takes.

"What mortal could possibly say no to your baking, Mr. Johnson?" Teffy licks the cream cheese frosting from her finger.

"How are your parents doing, Teffy?" Mr. Johnson gives her an uncomfortable smile.

It's one that Teffy has gotten used to the last few weeks, ever since her parents closed their store, Harrison by Design. "They're okay. Dad's back to work at his old marketing firm and Mom has basically taken over the entire first floor with her new Etsy store."

Teffy's mom has gone from never being at home to always being there. *Always*. It's been really inconvenient.

"Are you spending your summer at By the Book?" He hands Teffy the spatula with extra frosting.

"Yeah, I really like it there. I think I spend most of my paycheck on books, though." Teffy started working at the bookstore during the holiday season and they've kept her on. It's the perfect job for her—she gets to talk about books. When it's slow, she works on her lyrics and texts . . . people. And makes plans.

"Any summer vacations?" Mr. Johnson asks. "You usually go—" He stops, knowing he's hit a nerve.

Teffy's family used to go camping every summer with the Yoons, their next-door neighbors. Their parents were best friends and eventually business partners. Then they let business get in the way. Her parents even told her she couldn't hang out with Liam Yoon, her non-Taylors best friend.

That did *not* go over well.

"Yeah, no big plans this summer, pretty low-key in fact." Teffy licks the rest of the frosting before heading back into the living room.

But she can't help but smile to herself.

There are some things no one has to know.

Our Chat (The Taylors Version)

TEFFY📚: Let us know when you land, TS!

TAYLOR🐝: And take so many pictures it'll make us jealous!

TAY🎉: SO JEALOUS!

TAY🎉: I want to see my dresses living their BEST LIVES! DOING THE MOST! OR DON'T BOTHER COMING BACK

TEFFY📚: Tay, if one of us is going to call your bluff, it'll be TS.

TAY🎉: I TAKE IT BACK! COME BACK NOW! WE MISS YOU!

TWO
End Game

What TS misses most right now is sleep. And sleep is one of the most important parts of recovery for the body and mind. She tries to get eight hours each night. But she didn't sleep a wink during the flight from Chicago to London. So she's exhausted. But also excited. Not, like, Tay-level excited, but pretty close. Taylor Shaw is in *London*.

Well, she and Gemma are currently stuck in traffic on the way from the airport, but still.

"On a scale of one to a billion, how annoyed do you think the people next to us were on the flight?" Gemma asks, looking rested since she did manage to sleep. Although, TS will only ever look at Gemma and see her gorgeous girlfriend.

Yeah, TS has become a walking heart-eyes emoji.

Deal with it.

"Why would they be annoyed?" TS goes through all the amenity kits that were discarded in their business class cabin. She holds up the lavender peppermint spray and spritzes it in the back seat of the black car that picked them up. "It smells like relaxation . . . and money."

Gemma laughs, and it sounds just as sweet as a soccer ball

swishing into the back of the net. "I don't think they're used to someone being that excited about a long flight and free stuff."

"Are you saying that it's me, hi, I'm the problem, it's me?" TS holds up her feet, which are wearing the cozy socks that were in the little bag at her seat. "Because I think it's *them*! Who wouldn't want *these*? *And* there's a toothbrush and toothpaste. And, like, lotions and stuff. Question: Do you think I can count these as my souvenir gifts to the Taylors?"

Gemma simply shakes her head and places her hand on TS's shaking leg. TS has this restless energy. She's not used to being cooped up in a tiny place. First the two planes, one to Chicago and another to London. Now the car ride. TS likes to stay active and move around. Also, she has no idea what time it is back in Indianapolis. A yawn overtakes her as she peers out the car window, hoping to see something—anything—to let her know she's in London. Well, except for the fact that the driver is on the opposite side of the car and the car is on the left side of the road.

"I still can't believe your family paid for us to be in business class." TS had originally protested when she found out how expensive the flight was, but she agreed only on the condition that she'll clean up after herself and make breakfast every morning for Gemma's aunt, uncle, and cousins. She really hopes Gemma's family likes eggs, toast, and protein shakes. "I'm spoiled now and I can't go back to the simple life." TS leans back with her sunglasses on.

"I've created a monster." Gemma nudges TS playfully.

TS does a double take when she looks at Gemma. "Sorry, I still can't get used to . . ."

Gemma's colorful hair—it's been lavender, pink, and most recently blue—has gone back to a more natural brown. Gemma ruffles her hair. "Don't tell me that you feel nothing when you look at me now."

"I'm sorry, do I know you?" TS jokes. Although, TS feels *everything* when she looks at Gemma. She has these big green eyes and an open face that shows off her every emotion: determination when she's on the soccer field, happiness when she's hanging with her friends, and a lot of amusement when she's with TS.

She's perfect in every single way. And TS wants to find the right moment to tell her that.

Gemma's smile fades. "My gran can be a bit traditional, and she hates when I dye it." Her hand goes up to her long bangs and she swipes at them as if it's a reflex.

"But she's okay with us, right?" TS asks as her throat tightens. Her family and friends have always accepted TS. She's never had to hide who she is. She's never been forced to pretend she's anybody but herself.

Gemma laces her fingers between TS's. "Of course. Why wouldn't she be?"

"Well, you said traditional, and sometimes that can mean . . . homophobic." That word tastes bad in TS's mouth. She'll never understand why who she loves is anybody else's business.

"Shaw." Gemma turns to her, her brow furrowed. "My grandmother, my entire family, loves and supports me. They can be many things, like a wee bit pretentious, but they aren't ignorant. Besides, I'd never put you in that position." Gemma gives TS's hand an extra squeeze.

And almost on cue, "Enchanted" comes over the car speakers. No surprise, they made a special London-bound mix that was 100 percent Taylor Swift.

Gemma and TS start singing along and the driver turns up the music. When it gets to the chorus, Gemma pretends to drum and they go from softly singing to screaming along. Complete with hand gestures and using their phones as mics.

Add the car driver to the list of people TS has annoyed since departing home.

But she doesn't care. She's with Gemma, and being here, in London, feels sort of like the fairy tales Taylor Swift sings about.

"Okay, game plan!" TS says excitedly, ready to start this new chapter with Gemma.

"Oh, you have a game plan?" Gemma teases. "Really? You? Shaw, have you perhaps done your research and come up with a strategy for holidaying?"

"You *are* talking to the team MVP, thank you very much." TS flicks her ponytail while Gemma rolls her eyes. Even though Gemma jumped and cheered the loudest when TS's name was announced at the award ceremony. "So, yes, I've come up with a plan to make this trip as . . . awesome as possible." TS stops herself from saying *magical*.

But that's what she wants this trip to be. A wonderful, magical four weeks with Gemma. For TS to admit that Gemma is the MVP of her heart.

Wow, when did TS get so corny?

She lets out a little giggle. It's official: TS is jet-lagged. And, yes, in love.

"Okay, let's huddle it up. Hit me with the plan, Shaw," Gemma says, her eyes sparkling. She knows when to amuse TS, which is a lot, and when to make TS snap out of her overly intense nature when it comes to training.

"Tonight. You, me . . ." TS squeezes Gemma's hand. "Walking along the Thames on the South Bank to see the city lit up." TS has scrolled through so many pictures of St. Paul's Cathedral and the Elizabeth Tower and Parliament illuminated at night. It looks super romantic. Maybe this is when she'll tell Gemma exactly how she feels. Start the trip off the best way possible.

"Oh! That's one of my favorite walks. Sounds perfect." Gemma rests her head on TS's shoulder and TS takes a hit of Gemma's lavender scent. Even though TS is currently thousands of miles away from her family, being with Gemma, like this, makes her feel at home.

"And then, well, we can keep up with training: morning runs at Hyde Park, then we can do fun touristy things in the afternoon, in which I'm going to embarrass you by being a super loud American. I'm going to channel *Tay*."

"You could never embarrass me," Gemma says with a laugh. "Besides, I want nothing more than to see you attempt those high kicks."

"Challenge accepted." TS knows she'll have to stretch more. Tay has got some insane flexibility.

"Well, just know, my family might have some events for us to go to.

They were talking about some gallery opening." Gemma's eyes darken for a second, before she brightens up. Guess TS isn't the only one jet-lagged. "But! Don't feel pressure. You don't have to come to everything."

"Like I'm going to leave your side." TS gives Gemma a little nudge. She hopes that didn't come across as creepy, but why would she come to London to not spend every waking moment with the most wonderful girl in the world?

The car exits the freeway and the driver turns down the music. "Sorry to bother you, miss, but I wanted you to know that we're about twenty minutes away."

"Thanks, Nigel." Gemma lets out a long breath.

It's time for TS to get her game face on. "Okay, let's go over your family one more time. There's Freddie, the oldest."

"Yes, twenty-four but acts like an entitled child most of the time." Gemma sucks on her teeth. "He'll tell you to call him Duke of Huntington, but ignore him."

"Duke." TS snorts. Because how ridiculous is that.

"Yeah, he doesn't get that title until Uncle Ollie passes. The title comes with the estate and, of course, Buckingshire Castle."

TS blinks for a moment. She knew they'd be spending part of the summer at the huge estate that's been in Gemma's family for generations, but she didn't realize it was *an actual castle* with titles.

"Please tell me you're joking." TS's leg has gone into overdrive. When she feels out of sorts, she likes to go for a run or kick a ball around. Being stuck in traffic with no sleep and all this pent-up energy is probably not the best way to be introduced to Gemma's fancy extended family.

"It's fine, don't worry about it." Gemma waves her hand away. "My cousin Cressida can be a lot, but she's usually wrapped up in her own drama. She's also an elite athlete, dressage."

"Dressage?" Okay, TS was under the assumption that Americans and Brits spoke the same language, but it feels like Gemma is speaking Latin.

"Horses," she clarifies.

"Like racing?"

Gemma tilts her head, her brows furrowed. "Not exactly, it's sort of like watching a horse trot and dance, but it requires a lot of skill and mastery."

"Uh-huh." TS nods her head. It's something she assumes she'll be doing a lot of at various things she'll be clueless about during her stay.

"It'll be fine." Gemma pats her hand.

Of course it'll be fine. TS is with Gemma. In London. How could this be anything but perfect?

Not to state the obvious, but TS isn't in Indiana anymore. When Gemma mentioned that her aunt and uncle live in a nineteenth-century townhouse, she assumed it was like the ones in their neighborhood back home. Standard houses with two to three stories, just a lot older.

Wow. How wrong was TS. The five-story, ten-bed, seven-bath

townhouse has a gym and wine cellar. It sits across from Eaton Square, which TS has been informed is "one of the most sought-after locations" in the Belgravia neighborhood, which is very *posh*.

Posh is the British way to say someone is extremely fancy and rich. It's a word TS will be using a lot this summer.

TS is pretty sure her mouth hung open when they walked into a white marble and gold—*gold!*—entryway. The rest of the house looks like it belongs in a museum: oil paintings, antique wooden furniture, and rich tapestries on the walls.

Oh, and did TS forget to mention that there's a butler? An actual butler! His name is Reginald. He looks like he's a thousand years old, and he wears a suit and everything. He offered to unpack TS's suitcase, which she declined because that would be weird. Plus, she sort of shoved everything into it. She'd be embarrassed by the mess.

As TS looks at the clothes she's spread out on the canopy bed in the guest room, she wishes she would've packed Tay's entire closet. Her "presence has been requested for afternoon tea with the family on the outdoor patio at half two," which according to Google means two thirty. Since she doesn't think jeans and a T-shirt would be appropriate, she puts on a dark green wrap dress.

It's the first time TS is starting to wonder if *she'll* be considered appropriate for Gemma. TS is used to casual family meetings and this makes her feel out of her element. But at least she'll have Gemma. TS assumed Gemma would've knocked on her door to go down to meet her family, but it's nearly time and she doesn't want to be late and there's a good chance she'll get lost on the way down the two (or is it three?) flights of stairs to the backyard. TS sticks her head out of her room, and it's oddly quiet. She starts down the stairs and feels like she's in some fancy hotel, not a house.

"Good afternoon, Miss Shaw." A maid—in an actual uniform—is waiting at the foot of the stairs. "I'm to escort you out to the patio."

"Oh, um, thanks." Why does TS feel like she should bow? Curtsy?

TS has so much more googling to do.

No, she's Taylor Shaw. She doesn't hesitate. She's not timid. As she follows the maid to the backyard, she decides to have the same attitude she goes into a soccer match with: confident and purposeful. She belongs here. She belongs with Gemma. She's going to be just fine.

Then she arrives on the patio. Gemma is seated on an ornate metal chair in a light blue satin maxi dress, surrounded by people who look like they belong in the pages of a high-fashion magazine. The men, Gemma's uncle Ollie and her cousin Freddie, are in pastel polo shirts, dark pants, and brown leather shoes without socks. The women, her aunt Alexandra and cousin Cressida, are in floral maxi dresses. Cressida's black hair is curled to perfection, and it looks like her makeup has been professionally done. TS fiddles with her unwashed hair, which is up in its usual ponytail.

So much for being confident. TS suddenly feels so out of place. And Gemma . . . TS has never seen her look so sophisticated. She has on the most makeup she's ever seen Gemma wear: light blue shimmering eye shadow, eyeliner with a wing, and her lips in sparkling pink. Don't get TS wrong, she can't wait to kiss those lips, but it's just different.

"There she is!" Gemma jumps up and guides TS to a seat beside her. "Everyone, this is Taylor."

TS can't remember the last time anybody has called her Taylor, besides her parents. Gemma usually calls her Shaw, like most of her teammates. She's worried she's going to glance behind her when someone says Taylor, expecting to see Taylor Perez. TS starts to feel numb as she's introduced. The family all give her a polite smile, but she can see their gazes lingering on her messy hair and feet, which are in white canvas shoes. Then, like she isn't even there, the conversation goes to people and places unfamiliar to her. While TS's gaze keeps darting to the three-tiered selection of tiny sandwiches, scones, and desserts on the table in front of them. No one has touched anything, so TS keeps her hands in her lap while her stomach rumbles.

Apparently, TS is not being subtle, or her stomach was that loud. It's a toss-up, because TS's aunt finally addresses her.

"My dear, feel free to help yourself, you must be famished after your journey." Alexandra gives her what TS assumes is a warm smile, though her tight, line-free face doesn't really move.

"Thank you." TS places a couple sandwich pieces on her plate, but they're only an inch-wide strip each. She's still hungry after eating three. Since the family is busy talking about summering—TS wasn't aware *summer* could be used as a verb—and some charity event, TS keeps herself busy by eating. Waste not, want not.

"American, huh?" Freddie leans over to TS and looks at her with pale squinted eyes. His light brown hair looks freshly cut and he smells like wood. Expensive wood that's been drowned in musk. "I've spent some time in the States. In fact, I was just in Miami for a long weekend with some mates. We spent most of it on a yacht. Have you been?" TS isn't sure if he means on a yacht or to Miami, but it doesn't matter since the answer is no to both and Freddie carries on talking. "I much prefer more cosmopolitan cities with rich history, like London, although I was in Tokyo last month and the nightlife is beyond."

"Cool." TS smiles and nods.

Freddie smiles . . . No, it's more of a snarl. His accent is also different than Gemma's: It oozes money. And entitlement.

So far, TS is not a fan.

"Don't hog our guest, Frederick," Gemma's uncle Ollie says with a forced laugh. He swirls brown liquid in a crystal glass. "I hear your mother is in academia like my sister."

"Oh yes, she's a kindergarten teacher." While Gemma's mother has a PhD and teaches engineering at Purdue University.

Ollie pauses for a moment. His nose twitches around as if he doesn't understand TS. "Why, isn't that just adorable. And what is your father's profession?"

"He's in . . . tech." TS's dad works in the IT department of a large advertising firm, but she figured "tech" sounds better.

Huh. TS has never felt the need to exaggerate what her parents do before.

"Adorable," Ollie repeats with a dismissive sniff.

TS can't remember the last time anybody referred to her as adorable. TS is tough. TS is focused. She and her parents' careers are not adorable.

TS glances at Gemma. She's shifting uncomfortably in her seat. She gives TS a tight smile before mouthing, "Sorry."

"Enough of this boring dribble," Cressida says with a wave of her expertly manicured hand. "We need to discuss important matters, for instance what we're doing tonight. It's Friday night. Gems, you're in London, we *must* take you out."

"Oh." Gemma's eyes dart to TS. "Well, we're sort of tired, and TS and I were thinking about having just a chill evening and—"

"Nonsense." Cressida wraps a finger around her silky hair. "A night out will keep you awake. We can start at the club, then go to a *real* club."

"You're so predictable, Cressida," Freddie says with a sneer. "You just want to go where the drama is."

"I can't help it if drama just loves me." Cressida picks up her gold iPhone and starts typing. "I'll sort out plans."

"Oh, um . . ." Gemma gives TS a pleading look.

Despite what some people think, TS does know how to have fun. *However*, going to any kind of club with Cressida and Freddie sounds like the opposite of fun, especially on no sleep. She wants to spend tonight alone with Gemma.

TS notices everybody's eyes are now on her.

"Sounds great!" TS says with a smile that costs so much effort, it feels like her face is going to shatter.

But really, it's not that big a deal.

After all, it's just one night.

TS has learned to trust her gut over the years. She has this sixth sense when she's on the field, where she can anticipate her opponent's next move.

So it doesn't surprise TS that the Houndstooth, a private club where TS is fairly positive the membership requirements are having a ton of money and being a snob, is the last place she'd want to spend her first night in London with Gemma. Techno music fills the first floor, with its low lighting, dark wood, red velvet seats, and checkered wallpaper. Since they arrived—TS wearing the satin green vest and shorts she wore to Homecoming and Gemma in a sequined rainbow minidress—TS has pretty much been ignored, sitting by herself at a corner table. Gemma keeps being whisked away by her cousins to talk to people named Mitz and Pips and Cols.

"Your hair!" A tall blond wisp of a woman collapses down next to TS and twirls her finger around a strand of TS's red hair. "I love it. Is the color real?"

"Um, yes and thanks." TS pulls her hair away. The woman leans in so close, she's practically in TS's face. "Hi. I'm TS, um, Taylor. Do you know Gemma?"

The woman blinks in this weird way, looking like she's half asleep. "I want it. How much?"

"How much what?" TS looks down at her outfit and wonders if

this woman thinks TS works here. The very attractive staff are in all black and blend into the background, only swooping in when someone's glass needs to be refilled.

The woman shakes her head. "Your hair. I want it."

"You . . . ? What?" TS searches the room for Gemma and spies her embracing a gorgeous girl with dark brown skin and shorn black hair.

The woman yanks at TS's hair.

"Ouch!" TS stands up, touching the tender part of her scalp. "My hair isn't for sale."

"Daaaaarliiiiing." The woman drawls the word out. "*Everything* is for sale."

Welp, TS has literally no response to that. Maybe people in this world think that's true, but TS has worked hard to get to where she is. If she wants something, she has to earn it.

Cressida comes over, wearing a leather minidress with a diamond and emerald necklace. She puts her arm around the woman, a mischievous look in her eyes. "Babes, I think Gordo is looking for you."

"Oh." The woman finally pulls her gaze away from TS. "Well, can't keep a lord waiting."

Mercifully, the woman walks away, and Cressida sits down and pats the place next to her. "Join me. You'll want to watch this. Gordo has quite the reputation of being a heartbreaker."

"Is he really a lord?" TS sits back down, even though her attention is on Gemma having an animated conversation with the stunning girl. "What does that even mean? *Lord*." TS tries not to roll her eyes, but *come on*.

Cressida scrunches up her nose. "Listen, TS, I'm saying this as a favor. If you're going to be around our family, you'll be meeting a lot of people with titles. It's common in our world. The important thing is for you to not be too . . . American."

"What does that mean?" TS asks yet again. She'll probably be asking that a lot this summer. While TS should be insulted, she wants to fit in with Gemma's family. She doesn't want to embarrass herself or Gemma.

Cressida puckers her painted pink mouth. "You know, loud. Brash. Naïve. Entitled."

TS lets out an actual snort. Cressida, who snapped at the car driver for not opening her door quickly enough, thinks *TS* is entitled.

Cressida lifts her perfectly sculpted eyebrow. "Exactly."

"Yeah, well, if you think I'm loud, you should meet my friends." It's not as if TS is a shrinking wallflower, but compared to Tay and Taylor, it's sometimes hard to get a word in. And people wonder why Teffy is so quiet.

"Speaking of friends, *dear* friends, I'm sure you've heard *all* about Zara." Cressida gestures at the girl with Gemma. TS tries not to get jealous as she watches Gemma talking with a wide smile on her face, her eyes sparkling. You wouldn't know that Gemma just flew in that morning, while TS feels more exhausted by the second.

"Um . . ." The thing is, TS has *not* heard of Zara.

Cressida crosses her toned and tanned legs. "They were the best of friends when they were wee ones. Then Zara's family moved to France, but they reconnected a couple years ago and, well, became more than friends." Cressida raises her eyebrows and puts a hand to her heart while TS realizes she's never been so jealous of anything in her life.

But no, that doesn't matter. Gemma is with TS now.

Well, not physically. Gemma is with Zara, who keeps touching Gemma's arm as they talk.

Cressida continues and it's like a dagger twisting in TS's heart. "Yes, poor Zara missed Gemma so much when she moved to the States."

TS doesn't ever want to know the feeling of missing Gemma. She's her everything. Her A-Team. On and off the field.

"It's so nice to see Gemma back in her element," Cressida continues, her eyes darting at TS. A satisfied smirk spreads across her lips. "Where she belongs. With the right kind of people."

TS tries to keep her expression neutral as Cressida leans forward, studying her face. TS will not let Cressida know she is getting to her. TS has years of practice of not showing emotion on her face.

Yeah, TS trusts her gut. And it's telling her that this world is too uptight and pretentious. These people are sort of horrid and vapid.

But that doesn't really matter. She's here with Gemma, who isn't any of those things. Gemma asked her to spend the summer in England for a reason—because they do belong together.

TS will give Gemma's cousins this evening since she has the next four weeks to be with Gemma and tell her she loves her.

Our Chat (The Taylors Version)

TS ⚽: Sorry I've missed all the messages . . . this time difference . . . don't want to wake any of you up

TAY🎉: WAKE US UP!

TAYLOR🐝: Have you been given a crown yet?

TAY🎉: The pic of you AND MY DRESS in front of Big Ben—GAH!

TS ⚽: It's technically called the Elizabeth Tower

TAYLOR🐝: She's already such a Brit

TS ⚽: What's going on? I need details

TAY🎉: YES!!! WHAT'S GOING ON, TEFFY!

TEFFY📚: Ummm . . .

TS ⚽: Wait

TS ⚽: WAIT

TS ⚽: Is it finally happening?????

TEFFY📚: Maybe.

TS ⚽: Love how our Teffy has become the Bad Girl of the group

TEFFY📚: Light me up. 🔥

THREE
I Did Something Bad

Teffy has become a bit of an expert on escaping from her house. After all, when you've spent the last eight months—*eight months!*—hiding a secret from your parents, you sort of become really good at keeping things to yourself. It's not like Teffy was ever someone who had to share every thought or emotion—that's what her songwriting is for.

And she has had *a lot* to write about lately.

But today, today is the day she's finally going to come clean. As much as she wants to back down, she's already set the wheels in motion.

There's no turning back now.

"I'm heading out for a quick run!" Teffy tells her mother Monday before dinner. At least she thinks she's telling her mom. The living room has become overcrowded with boxes and packing materials. "Mom? Where are you?"

Her mom's head pops up from behind a stack of padded envelopes. "Here! Just organizing everything for my run to the post office tomorrow."

"It looks like business is going well." Teffy's mom opened an online store for pet owners where she makes personalized wire paw prints, wooden frames, ornaments, and keychains. It's kept her mom busy and happy, so Teffy doesn't bring up the fact that their parents have refused her and her brother Charlie's request for a dog for years.

"Yes, it's really good." Her mom lights up as she gets another order notification on her phone. "And I'm impressed that you're keeping up with the running while TS is away."

"You know I'll never hear the end of it if I'm slower when she gets back," Teffy jokes.

You know what else Teffy has become really good at? Stretching the truth. Okay, she's lying. She feels guilty about it, but her parents have been so unreasonable, it's left her no choice.

"And I'm glad the store is going so well." Teffy starts shaking her legs out, like TS taught her. "It's truly amazing."

While it *is* amazing how quickly her mom's store took off, Teffy also wants her mother to be in the best mood possible for later.

Even the thought of that upcoming conversation makes Teffy feel a bit nauseous. Confrontation is not something Teffy likes. But enough is enough.

Or... The voice in her head tries to convince her that she can keep her secret for a few more months.

"Thank you, honey," her mom says before a buzzer goes off in the kitchen. "Dinner is in an hour, and please put your work schedule on the refrigerator so I can keep track of . . ." She gets distracted by her phone and walks aimlessly into the kitchen.

It's been like this for weeks now. Truthfully, having her mom get easily sidetracked has made things easier for Teffy. With a hammering heart, Teffy heads out of the house and starts running . . . the three whole blocks to the park. She walks over to the far corner where there's a bench you can't see from the road.

Teffy clenches at the side of her stomach, where a cramp has developed. This is what she gets for actually running to the park, but she couldn't wait to get here.

"Hey, Tefs." Liam Yoon stands up from the bench. He smiles at her for a moment, and she takes in his beautiful face—those dark eyes and full lips—as he runs a hand through his messy brown hair. Then he takes two quick strides and is right in front of Teffy.

"Hey, yourself." She bites her lip as she can't help but stare at his mouth. That mouth that she spent years daydreaming about. The one she fantasized about kissing. The one she was sure she'd never have.

Liam licks his lips as he tenderly cups Teffy's face with his hand. Her heart flutters in its familiar pattern when she's with him. Liam leans in and Teffy closes her eyes as Liam kisses her. He wraps his arms around her, and she leans into him. She still can't believe that this is real.

But it is.

Liam pulls away and puts his forehead against hers. "Are you ready for this?"

Is she? She thought she was, but now . . .

A harsh reality crashes around her. While, yes, being with Liam has been amazing and everything Teffy hoped it would be, there's been one teeny, tiny problem.

Teffy buries her head into his chest. "Maybe we can put this off for another week. Or month? How about a year?"

"Tefs . . ." Liam gives her a kiss on the forehead. "You can't keep lying to your parents."

"You sure about that? I've become really good at it. Expert level, in fact. I'm the TS of keeping things from my parents." While Teffy is somewhat joking, she can't help but wonder, if being with Liam is so wrong, why does it feel so right? Why mess up how amazing things have been with Liam by telling her parents, who could ruin everything?

Teffy's wildest dreams have come true: She's with Liam. They had been the closest of friends since she could remember, but Teffy's feelings for Liam continued to grow, even though he had a girlfriend. Teffy had been convinced he'd never see her "that" way. Then came Homecoming, when Teffy confessed her feelings to Liam.

Teffy smiles as she thinks about Liam coming up to her at the Homecoming dance and taking her by the hand. "You cut me off before, and I would like the opportunity to tell you exactly how I feel about you, Tefs," he said.

Teffy had walked outside with him, this hopeful feeling in her belly. And then all the songs she'd ever written were nothing compared to what happened next.

"You know what my favorite part of my days has been?" Liam began. "Spending time with you. I looked at my days—my weeks—and broke them down to when I got to be with you. When you stopped talking to me, I felt like I lost a part of myself. I'm sorry it took losing you to realize how much you truly mean to me. Tefs, you just get me. And you, well . . . I want to know every single thing about you and your day and I just . . . I want to kiss you right now. Tefs, can I kiss you?"

Teffy had given the slightest nod, worried that she'd misheard Liam. But then Liam had leaned in, and they shared their first kiss. Teffy prides herself on being well-read and a bit of a writer, but there were no words available to describe the feeling that erupted inside her. Her lips felt like they were on fire, her heart like it was going to explode from happiness.

After Homecoming, Liam and Teffy started dating, using the Taylors as decoys: music sessions with Tay, studying with Taylor, and runs with TS. Teffy was supposed to tell her parents, but she kept making excuses because she was worried her parents would take Liam away from her. Liam's family found out before Liam's birthday in December and were supportive, even though they didn't agree with Teffy lying to her parents.

But honestly, her parents should know that Teffy isn't a runner. It's sort of their fault for being so gullible.

Liam gives Teffy a gentle squeeze now. "Well, *I* don't want to have to keep hiding. I want to shout to the world that we're together. I want to walk down the sidewalk with your hand in mine. I want to take you out to dinner with candles and stuff. Like, I want to properly woo you, Tefs. Go totally romantic on you."

"I want that, too." Of course she does. Teffy wants to have Liam over to her house. She wants to have him be part of her world. She doesn't want to have to keep lying.

Liam wraps his arms around her. "And I can't wait to take you out with my friends. I hate having to lie to them about not being able to hang. Now you can come to parties. Be in the crew."

Okay, there is one benefit to keeping their relationship a secret. Teffy doesn't really want to "hang" with Liam's crew. They're fine and all, it's just she likes having Liam to herself. Where she can just be Teffy. Where she doesn't have to try to impress the cool kids.

"Come on, Tefs. You already sent Charlie away for the evening so we've got your parents all to ourselves. We can do this. I've got you." Liam holds out his hand to Teffy and she takes it as they walk home.

Her heart speeds up as they approach her house. Her plan is to have them both sit down with her parents and make them listen, make them understand that their personal—and let's be honest, petty—feud with the Yoons shouldn't get in the way of Teffy's happiness.

Liam gives Teffy's hand an extra squeeze as they walk through the front door.

"Is that you, Teffy?" her mom calls out from the kitchen. "Can you come in here and get the salad ready?"

Her dad comes down the stairs. "I can hel—" He stops cold when he sees Liam holding Teffy's hand. His eyes, the same wide brown ones that Teffy has, are blinking at the sight. It's obvious he didn't see this coming.

Teffy's mom pops her head out from the kitchen. "If you—" She drops the towel in her hand. "What's going on? What is—?" she starts, but Teffy cuts her off.

"We need to have a talk."

"Hi, Mr. and Mrs. Bennett," Liam says, a slight waver in his voice. "I know it's been a while."

Teffy tries to stay calm and in control. "Mom, Dad, please sit down."

Teffy's mom looks between Teffy and Liam. "Need I remind you, Taylor Elizabeth Bennett, that we are the parents and you cannot—wait, have you even been running?" The lines around her mother's mouth deepen. "Exactly how much have you been lying to us, young lady? And for how long?"

Teffy isn't great at speaking out as much as the other Taylors, but this is too important to her. She channels TS's confidence by standing tall. "I wasn't given much of a choice, Mother. I'm not going to throw away one of the best things to happen to me because you can't forgive your friends. So, let's talk."

Liam looks at Teffy with such affection, she knows that he is worth this incredibly uncomfortable conversation. Liam guides Teffy by the hand as they sit down on the couch.

Teffy wills her brave face not to falter as her parents stare at her, both blinking as if they don't believe their eyes. Teffy will not budge. She crosses her arms. It feels like an eternity before her parents finally relent and sit down on the opposite chairs.

"Exactly how long has . . ." her mom begins, but shakes her head. "How did you . . ."

"I'll tell you everything, but first I have a question for you both." She had practiced her speech with the Taylors over and over again.

They even acted out the parts. Taylor played her mom and Tay her dad. At first it was hilarious since Tay kept doing a low voice to imitate her dad, but Taylor was Taylor, so she was extra and it was pretty terrifying. This should be easy in comparison. Oh, how Teffy hopes.

She dives right in. "Aren't things much better now? Mom, you love your new business. Dad, you were saying the other day how much you missed the consistency of working for a company—the benefits, the regular pay, not being in charge. And you're both home. We're back to having family dinners. I'm really sorry about what happened to Harrison by Design, but you didn't seem that happy with the store this past year."

Her parents both look down at the floor. She knows how upset they were to lose the business, something they had built with their best friends, but it's not a life. It's work.

"When I'm with Liam, I'm reminded of all the good times we've had with the Yoons. I know how upset you were when they pulled out of the business, but the past is the past. I want to focus on my future, and my future includes Liam."

The silence in the room is torture. Teffy usually prefers the quiet, but not this kind, which is charged and heavy.

"Mr. and Mrs. Bennett," Liam starts. "I can't speak for my parents, but I know that there's this hole that's been missing since you fell out. And I'm really sorry about how everything went down, but Teffy and I shouldn't be punished. I care for your daughter a lot, and she's extraordinary."

Teffy's heart starts beating faster. She still can't believe that he chose her.

"And I'm happy, really happy," Teffy shares with a smile. Liam was right. She can't keep this a secret any longer. She shouldn't have to. "Doesn't my happiness matter to you?"

"Of course," Teffy's mom says, her voice a whisper.

"Then give me one reason—one *good* reason—why I can't be with Liam. Why I should let *your* issues with Liam's parents get in the way of *my* happiness." Teffy keeps eye contact with her mother, and that's when she sees the wetness form around her eyes, the tremble in her chin.

"It's been really hard, not talking to your parents, Liam," her mother admits. "Your mom was my best friend, and well, it hurts." She closes her eyes and takes a deep breath.

Teffy feels guilty bringing all this emotion up in her mother, but maybe they can repair what they once had.

"Mrs. Bennett, I know my mom misses you." Liam gets up and gives her mom a hug, which she holds on to tightly.

"I just don't know, Teffy," her dad says, his cheeks red. "We've been put in a tight spot."

The Bennetts don't have as much money as the Yoons, but it never got in the way of their friendship before. Teffy could tell her dad sometimes got embarrassed by not having as much as they did, but it didn't matter to her.

"I know." Teffy stands up, feeling a bit wobbly, but determined.

"But, Dad, I'd like my boyfriend to join us for dinner. So either you can invite him to sit at the table, or we can go somewhere else. I'm done hiding the truth."

The room is quiet. Liam's got his arm around her mother, who is fighting back tears. Her father runs his hands through his thinning hair.

Maybe they'll say no and she'll have to . . . what? Teffy can't imagine her life without Liam. Her parents have to understand that.

Her dad sighs, a heaviness in him that makes Teffy's heart ache. Her parents have lost so much, but it's something they can fix. This is just one tiny step.

"While I don't appreciate you lying to us, Teffy, I understand this has also been difficult for you." Her dad nods to himself and then he looks at Liam. "Liam, would you like to stay for dinner?"

"Really?" Teffy bounces on her heels in a very Tay-like manner. She throws her arms around her dad.

She did it. *They* did it. Teffy no longer has to keep Liam a secret.

"No more hiding," Liam says as he picks Teffy up in a hug.

"No more hiding." It's almost as if Teffy doesn't know what to do next. They're no longer limited to sneaking around. They can be a real couple.

"So." Liam's dark eyes are sparkling. "I think it's time my crew met my amazing girlfriend."

"Oh yeah, I mean, yay!" Teffy forces a smile.

But honestly, after surviving the talk with her parents, how bad could hanging with her fellow classmates really be?

Our Chat (The Taylors Version)

TAYLOR🐝: Hey, Teffy . . . How's your BOYFRIEND LIAM?

TAY🎉: YES!!! YOUR BOYFRIEND LIAM!!!!

TS ⚽: Wait 😮

TS ⚽: Is this a trap? Can we finally text about it?!?!?!?

TEFFY📚: LIAM 🥰

TS ⚽: Okay, we need a group FaceTime ASAP

TAY🎉: YES!!!!! We'll call you at the Archers rehearsal

TS ⚽: And stop having things happen without me

TAYLOR🐝: Definitely nothing can happen when I'm at camp!

TAY🎉: What's the fun in that?

TEFFY📚: So you WANT drama, Tay?

TAY🎉: No!

TS ⚽: And how are things with Harrison High's premier garage band?

TAY🎉: Good!

FOUR
Out of the Woods

Tay wants everything to go perfectly.

She always loves performing with the Archers, even if it's just a rehearsal. But her best friends (minus TS) are coming over to watch and she wants everybody to get along. It's not like there's a rift or anything, it's just Tay wishes that her friends and Reece were closer. That things could be a bit easier for her. That she wouldn't have to always worry. It shouldn't be too much to ask. Just for everybody to be as happy and excited about things as her—okay, maybe not *as* excited, since Tay has enough enthusiasm to power a small city—but at least that everybody could just be . . . cool.

"Tay, it's fine," Reece says from the couch while the rest of the band starts warming up in the basement of Reece's house, which has a recording studio, an entertainment section with the biggest TV Tay has ever seen, a kitchen, *and* still has enough room for the band to rehearse in the corner. Reece reaches out to grab Tay's hand and drags her to sit with him. "There's plenty of food. The band sounds great. Relax." Reece nuzzles his face into her neck.

"You're telling *me* to relax?" Tay playfully swats his arm. Between the two of them, it's Reece that gets nervous talking to people—something Tay finds as easy as breathing. It's Reece who overanalyzes the setlist and basically everything about the band. It's Tay who worries about . . . them.

"Here." Reece holds up his phone and puts it on selfie mode as he snaps a picture of them. Reece's jet-black hair has grown out to his collarbone, so he now tucks his hair behind his ears, revealing pale blue eyes that Tay finds herself getting lost in. "Look at you."

Reece zooms in on a beaming Tay. She's got her hair pulled back into pom-pom buns. Her teal romper stands out against her brown skin.

"We need to post this on our socials to promote this weekend's gig." Reece tags both of them as he shares details about their performance at the Hancock County Fair with the hashtag #musicpowercouple. "Hey, do you think Teffy would mind showing me the chord progression in that song you were singing the other day?"

Tay jumps up from the couch. "Oh, yes! It's so good, right?" Teffy has been writing a lot lately, which isn't a surprise since she had a *secret romance* with her *childhood crush*. It's like the stuff of rom-com dreams.

Then again, so is dating a guy in a band.

GAH! And people wonder why Tay is so excited. Do you blame her? She's in a band! With her boyfriend!

So it's no wonder she doesn't want anything to mess it up.

"Yeah, she's a really good songwriter." Reece plays with THE ARCHERS bracelet Tay made him.

There's something Tay has been wanting to bring up to Reece for a while, but she's worried how he'll react. Here's the thing: Tay loves Teffy's songs so much. She comes alive when she performs them. And she really wants the band to start playing Teffy's songs, but it's just that she knows Reece can be a bit sensitive about his music. About everything, really. But that's what makes *him* such a great lyricist.

"Do you think . . ." Tay starts.

"Yeah?" Reece leans in and gives her a quick kiss on the cheek.

"I was just . . ."

"Hey!" Taylor enters the living room with Teffy behind her, charging in like she owns the place. "I didn't have lunch because I knew you'd be stocked with snacks, and wow, you did not disappoint. I also dressed for the occasion." Taylor gestures at her HARRISON HIGH SPRING FESTIVAL T-shirt and jean shorts. "I was hoping there would be corn dogs and cotton candy to fully prepare us for your fair gig, but this'll do." Taylor takes a handful of pretzels and looks over at the spread of chips and guacamole, cheese, and cookies.

Reece lets out a laugh. "Hey, Taylor. Teffy." He gives them each a nod before he gets up and grabs his guitar to start tuning.

Probably wasn't the best timing to bring up Tay's idea, anyway.

"Hey!" Teffy waves at the other band members before sitting down next to Tay. "How's it going?"

"Good." Tay pushes down the desire to ask about her songs and turns to more swoony, romantic matters. "Um, Teffy! You have to tell us everything going on with you and Liam!"

Teffy blushes as she pulls out her phone. "Oh, you didn't see my post?" Teffy shows her profile with a picture of her and Liam, cheek to cheek. "No more hiding!"

"And you lived to tell the tale." Taylor comes over with a plate heaped with food and holds it out to her friends to help themselves. "So are your parents cool or . . ."

Teffy looks thoughtful for a moment. "*Or.* They still aren't talking to Liam's parents, but we had a pretty good dinner. It was a bit awkward, but I think it's going to take time. Although . . ." Teffy bites her lip. "Now that we're not sneaking around anymore, Liam wants me to hang out with his friends from the football team." Teffy pretends to shiver.

"The same ones who tried to take *the hat* at that first party at the beginning of the year?" Taylor sneers for a moment, before she tilts her head. "That seems so long ago, right? Like, wow. If I could go back in time and have a talk with *that* Taylor."

Tay only nods. She doesn't want to remind Taylor that they tried to talk to her about Hunter and she wouldn't listen.

Besides, that's all in the past!

"Well, I'm so happy for you and Liam!" Tay wraps her arms around Teffy. Things just seem so easy between Teffy and Liam, even when they had to sneak around.

Teffy buries her head in her hands as heat creeps up on her pale cheeks.

Taylor leans back on the couch. "Speaking of happy couples, do we have time to call TS before you start playing?"

"I think so . . ." Tay looks around at the band, who have become her good friends since she joined. Owen is tuning his guitar, and Corey, the bassist, is busy chatting away with Kai, who is seated behind his drum kit. Reece is scribbling in a notebook. "Yeah, let's call her, I can't wait to hear all about London!"

"Get in close!" Taylor says as she lines them up in her phone frame. "Aww, look how cute we are. I'm going to miss this so much."

"Same." Tay puts her head on Teffy's as they wait for TS to pick up.

The screen lights up with TS's sweat-stained face. "'Ello, luvs!" she says in a fake British accent. At least Tay thinks it's fake. With how quickly TS can pick up on all things soccer, it wouldn't totally surprise Tay if she came back with an accent.

"Oh my goodness, hi! Where are you?" Tay leans in. "Please tell me you're in a palace and being knighted."

TS lets out a laugh. "Not yet. I'm in Hyde Park." TS flips her camera so they can see a large green field with a group of older guys running around. "I wanted to see if I could find any pickup soccer games and luckily found these guys."

"TS, how old are they?" Teffy asks.

TS brings the camera back to her. "They're, like, in their twenties and thirties and not even that good." She shakes her head in disappointment. "Of course, when I asked them if I could join, they gave me that look like, *you think you can hang with us*, and then I destroyed them." TS lets out a delightful cackle.

"Is Gemma with you? I want to say hi!" Gemma has become an

honorary Taylor. Tay likes her not just because of her accent, but because she makes TS so happy. There's this lightness in TS when Gemma's around. TS isn't so serious and focused.

TS grimaces. "No, her aunt wanted her to go to some museum exhibit. Just like yesterday, when her cousin dragged her to some charity event. And the day before that . . ." TS sticks her tongue out.

"Weren't you invited?" Teffy asks with a frown.

TS lets out a long breath of air. "I mean, saying I was as an afterthought is being generous, but I don't want to have to dress up and pretend to be interested in things and people that I am not. But! Next week we go to her grandparents' house—oh, I'm sorry, *castle*—and Gemma's parents are coming and that'll be nice because they are . . . normal."

Tay knows TS doesn't play things up and get all dramatic like Taylor or overemotional like her, but there's this hardness in her that makes Tay worried about her friend.

She's not the only one.

Teffy takes the phone in her hand. "You okay, TS? Really?"

She shrugs. "Yeah, I mean, I'm in London. With my gorgeous girlfriend. I can't really complain."

"But you're allowed to, you know that, right?" Taylor says, that protective edge in her voice. "I'm sure it's a lot, and just know that we're here for you."

"Whatever you need," Tay adds.

TS stares out at the field. "I appreciate you all, but it's fine. You know I don't like to get into drama so I'm just trying to keep to myself, get some practice in, and hang with my hot girlfriend when she isn't being whisked away. I'll survive."

Of course TS will survive, but Tay wants her to be happy, and instead she seems stressed.

"But do—" Tay starts, but TS cuts her off. "Hey, Taylor, when are you leaving for Camp Cash Money?"

"It's *Whispering Pines*." Taylor lets out a groan. "Tomorrow. I heard cell reception is spotty and counselors aren't allowed to have their phones on them during activities. So when you do hear from me, get ready for it to be *a lot*."

"Oh, and you're quiet and demure now?" TS gives her a smirk. "Can we please talk about how Teffy is now officially with—"

Their call is interrupted by an earsplitting grinding of guitar chords. Reece has his back to them while he warms up. Loudly.

"Um, I think we're starting soon." Tay gives TS an apologetic smile.

"No worries, I gotta get back to showing these Brits how to actually play soccer." TS blows them a kiss as the group says their goodbyes.

When they hang up, Tay gets this pang. She's happy for TS and Taylor to have these opportunities, but it means the group is splitting up.

"You ready, Tay?" Reece asks.

At least she has the Archers. And Reece.

"Woo!" Taylor lets out a cheer. "I'm going to channel my inner midwestern mom exhausted from carting kids around a fair all day." She falls back on the couch dramatically.

Tay walks over to the microphone in the middle of the band, warming up her vocals.

Reece holds up his hand, signaling the rest of the band to stop. "Before we start, I think we need to talk about our look. We aren't cohesive as a band."

Reece has a point. While Reece is always in all black, Tay prefers colors, and she's been wearing a lot of shades of blue lately. Corey and Owen are fairly interchangeable. They both are tall, white, have short brown hair, and are usually in jeans and T-shirts. Kai has a preppy vibe, and he's currently in a teal polo shirt and khaki shorts, which stand out against his dark brown skin. He's also bigger, like a teddy bear, with his black hair in a tight fade. "We need to look professional."

"Dude, we're sixteen, we *aren't* professional," Corey replies. "What? You want us to dress in all black? Or are you going to—shocker—wear some color for once?"

"Hey." Kai stands up behind his kit. "Let's be real, nobody is going to be looking at us, they'll be looking at Tay, and that girl's got style, so she can do whatever she wants and the rest of us will simply fade into the background."

Tay blushes at the compliment, but as she glances at Reece, she can tell he isn't taking it well. His jaw is set tight. His brow is furrowed. It's the first sign of trouble. Tay's belly starts to churn. See, this is exactly what she was worried about.

"So what am I, then?" Reece asks. "Just the songwriter. Just the lead guitarist. Just the person who put this band together."

"Relax. *You* are the one who wears black," Owen states before gesturing at Tay. "And I agree with Kai, all eyes will be on Tay, which is a good thing."

Tay shifts on her feet. This isn't the kind of attention she likes. She can tell Reece is starting to fold in on himself. His confidence is fragile. It had to be hard for him to turn over the lead to her, but he did it because it was best for the band. Tay knows she has to defuse this. It's something she's gotten used to doing with the band. And Reece and her dad.

"You know what, I think Reece has a point." Tay measures her words. She doesn't want to change her appearance for Reece—she did that when they first started hanging out. But it would make sense for the band to look more like . . . a band. Then an idea comes to her. "Oh! You know what I'd love to do! Have, like, an onstage persona. Like Beyonce and Sasha Fierce. When I'm onstage I can have more of a rocker vibe—distressed jeans, rock tees—that would fit with the rest of you." She fiddles with the black leather bracelet Reece gave her. "Teffy and Taylor? What do you think?"

"You make anything look good, Tay," Taylor replies with a snap of her fingers. "And I'm here for your rock star era."

Teffy jumps in. "And I'm sure Charlie wouldn't mind you borrowing some of his vintage rock T-shirts, he has plenty to go around."

"Okay!" Tay claps her hands and looks around to the band. See, this all worked out for the best! She's excited to come up with a stage persona. "Sound good, everybody?"

Owen, Corey, and Kai all nod while Reece's gaze is on the ground.

Tay approaches him cautiously. She often feels like she's on a tightrope with the band. Things will be going well and then something happens and she finds herself feeling unsteady.

"Reece." Tay wraps her fingers around his. "Are you okay? I can send you some pics of outfit ideas. I'll totally take inspiration from when Taylor rocked out on the electric guitar to 'We Are Never Ever Getting Back Together' during the 1989 tour."

Reece looks up at Tay with those light blue eyes, and his tension melts away. "Of course, I trust you. Whatever you think is best."

See, Tay really had nothing to worry about. It's all good.

Our Chat (The Taylors Version)

TS ⚽: I'm about to say something I never thought I'd say

TAYLOR🐝: That soccer is boring 😉

TS ⚽: 😡 😡 😡 😡 😡 😡

TS ⚽: It's a good thing there's an ocean between us

TS ⚽: I miss Cheetos, like, real American Cheetos with their glorious chemicals

TAY🎉: AND US!

TS ⚽: Of course

TS ⚽: (I'm not going to forget that soccer comment, Taylor)

TAYLOR🐝: 😅

TAYLOR🐝: Well, look at that! Almost at Whispering Pines. Where I won't have much reception. Ahem

TEFFY📚: Good luck! Try to fill us in when you can.

TAY🎉: DON'T FORGET ABOUT US!

TAYLOR🐝: I could never do that . . . no matter how hard I try 😂

FIVE
All Too Well

Taylor doesn't know how she got so lucky. She not only got this amazing summer job, but she's also been assigned to the Red Team, and *Red* just happens to be one of her favorite Taylor Swift albums. Then again, they're all favorites. That also means her uniform consists of a red Whispering Pines T-shirt or polo, which matches with her signature bright red lip. She brought a bunch of comfortable shorts and skirts to match. And her red Converse. She may be running after kids, but she'll be stylish while she does it.

Taylor surveys the large open space she'll be sharing with a co-counselor and the ten nine-to-ten-year-olds they'll oversee. There's a large seating area in the middle of the room with a sectional couch and beanbags. Along the walls are bunk beds, and in the corner closest to the front door is a larger bunk bed she'll be sharing with another counselor.

There's a knock on the door and Taylor sees a red-shirt-wearing counselor around her age. She's got long, straight black hair, skin slightly darker than Taylor's, and arms full of both beaded and brass bracelets. "Hi, I'm Mia! She/her. We're going to be cabinmates for the summer!"

"Hi, Mia! Taylor, she/her!" Taylor hands Mia her own goody bag.

"Oh, presents already, we're going to be fast friends." Mia plops down on a bright rainbow rug, her white Vans covered in ink drawings of flowers. "I didn't know if you wanted the top or bottom bunk so I haven't unpacked yet." Mia gestures at her two suitcases by their bunk.

"I'm good with either." Taylor grew up sharing a room with her sister, who snored very loudly, so the summer on a bunk bed surrounded by nearly a dozen other people will be nothing.

"Oh, this is sweet. Thank you!" Mia pulls a friendship bracelet from the bag and puts it on her right wrist. "If it's okay with you, I'll take the bottom. I like to feel grounded."

"Works for me." Taylor throws her backpack on the top bunk. "This is my first year here. You?" Taylor's excited to make new friends. She realizes no one will compete with the Taylors, but she wants to have a summer camp crew.

Mia wiggles her shoulders around—it's a very energetic, Tay move. "Well, it's my second year as a counselor, but I've been a camper twice, so I guess this is my fourth year. It's the best, no way I wasn't coming back. And when you see the art studio, you'll understand why. It's amazing. My mind just whirls with possibilities when I walk in."

"Is art your specialty?" Taylor asks. Each counselor is assigned to a different area of interest.

"Yeah, and music, you?"

"Well, I'll be overseeing the group's games, even though I'm not sporty. I'm good at organizing and telling people what to do." Which is true. Taylor won't have any trouble rounding up a group of kids and making sure they have everything they need. She probably got it from watching her mom wrangle her and her four siblings. And, let's be honest, her dad, who can be a bit of a kid himself.

Mia lets out a laugh. "I think we're going to get along. Have you met anybody else yet?" Taylor shakes her head. "We have two other Red Team counselors—Noah, they/them, and Caleb, he/him—I know them from previous years and they're both super cool and chill. Well, Caleb is such a big kid, so maybe not as chill. Or, come to think of it, not that cool, but a total sweetie. *And* I just caught a glimpse of our senior counselor, and I don't know what his deal is yet, except yum-*my*." Mia pretends to fan herself. "You in a relationship?"

Taylor shakes her head again. She's usually not at a loss for words, but whenever relationships are brought up, she tries not to think about what happened at the beginning of the school year. It's like a bruise you forget about until you press on it. "Well!" Taylor exclaims, to stop those feelings from resurfacing. "I know we have our orientation with our section soon. Care to give me a tour until then?"

"Absolutely!" Mia jumps up and links her arm with Taylor as they head outside. "You should know the food is really good, and I'm saying that as a vegan. Okay, what else? Mr. Mason, who runs the place, is super nice. You've met him, right?"

"Yeah, during my interview."

"Of course." Mia nods. "Oh, and we get extra competitive during Color War, so we'll want to start training our team early with drills and also puzzles. It's so fun!"

Taylor is getting excited thinking about it. She also hopes she'll be so busy she won't get homesick. This is the longest she'll have ever been away from her family. And the Taylors.

Mia gives Taylor a tour of the massive grounds. The lodges are tucked away beneath a canopy of pine trees. Down one path from the lodges toward the lake are the activity facilities: a theatre and art studio, along with a soccer field, baseball diamond, two basketball courts, two tennis courts, and a boathouse. The other path leads to a large open field, opposite the spacious dining and rec halls.

Perhaps this really is Camp Cash Money.

Not like Taylor is complaining.

Mia also fills Taylor in on all the important inside information—like to get to the dining hall early on tater tot casserole night and to take advantage of morning yoga at the lake, as it's the only quiet time they'll get.

As they wind their way to the rec hall, there are two people waiting outside the door, both wearing red shirts. One has dark brown skin with short-trimmed black hair, the other is a tall, skinny, pale white guy with curly reddish-brown hair.

"Hey, Caleb and Noah! This is Taylor. She's new." Mia gives them both a big hug and Taylor just knows she's on the right team.

"I'm Noah, welcome to Camp Whispering Pines!" Their nails are painted in classic red and Taylor is transfixed by their lashes and expertly applied cat eyeliner. She needs to get pointers.

"Thanks!" Taylor gives them a confident nod. "Although, this is probably really unfair. Do the other teams even stand a chance against us?"

Noah lets out a loud laugh. "Oh, I like you. And speaking of liking . . . did you see our supervisor? Looks like it's going to be Hot Boy Summer." Noah pretends to flip their hair.

Yeah, they and Taylor will get along just fine.

"Hi!" She waves at the tall one. "Caleb, right?"

"Yeah, hi—" Caleb's voice breaks, then he clears his throat. "Yeah, hey," he tries again with a deeper voice, but Taylor can see him internally cringe.

Noah puts their arm around Caleb. "It takes him a while to warm up to new people," they stage-whisper. "Are you ready for today's joke?"

"I've been waiting!" Mia says with a shake of her head. "Is it really summer without a dad joke from Caleb?"

Caleb's eyes dart to Taylor. "Oh, um, I . . ."

Taylor gives him an encouraging smile. She didn't think counselors could be shy. "I love a good dad joke, my dad practically speaks in them. He can be so embarrassing." Even though there's a part of Taylor that knows she'll miss her dad, punny jokes aside.

"Oh, well, the kids like them." Caleb's cheeks are flushed. "So, yeah, okay . . . What did the pig say on a hot summer day?"

Mia and Noah reply in unison, "I don't know, what did the pig say on a hot summer day?" They're both already giggling.

Caleb's light brown eyes start to sparkle. "I'm bacon!" he exclaims before letting out a huge laugh.

The joke itself isn't *that* funny, but Taylor can't help but laugh along with her fellow counselors.

Noah pats Caleb on the shoulder. "The kids eat this up. Honestly, Caleb is their favorite, between the jokes and treating him like a jungle gym, and then I have to be all, 'No climbing on the counselors, kids,' but—" Noah looks around the empty field. "There are no kids around now!" With that, Noah jumps on Caleb's back, to which Caleb runs around a nearby tree with a laughing Noah hanging on.

"Well, it's nice to know that some things never change." Mr. Mason has stepped outside, looking at Taylor's fellow Red Team counselors with an amused expression. He's wearing a hunter-green Whispering Pines polo shirt with a matching baseball hat. His salt-and-pepper curly hair peeks out. "Red Team, it's your turn."

"Hi, Mr. Mason. Taylor Perez." Taylor extends her hand, since her interview was done over video chat. She's surprised he's much shorter in person.

"Taylor, yes, welcome!" He smiles warmly at her. "I should've mentioned you've got two very big kids on your team."

Caleb sets Noah down, his pale cheeks red. "Oh, hey, Mr. Mason," he tries to say in a relaxed manner, but he's a little out of breath.

"Maybe save all that energy for the kids." Mr. Mason chuckles. "But of course I've got to know, what's today's joke, Caleb?"

"Oh . . ." This time when Caleb tells it, Taylor joins in on the chorus with the rest of them.

This summer is going to be so much fun. She already loves her team. And she can't wait to share some of Caleb's jokes with her dad. Unless that'll just encourage him.

Mr. Mason gestures at the front door. "Okay, okay. Get in here, Red Team!"

Taylor walks into the large reception hall, where the camp hosts their indoor activities when it rains. It has large wooden beams and a mural painted by last year's campers.

Mr. Mason gestures at the chairs circled up in the center of the room. "Have a seat."

Taylor sits down with her team and notices one seat is empty.

"We're just waiting on—oh, here he is." Mr. Mason gives a nod over Taylor's shoulder. "Red Team, meet your supervisor for this summer."

Taylor turns around and feels as if the ground has swallowed her up. Mr. Mason is talking, but Taylor's head is swimming as she takes in the person who will be overseeing her this summer. It just so happens to be the one who took her heart and stomped all over it.

Hunter Brown.

This can't be happening.

How? How is this possible?

Just a minute ago, Taylor thought she was so lucky, with her team and laughing and having fun, and now . . .

Hunter strides over to the chairs in his red shirt, his sandy-brown hair a bit longer and curlier than the last time she saw him. Hunter's hazel eyes bore into her, and his lips curl up in a wolfish grin. When he sits down next to her, Taylor shifts her gaze straight ahead. She doesn't want to look at him. She doesn't even want to breathe the same air.

Taylor tries to steady her pounding heart as Hunter introduces himself to the group. Mia's gazing at him with wide eyes and Noah has their elbows on their legs, hanging on every word spewing out of Hunter's mouth. Caleb gives him an enthusiastic high five.

Great. So much for being part of a team.

Memories start flashing back to Taylor. How after she bumped into Hunter on her first day of school, he was all she could think about. How he seemed so perfect. He said all the right things to Taylor. He told her he loved her. She'd loved him. So much.

But he also manipulated her. He treated her like a queen until she wanted to do something that didn't revolve around him. She gave up her campaign to be freshman class president for Hunter. She got into a fight with Teffy because she didn't want to believe that Hunter wasn't this perfect guy she had made up in her mind. She gave up a lot for Hunter.

And then he cheated on her. And tossed her aside like she was nothing. Like she meant nothing.

Taylor feels a burn behind her eyes, the emotions flooding in.

She feels a tap against her knee. It's Caleb. "Hey, are you okay?" he whispers. His eyebrows are furrowed as he studies Taylor.

Taylor can only nod. But if Caleb, who has only known Taylor for about two minutes, can tell there's something wrong, she has to get herself together. She can't let Hunter think that he means anything to her. Because he doesn't. It's just . . . hard. To have to be around the person who took advantage of her. To have to be on a *team* with him.

Taylor tries to bring herself back to the group conversation but then tenses up as Hunter flings his arm around her. "And I know this one. We go to the same school, or I should say, *went*. I graduated. Yeah, Taylor and I go waaaay back."

Taylor jerks forward so Hunter drops his arm, but he lets it skim her back. Taylor wants to take a shower. She feels dirty. It used to be that all Taylor wanted was Hunter's touch, but now it makes her sick to her stomach.

There's more conversation happening around her, but it's taking everything in Taylor to not storm out of the room. To try to figure out how this has happened. Her mind goes back to all the talking Hunter did—so much talking—and he had mentioned summer camps, going to them, being a counselor, but she would've remembered if he had mentioned Whispering Pines. She never would've applied for this job if she knew he would be here. Never.

"Okay, great, team!" Mr. Mason says with a clap of his hands, causing Taylor to come out of her daze. She has basically missed everything that was said. "See you at dinner. Get an early night tonight, the campers arrive tomorrow morning and then the fun really begins."

Taylor stands up to follow Mr. Mason, but Hunter steps in her way. "It's great to see you, Taylor." He goes to run his fingers through his hair, and that's when Taylor notices the red beaded bracelet that she made him when they were together.

"Why do you still have that?" she blurts out. "I want it back."

"Aw, Taylor." Hunter puts his hand to his heart like he's in pain. "Of course I still have it. It was a gift. You know that you can't get back the things you gave me."

Taylor doesn't think it's possible to hate another person as much as she hates Hunter Brown in this moment.

"I'm just surprised you didn't break it, like you do with your promises," Taylor fires back. She's sure to stand tall, even though Hunter's a foot taller than her. She will not let him get to her. She will not let him make her feel smaller.

That old Taylor can't come to the phone, because she's dead.

Hunter tsks. "So childish. Things probably could've worked out if you were older."

"Please. You liked that I was young. I was too naïve to see through your lies and manipulation. But I'm fifteen and a half now and know better." Taylor turns on her heels and heads straight to the main office to talk to Mr. Mason. There is no way she can be on the same team as Hunter. She doesn't want to even be in the same camp. She was able to avoid him after they split by steering clear of any hallways or classrooms he'd be in.

"Wait a minute!" Hunter grabs Taylor by the elbow and she pulls it away.

"Don't you dare touch me!" she hisses. "Don't you ever touch me again!"

"Hey!" Mia comes over, with Noah and Caleb standing protectively behind her. "What's going on?"

"Nothing!" Hunter smiles that smile that used to get him whatever he wanted. "We're just catching up. Right, Taylor?"

"Taylor?" Caleb asks, his jaw clenched.

Her three co-counselors are studying Taylor with concern, and neither Mia nor Noah looks to be fawning over Hunter anymore.

Taylor weighs her options. She was planning on marching to Mr. Mason's office to tell him she can't be on the Red Team. She can't work with Hunter.

Although, would that be the best thing for her to do on her first day? Taylor has to think this through. If she did that, she'd be leaving the Red Team vulnerable to Hunter's manipulating ways. Keep your enemies close and all that.

"I'm fine," Taylor says, and notices that Hunter relaxes slightly next to her. "*However*, I need to have a word with Hunter, but I'd appreciate if you would all stay close by." She then makes eye contact with Hunter. "Just in case I need backup."

The corner of Hunter's lips twitches. Ugh. Taylor forgot how conceited he is.

"You sure?" Mia asks.

Taylor nods as she leans in to Hunter to say in a low voice, "You think you have everybody fooled, but I know better. I'm only going to say this once, you better not pull any of that crap on any other counselor or camper. You better watch your back, Hunter. I'm older and wiser."

Taylor turns on her heel and flips her hair.

"Let's go," Taylor says to her fellow counselors, who follow her out of the lodge.

Turns out, this won't be Hot Boy Summer.

It's going to be the Summer of Revenge.

Our Chat (The Taylors Version)

TEFFY📚: You hanging in there, Taylor?

TS ⚽: I can't believe that creep is allowed to be around people

TAYLOR🎀: I'm focusing on my kids, who are great, all Taylor fans

TAYLOR🎀: they also like Taylor Swift 😉

TAY🎉: WHO ISN'T A FAN? They're Swifties AND . . . Perezheads?

TAYLOR🎀: I LIKE IT

TS ⚽: You're creating a monster, Tay

TEFFY📚: It's TAY who is going to have so many fans after today!

TAY🎉: GAH!! I CAN'T WAIT FOR YOU TO SEE MY NEW ROCKER LOOK: straight black hair, nose ring, sleeve full of tats . . . I WENT ALL IN

TEFFY📚: Um . . .

TAYLOR🎀: TAY!

TS ⚽: I leave the country for a week . . .

TAY🎉: KIDDING! I wish I could see your faces 😂

SIX

But Daddy I Love Him

Everybody has to start somewhere, Tay reminds herself as she looks out at the empty seats in front of the stage at the Hancock County Fair. They're performing in an area tucked away in a corner by the food trucks.

"Once you start singing, Tay, this place will get packed," her dad says as if he could read her mind.

Tay can only smile as she needs to remain positive about their performance. The band often looks to her for support, and she knows that they'll rock even if it's only their friends and family in the audience.

"Hey, Tay!" Teffy comes over with Liam, their hands full of the finest food a county fair can offer: nachos and hot dogs. "You look amazing!"

"Thanks!" Tay spins around in her outfit: gray distressed jeans, a LONDON CALLING T-shirt (so TS could be there in spirit) that she borrowed from Teffy's brother, black Converse, and she pulled her hair up on the sides so her curls form a sort of mohawk. She looks fierce. Even Kai has swapped out his colorful shirts for a black tee. The Archers are totally giving off rocker vibes and Tay is here for it.

Tay gives Teffy a hug before turning to Liam. "Thanks for coming, TEFFY'S BOYFRIEND LIAM." Tay loves not having to keep that secret anymore. When her friends are happy and have good news, she wants to shout it to the world!

"Are you kidding me?" Liam ruffles his messy dark hair. "I can't wait to say that I knew you when. Today: Hancock County Fair, tomorrow: Lucas Oil Stadium."

The dream. Tay's stomach does a roundoff. This is why she's here. To start something. To build an audience. To get in front of people.

If only she were doing it with Teffy.

Tay's dad starts setting up his tripod. "I'm going to get a good spot in the front row so I can record for your socials. Look at me, *socials*. I'm so hip, yo."

"Daddy!" Tay puts her head in her hands, even though she loves how encouraging he is. Sure, he may not be that supportive of Reece, but he's become one of the Archers' biggest fans. He wanted to get a bunch of merch printed before Harrison by Design closed, but the group couldn't agree on a logo.

"Your dad is super cool, Tay." Liam takes a huge bite of a hot dog, leaving a smudge of ketchup on his chin.

Teffy smiles at Liam as she gently wipes it off his face. "You're hopeless."

"Utterly." Liam goes in to kiss Teffy, but she swats him away.

"Liam! Your mouth is full. Gross." Teffy laughs as she tries to get away from him.

Liam takes an even bigger bite. "What are you saying, babe?" he says with a full mouth.

Teffy shakes her head, but Tay can tell how smitten Teffy is. She's so happy they're finally out in the open. Tay swears she nearly burst a blood vessel keeping that secret.

"You ready?" Teffy asks as she holds out her nachos to Tay.

Tay declines, not wanting to be jumping around stage with a full belly. "Yeah, I'm a little nervous about our songs. Reece's are just . . . a little melancholy. We wanted to do covers, but Reece was pretty insistent on doing the ones he wrote."

"Not everybody can write a song like Teffy Bennett." Liam beams with pride.

Doesn't Tay know.

"You are going to be amazing, Tay. You were born to be on a stage." Teffy reaches her arms out wide. "And you can make any song a bop by being your bright, shiny, spectacular self."

"Aw, Teffy." Tay gives her a hug. What she would give for Teffy to have half as much confidence in herself.

"Hey!" Reece comes out from behind the stage. "Oh, hey, Liam and Teffy, thanks for coming."

"Of course, man." Liam holds his hand up for Reece, who—thankfully—gives Liam a high five. Reece can sometimes be awkward in social settings.

"We go on in five, Tay." Reece fiddles with THE ARCHERS bracelet. Tay needs to make him a new one, as it's starting to fray from all his pulling.

"Okay, great. Hey, can you go say hi to my dad?" Tay asks. "It would mean a lot."

Reece looks over at where Tay's dad is busy setting up his phone. "What kind of mood is he in?"

"It'll be fine." Tay isn't so sure about that, but she wants her dad to give Reece a chance.

"I will, for you." Reece then plasters on a smile as he approaches Tay's dad.

Liam puts his arm around Teffy. "Tay, we know a thing or two about parents not approving. It'll be okay."

"Yeah." But the thing is, Mr. and Mrs. Bennett's issue isn't with Liam, it's with his parents. They love Liam. They're just . . . stubborn. Tay just wishes her father would come to his senses.

Tay watches as Reece approaches her dad. She wants to rush over and help, but she also knows they need to become more comfortable around each other without her having to always intervene. Her dad glances up with a shake of his head. Reece asks her dad a question, and her dad's eyes light up as he starts showing Reece his recording setup. Tay can exhale a bit.

"I should go." That excited feeling she gets before she performs starts growing in her bones. She wishes they were starting with a banger that would get people dancing, but Reece insisted it should be this slower emo song. But it's a Sunday afternoon. She can only hope that people will want to have a seat and feel . . . angst?

"We'll be up in front cheering!" Teffy gives her another hug.

Tay heads backstage, and the band has a quick moment in a circle before they take the stage. There isn't anybody there to introduce them, so it's up to Tay. The guys go out first, then Tay runs out onstage to loud applause from the few people who came for them, and tepid applause from the other dozen people seated.

"Hello, Hancock County! We're the Archers from Indianapolis and have some original songs we're going to play. Hit it!" Tay throws her hands up in the air as Reece starts strumming his guitar and Kai kicks in the beat. Tay does her best to work the stage, but the song is a bit too slow, so she can't really let loose and dance. She needs to control her vocals for the "*love will break you in two*" she basically shouts during the chorus. The song is definitely a mood.

It's not hard to notice in the daylight that a few people have already left. The Archers go on to the next song, which is even more depressing: "Dying Without You."

And now it's just the nine people who personally know the band members.

This was definitely not part of Tay's dream.

"Hey!" Kai calls out from the drums. "*We* are dying with these songs. We gotta switch to covers."

Reece shakes his head. "Why are you surprised these fair folks have no taste?"

"We're not going to get more gigs if people flee," Owen replies.

The silence coming from the stage is uncomfortable and Tay knows it's up to her to get the band back on track. "Why don't we try a couple covers and see what happens?"

"Yeah, let's have some fun." Kai starts twirling around his drumsticks. "What are we doing, boss?"

Kai, Owen, and Corey look to Tay in anticipation while Reece is glaring at the ground. She knows what she's going to do next won't go over well with Reece, but she's the one with the microphone in her hand.

"'Bejeweled'—our rock version." When they're goofing around, the band will take some of their favorite Taylor Swift songs and turn them into rock songs. It's honestly Tay's favorite part of their rehearsal, and she's been dreaming of the day when they could perform them onstage.

Today is that day.

Kai starts with a drumbeat and she looks to Reece, who pauses, but then plays the guitar chords. Tay turns to the sparse audience. When the first line comes out, Teffy stands up and starts cheering. Tay's dad and Liam come up next. Teffy is singing along and Tay can't help but notice people are starting to come over, many singing along to the Archers' version of the Taylor classic.

Tay lets loose, jumping up and down, even getting the growing audience to clap along when they get to a part of the verse they strip back with just drums and a guitar.

The crowd has doubled by the end of the song. Hey, it may be only twenty people, but Tay feels this wild joy being onstage. She feels in control. She feels free. She feels like herself. And she wants to turn this up to eleven.

"'Cruel Summer,'" she tells the band, and they don't even hesitate and go right into it.

Tay sneaks a few glances at Reece and he seems to be enjoying himself. His eyes get wide as more people start filling in the seats. At one point, Tay comes over to Reece and leans her back against him as he does a killer guitar solo, which is a lot longer than he usually goes for. "Thank you," he mouths to her as the crowd goes wild after his solo.

"Okay, Hancock County," she says halfway through the song, "we all know the bridge to this song, right? Let's hear it!" Tay holds out the microphone as the crowd sings along. Teffy is practically pressed against the stage as she screams. The seats are all now full and people are standing.

Standing room only!

This, Tay thinks. *This is what performing should be like.* They continue performing their covers: "Anti-Hero," "Style," "Maroon" (all Archers' Rock Versions) and they are killing it. By the end, the area is packed—people are singing along and having *fun*.

"Thank you, Hancock County!" Tay says after the last song. "We're the Archers!"

The crowd is on their feet. Tay can't believe it. She wants to do this every minute of every day. Reece comes over and picks her up and twirls her around. "You're amazing, you know that, right?"

Tay blushes. See, *this* is why she's with Reece. Yes, there are times it can be a lot of work having to speak for someone, but he appreciates her. It's her choice to be with him. She takes his hand as they get off the stage.

"That was incredible!" Kai says as the band exchanges high fives and hugs. "This is what we get listening to Tay."

"Ah, what's happening?" Corey asks as he turns back to the stage, where there's a bit of a commotion.

It's then that Tay realizes the crowded is chanting, "Encore!"

"They want *more*?" Reece's jaw is practically on the floor.

"Well, we should give the crowd what they want, right?" Kai throws a drumstick in the air and catches it.

"Uh, are we even allowed?" Tay looks over to one of the fair organizers off to the side of the stage. He gives them a thumbs-up.

"Okay!" Reece claps his hands. "We need to do an original now that we've got more people."

"Are you kidding?" Corey shakes his head. "Dude, they want to sing along to Taylor Swift. They want to dance. We can't do a one-eighty and do some mopey song."

"My songs aren't mopey, they're art." Reece's cheeks get flushed.

"Of course they are!" Tay says, but she also knows switching gears now wouldn't be a wise move. "But they're expecting more Taylor."

"And Tay," Kai replies with a wink. "What do you say, boss?"

There's only one response for Tay. "'I Knew You Were Trouble.'"

"Yeah, you are." Kai runs back out onstage with the rest of the band behind him. Tay can't believe the cheers when she gets in front of the microphone.

So this is what it's like to have your dreams start coming true.

"One, two, three—" Tay counts off, and in the front row comes the loudest scream she's ever heard from Teffy.

"LET'S GO, TAY!"

♥♥♥♥

Tay likes to smile. A lot. She has never done it so much that her face hurts, until this gig. Not only is Tay beyond thrilled with the reaction, but they had people waiting for them off to the side of the stage when they finished. To get pictures! With her! Because they like her singing!

"You're so cool!" a young girl coos to Tay as she takes a selfie.

"Oh my goodness, thank you!" Tay feels like she's on cloud gazillion.

"Do I need to be your security?" her dad jokes as he beams.

"He has a point." Teffy folds her arms and tries to look all serious and threatening, but then just doubles over in laughter. "But for real, that was incredible! You guys need to become a Taylor Swift rock cover band. You were glowing! You're *still* glowing!"

"Yeah, you're such a rock star, Tay!" Liam starts playing air guitar as he bangs his head.

Tay isn't the only one getting attention. Reece is also surrounded by fans—they have fans now! She tries to not get jealous that it's all girls. She doesn't blame them, he's a cute guitarist who plays Taylor Swift songs.

Swoon!

Reece finally comes over and picks Tay up. "Well, I guess we need to listen to you more often."

"That, my boy"—Tay's dad clamps a hand on his shoulder—"is the smartest thing anybody could say about my daughter."

"We did it!" Tay can't believe it.

But no, they didn't just do it. They crushed it.

♥♥♥♥

No surprise, Tay is still on a performance high later that evening.

"You better not be too big to do dishes, Miss Superstar," her dad teases as he picks up her plate after dinner.

"Excuse me, did you just make eye contact? Do you *not* know who I am?" Tay pretends to scoff, then erupts into laughter. Giddy laughter.

This is seriously the best feeling in the world.

She doesn't even mind doing dishes. Everything has a new shine on it. Tay fills the sink with hot soapy water, humming to herself. She doesn't think she'll ever stop smiling.

"You know who I really like?" her dad says as he takes a wet pan from her. "Kai. He's a cool dude. And really nice."

"Did you just say *cool dude*?" Tay laughs. "Yeah, Kai is great. All the guys are."

Her dad makes a noise that makes it clear he doesn't agree.

"And you know who is *really great*? Reece. He's nice. You know who isn't nice? *You* to Reece." She shuts the water off. "And I'm really tired of this. I know you don't like Reece and that you've built in your head the kind of guy you want me to be with and it's not him, but he's the person *I* want to be with. He brought me into the band. He's responsible for what happened today. The joy that comes with it. He makes me happy. And I'm growing up, so you need to respect my choices, and I choose Reece, Daddy."

Her dad grips his towel tightly. "I know you do, honey, but I don't want you to get hurt."

"Let me tell you something, right now the only one hurting me is *you*." Tay throws the sponge into the sink and stomps to her bedroom and slams the door.

Well, it seems like something can wipe the smile off Tay's face after all.

Our Chat (The Taylors Version)

TS ⚽: Tay, you have some explaining to do

TAY🎉: 👀👀👀

TS ⚽: Can't believe you hid how rockin' the Archers are, those videos 🔥

TEFFY📚: And in person it was 🔥🔥🔥!

TAYLOR🐝: The Red Team is obsessed! OBSESSED! I got such cool points for knowing you

TAY🎉: AWWW, THANKS!!! I STILL CAN'T BELIEVE IT! 🥰

TS ⚽: On the way to the posh country house and we've been playing you on repeat

TAYLOR🐝: You and a zillion other people—have you seen the hits it's gotten? 10K!! Please tell me Reece is thrilled

TAY🎉: HE IS!!! WE'RE ADDING EVEN MORE SONGS!!! ANY REQUESTS?

TAYLOR🐝: WHERE DO I EVEN START? All of them! EVERY SONG

TEFFY📚: Better begin conditioning on the treadmill for your 3.5 hour long concert.

TS ⚽: LET ME BE YOUR TRAINER!

TAY🎉: You all would make THE BEST entourage!

TS ⚽: OH MY

TS ⚽: Y'ALL

TS ⚽: 😳

TAYLOR🐝: What? WHAT? I have to lock up my phone soon. WHAAAT?

TS ⚽: This house, wait, no, this CASTLE. What am I doing here? FOR REAL

SEVEN
Question . . . ?

TS did her research before heading off to London. She had tackled it like she does most things in her life: study, plan, and be prepared.

What TS didn't prepare for was how homesick she'd be. Or that instead of becoming closer to Gemma, TS feels . . . adrift. She came into this trip thinking she and Gemma would be inseparable, but it's been the opposite. TS can take some of the blame: She's used any excuse during their two weeks in London to go to the park to play soccer. To go for runs. To escape the pretentiousness and judgmental glares of Gemma's aunt, uncle, and cousins. But it's not like TS hasn't tried. Every morning, and it's been *every morning*, whatever plan TS had come up with to spend alone time with Gemma—taking a day trip to Windsor Castle, going on a bus for high tea, hitting Camden Market in the afternoon—got usurped by some boring, stuffy plan from Gemma's aunt or cousins.

Hopefully being in the country means escaping from the zillions of events Gemma has been dragged to. Although, it isn't lost on TS that Gemma could've said no. Gemma could've joined TS in the park. Or on a walk. TS even went to the Black Dog by herself. At least she didn't have to share the nachos made with waffle fries.

She hopes the countryside will give them a new start. Maybe now she and Gemma can spend more time together. TS has never been this physically close to Gemma, sleeping just down the hall, but she feels so far away.

That was until they pulled up to the castle. An actual castle. The thing is, you can only prepare yourself so much. TS had, of course, looked up Buckingshire Castle. She knew the facts: It was built in the early 1600s by the first Duke of Huntington. It boasts over *three hundred* different rooms, including a grand ballroom. Seeing it in person, however, is an entirely different thing.

The outside is intimidating: With several stories of rich, dark, ornate details, it looks like the fanciest wedding cake with an imposing central tower, classical columns, and huge arched stained-glass windows. The inside feels like a movie set featuring kings and queens—at least the several dozen rooms TS saw during her tour, which was only a portion of the estate. It's lavishly decorated with elaborate plasterwork, fireplaces, marble statues, and furniture that looks so old—and priceless—that TS is afraid to sit down. Or touch anything.

"Hey!" Gemma knocks on the door of TS's guest room, where TS has been standing awkwardly. She's not joking about being afraid to sit down.

The guest room is bigger than the first floor of TS's house. The large canopy bed could easily fit all of the Taylors. It has four carved wooden posts and is draped with maroon velvet that matches the curtains on the floor-length windows that look out on the rose garden. There's a chaise lounge in one corner and a dressing area in another.

Yeah, it's a lot.

"Are you ready for dinner?" Gemma glances down at TS's pink sundress. TS notices a slight expression on Gemma's face, one that she's become accustomed to receiving from Gemma's cousins: judgment. She's never felt judged by Gemma before. Until now.

"Uh, yeah?"

TS knows her dress is nothing like the purple floor-length silk gown Gemma is wearing, but she also wasn't told to pack a prom dress. TS was informed when they arrived that dinner was a "formal affair" as there would be guests. When TS's family has guests, it usually means a couple friends and family, but when she saw the longest dining table of her life and staff rushing around getting ready, she knew this was going to be more than having the Taylors over for pizza.

"Oh, okay." Gemma smiles, but there's a strain. "Would you maybe . . . like to borrow something to wear? You might be more comfortable."

TS can feel her back tensing up. It would've been nice to be warned that sundresses wouldn't cut it for this trip. TS doesn't want to get into a fight, she really doesn't, but she can't help but feel like Gemma didn't prepare her. And we all know how much TS likes to be prepared.

"If it would make *you* more comfortable," TS says between clenched teeth.

"Oh, no!" Gemma bites her lip. "I just, I think you look gorgeous and I didn't even think about tonight and my grandmother and . . ." TS can see the tension on Gemma's face.

TS knows Gemma's family has been stressing her out, so she'll be a team player. "You know what, a different dress would be great, thanks."

TS is firmly Team Gemma, so that means she'll smile and wear a fancy dress. Because she really does want to make a good first impression on Gemma's grandmother. The one who doesn't like Gemma's colorful hair. The one who was busy "instructing the staff" when they first arrived.

To be honest, TS is sort of dreading meeting her. The second TS saw the castle, she realized the thank-you gift she brought of Indiana souvenirs—a magnet, mug, and tea towel, along with an Indy 500 toy car—would be staying in her suitcase. It doesn't fit the old-money vibe. TS is wondering if *she* fits the vibe. Her wardrobe—oh, who is she kidding, Tay's wardrobe—isn't cutting it.

"Let's pick something out!" Gemma says a little too brightly. TS can tell she's trying to be extra positive to offset TS's mood. She takes TS by the hand to her bedroom. She flings open a large antique dresser and starts going through all the gowns she has.

TS didn't know Gemma had so many dresses.

Do you even know Gemma? scratches in the back of TS's mind. She's been different since they arrived in England. Her accent has morphed to where she sounds more like Freddie. She laughs at jokes that aren't remotely funny. She hasn't gone for a run or done any training. While, yeah, she looks beautiful no matter what—even though she's turning into a mini Cressida with her hair, makeup, and outfits runway ready—it's the dirty and sweating Gemma running around a soccer field that TS thinks is super hot.

"What about this one?" Gemma holds out a maroon chiffon dress with a scoop neckline and flutter sleeves.

Fine. Whatever.

TS takes the dress and goes behind an antique screen in the corner to change her clothes. Although, TS can't help but think that Gemma's asking TS to change as a person.

All TS knows is that this better be worth it.

"So," TS says from the privacy of the screen. "Do I get to finally have some time alone with you?" Her voice comes out harder than intended.

"Of course." There's a pause. "I know my family has been a lot. They can be exhausting."

"Would've been nice to have been warned." It's like with the dresses. If TS had any idea what she was getting herself into . . .

Would she really have not come? Of course she would have. She'd do anything for Gemma. So if putting a dress on makes her happy, she'll do it. No need to make a big deal out of it.

"TS . . ." Gemma's voice sounds strained. "I'm so glad you're here. I knew the only way I could really deal with my family would be to have you beside me."

But TS *hasn't* been beside her.

TS comes from behind the screen. "Can you zip me up?"

"Of course!" Gemma struggles with the zipper. TS didn't realize she was bigger on top than Gemma. "Almost got it!"

The second the zipper finally goes up, TS feels constricted. But what's that saying, *beauty is pain*? TS can't help but think this entire evening is going to be one big pain in the—

No, be positive, TS tells herself. She's going to channel Tay and be bright and sparkly and . . . wow, it must be exhausting to be Tay.

TS looks in the mirror. The dress skims her knees since she's a couple inches taller than Gemma as well, but still. She does look nice.

"Gorgeous." Gemma wraps her arms around TS's waist and places her chin on her shoulder. "I'm sorry about everything. I really am. You know how much you mean to me, right? How much you matter to me?"

TS studies Gemma in the mirror: her brow is furrowed, and it's clear she's worried about TS. That she cares about her.

"Shaw?" Gemma turns TS around so they're eye to eye. She has a pleading look on her face.

TS opens her mouth, but then closes it. She had all these grand plans to confess her love to Gemma on this trip. Here's the perfect moment to tell her, but the words are caught in her throat. Not because she's scared, but being introduced to this part of Gemma has made TS pause. Taylor Shaw doesn't hesitate without a reason.

TS just doesn't know anymore. About anything. And TS is rarely unsure of herself. That in itself has added to the growing frustration she's had since she landed two weeks ago. *Two weeks.*

TS can feel her shoulders tensing again. As much as she wants to believe what Gemma is telling her, there are words and there are actions. Her actions are telling TS something entirely . . .

Do not start a fight, TS tells herself. *You're reading too much into it. Do* not *be the drama.*

TS needs to approach this trip with a new strategy. If there's one thing TS knows, it's strategy. So far, she's been on offense: creating moments for her and Gemma (only to be rejected) and trying to fit in with her family (see: dress). Maybe what TS needs to start doing is play some defense. Start anticipating problems and getting ahead of them.

TS rolls out her shoulders and decides to play it lightly. Make Gemma smile instead of frown. "Of course you mean a lot to me. It's the only reason I haven't punched Freddie in the mouth when he asks me to fetch stuff."

Gemma lets out a little laugh and she starts to relax. *Mission accomplished!* Even though TS isn't joking. While she had originally offered to make breakfast, the family's personal chef insisted he cook instead. When TS saw the spread that first morning—fruit artfully displayed, freshly baked scones, yogurt, granola, eggs, sausages—she knew anything she did would be inferior. Instead, Freddie would often ask TS to "fetch" things for him. He'd actually used the word *fetch*. "TS, make yourself useful and fetch Freddie another tea." And yep, Freddie refers to himself in the third person.

TS can think of a few other choice words to describe Freddie.

"Oh, I know the feeling." Gemma smiles that bright smile at TS. Maybe bonding over Gemma's horrific cousins will bring Gemma back to Team TS. "At least Cressida isn't that bad."

Seriously? TS literally bites her tongue. She thinks Cressida might be worse. She's constantly trying to make TS jealous. TS went for a run instead of attending some boring gallery opening with Cressida and Gemma. When they returned, Cressida kept mentioning how happy Gemma was to see Zara again.

Whatever. At least they're now two hours away from London and that drama.

"Oh!" Gemma shakes her head. "And I should've mentioned this earlier because I know it'll make you happy: My parents are here! Come on, they're dying to see you!"

For the first time in two weeks, TS is excited about being around Gemma's family, as Gemma's parents are nice and normal. They are firmly on Team TS. Now, if Freddie and Cressida could get lost in the woods . . .

A new start . . . TS says to herself as she descends the grand staircase with Gemma's hand in hers, voices drifting up from the reception hall. When she turns the corner, TS can see dozens of people—the men in tuxes, the woman in formal dresses. TS stops cold.

She is *so* out of her element.

"There she is!" Gemma's dad walks over, dressed in a tux. He has the same green eyes as Gemma. He embraces TS warmly. "It's so good to see you! How are you holding up? I see you're still in one piece."

"I'm really glad you're here." TS feels herself relax slightly, since she now has another person on her side.

"TS!" Gemma's mom comes over in a black beaded dress, her brown hair—the color Gemma's now is—is pulled back by large pearl combs. "Are you totally bored by all this? Do you regret coming?"

"Not at all." TS can't tell if that's a lie or not. She wants to be here with Gemma, but after watching Tay's videos on repeat, she wishes she were back in Indiana with the Taylors.

This is all so . . . foreign. In every sense of the word.

"Well, we're so happy you're here," her mom replies. She then waves at an older woman with white hair swept up in an intricate bun, wearing an elegant, beaded cream dress. "Mother! You must meet TS!"

Here we go. TS straightens her back, lifts her chin. She plasters on a smile as the woman comes over. Guests move out of her way like a parting of the sea. Her pale eyes are focused on TS, her face neutral. TS can't tell what she's thinking.

"Gran!" Gemma gives her a cautious hug—maybe she's worried she'll mess up her dress. Her grandmother is also very thin and looks a bit fragile, but still tough. Huh. TS can't get a read on her. "This is Taylor."

Gemma's grandmother steps in front of TS, appraising her.

"Hello, thank you for having me." TS's body has never betrayed her before—it knows when to pivot, kick, and fake, but it's at this moment when it decides to go rogue: She dips her head down and, yep, she's curtsying.

There's a polite chuckle from Gemma's dad while Gemma's eyes are wide as she recoils slightly.

"Oh, um." TS stands back up. "I . . ." *am an idiot*, she wants to finish. Instead, she smiles even wider. "You have a lovely home."

Home? HOME! This isn't some cozy two-bedroom house, it's a castle! Just stop talking.

Her grandmother gives her a nod, not a smidge of warmth on her face. When TS thinks of grandmothers, she thinks of her own: baking cookies, cheering for her on the field, big family dinners. Gemma's grandmother . . . is, ah, *different*. (Among the many things TS's family, including her grandmothers, have taught her is to be polite.)

"Thank you." Her voice is the kind that commands attention. "I must get back to my distinguished guests."

"Oh, of—" TS starts to reply, but she's already turned her back.

TS can't believe she was going to give this woman a Hot Wheels car.

"She can be a bit intimidating," Gemma's dad says with a laugh. "You'll get used to it."

"I'm so . . ." Humiliated? Embarrassed? Flustered?

Gemma takes her by the hand. "It's okay." But by the grimace on Gemma's face, TS can tell it isn't.

Gemma had told TS she could never embarrass her, but then Gemma asked her to change her clothes. She openly cringed at TS's interaction with her grandmother.

Before TS can recover from that horrifying experience, Cressida comes gliding over in a strapless black silk minidress, walking on impossibly high heels like they're nothing. "Aunt and Uncle! We're so glad to have you back on the right side of the pond!" She stops and looks TS up and down. "Oh, Gemma, you're so generous, donating your dress."

And Gemma thinks Cressida isn't that bad?

Gemma goes to open her mouth, but Cressida continues, "We have a surprise for our Gemma." The mischievous glint in Cressida's eyes makes TS nervous.

She hasn't even been downstairs for ten minutes and her emotions are all over the place, something else TS isn't used to.

"What surprise?" Gemma asks as she takes a piece of shrimp from a passing waiter.

"Look who's here!" Cressida waves her arms to the side and TS's instincts were right.

It's a bad surprise.

"Zara?" Gemma says. "Oh! Um . . ." Gemma sneaks a glance at TS. "Hi! Come meet TS!"

TS only saw Zara from afar that first night, but as she approaches, TS can see how absolutely gorgeous and glamorous she is. She's wearing a bright yellow satin empire-waist dress. Her dark brown skin is flawless. Her makeup looks professionally done while TS is in a borrowed dress and thought she was being fancy by wearing her hair down. There's not a splotch of makeup on her.

"TS!" Zara smiles, and TS can only stare at her impossibly straight, white teeth. "I've heard so much about you." She does that double-kiss thing on the cheeks that TS always fumbles. Is she supposed to air-kiss or kiss-kiss? She doesn't know so she sort of just awkwardly touches her cheek to Zara's.

At least it's better than a curtsy.

"Hi." TS can't tell if her voice has become small, or if this room is too loud. People are talking and there's clinking of glasses and plates being passed around. TS never has a problem focusing during the chaos of the soccer field, but here she's been thrown off her game.

Literally.

Cressida lets out a laugh, even though nobody's made a joke. "We were able to convince Zara to play in the match tomorrow."

"Really?" Gemma lights up.

Okay, there's a lot that TS could be jealous of when it comes to Zara: her beauty, the way she effortlessly seems to fit in, the way Gemma's family adores her. However, TS has also heard about what a good soccer player Zara is. *That* is a bitter pill to swallow.

"Yes, but your team is full so she'll be playing for the Lions." Cressida smiles as she takes a sip from a crystal champagne flute.

"Oh, well, it's all for charity!" Gemma's mom says cheerfully, but her eyes dart to TS.

"Yes." Zara's gaze settles on TS. "I can't wait."

The soccer game was something TS had been looking forward to. It's part of a big garden weekend, whatever that means. Cressida is participating in some dressage event tomorrow afternoon, but in the morning there's a charity soccer match: the Lions vs. the Roses. TS can't wait to get on a field. And, yeah, it would be nice to show off to Freddie and Cressida. And Gemma's grandmother, although TS bets she's not a big sports fan.

A bell rings and a waiter announces it's time to take their seats. It goes without saying that TS has never been at a dinner this fancy. The only time she's ever been anywhere with name cards was at a wedding. As TS looks at the table that seats well over forty people, she can only hope she'll be lucky enough to be seated next to Gemma.

Zara has taken Gemma by the elbow to find their names, and her parents have been stopped by someone they know, which leaves TS to find her place by herself. She looks at different names—lots of *Lords* and *Ladies*—and then TS finally spots her place . . . right next to Freddie's. So much for luck. As she sits down, she notices how far away the people seated on the opposite side of the table are. So she'll have to make do talking to Freddie or the elderly man to her right.

TS doesn't know why she's even remotely surprised she's seated as far away as possible from Gemma, who, of course, is next to Zara.

TS can't help but wonder if Cressida had anything to do with the seating arrangement.

Freddie sits down and launches into a heated debate with the person on his left, leaving TS to study the evening's menu, which is filled with words like pâté, foam, confit, and consommé.

TS really wants a cheeseburger.

"Freddie!" Gemma's dad walks over and plants his hand on Freddie's shoulder. "Switch seats with me so I can keep TS company."

TS has never been so grateful to another human as she is in this moment to Mr. Walker.

"Oh, well . . ." Freddie sniffs. "The thing is, I'm in a rather important—"

"Now." Mr. Walker pulls out the seat. Freddie stares at him for a moment. TS doubts people usually tell Freddie what to do. "Unless you'd like me to tell your mother about the—"

Freddie stands up quickly. "Yes, well . . ." He gives TS a quick nod.

Gemma's dad sits down with a headshake. "I don't have anything on him, but a guy like Freddie likely has a lot he's hiding."

"Thanks." There's an ache in the back of TS's throat that surprises her. Maybe it's because it's the first kind gesture she's received since she arrived.

"No, thank *you*. These affairs can be quite painful." He then opens his dinner jacket and shows TS that he has a stash of candy bars hidden in an inside pocket.

"I mean this with every fiber of my being, Mr. Walker, you are my favorite person in the history of humanity."

He lets out a delighted laugh. "TS, I know how hard it can be, being introduced to the family. They don't like outsiders. I come from up north, had a Geordie accent, and they didn't think I was good enough for Charlotte. I can only imagine how they're treating an American."

TS thinks back to her conversation with Gemma when they first landed. "Do you think they also don't like me because I'm gay?"

Mr. Walker tilts his head. "I'd certainly hope that isn't the case, and if anybody—and I mean *anybody*—says or does anything to make you think that, you tell me right away, yeah? Because you make my daughter happy and that's all that matters. I only wish we had time for you to meet my family, they'd welcome you with open arms.

Charlotte's, on the other hand, you'll have to earn your place, which you will. Especially when you wipe the floor with them tomorrow on the pitch."

TS nods along. She can't wait for the game and to show them all what she's truly made of.

This is my turf. As TS hits the soccer field the following morning, with Gemma beside her, she realizes how much she needed this. It's just the boost TS needs.

While the field is the same, everything else is very different. The sidelines are filled with spectators dressed in suits and floral maxi dresses, and some of the women are wearing hats or fascinators. Uniformed waiters pass around food and drinks.

Gemma jogs with her knees up. "I'm so out of practice."

TS stays silent as she takes the ball and starts tapping it with her feet. She doesn't want to remind Gemma that she could've gone with her to the park instead of choosing her cousins or aunt time and time again.

Today is the chance for TS to prove herself. The last thing she needs is to let anything get in her head.

A whistle comes from their captain, a guy named Charlie who was introduced as, and TS is not kidding, Charles Anderson Covington the Third, Earl of Wadsforth. TS can only guess from his uninspired drills and plays that he got the role of captain because of his title.

"All right, chaps!" Charlie gestures for their team of twenty to gather around. Gemma and TS are the youngest players while the rest are in their twenties and thirties. They're all dressed in white uniforms with a rose emblem on their sleeve. "Now, we know this is all in good fun, just like my time at Oxford." Charlie has made sure to mention Oxford as much as being an earl. "We are the friendly warm-up for the dressage event later on, but that doesn't mean we're going to let the Lions win. I have my pride . . . and a pretty purse on this event. Don't make me embarrassed to go to the club. Har-har."

Now, Charlie doesn't actually laugh. He literally says, "Har-har."

As Charlie goes through the starting lineup, TS is confused about why her name isn't mentioned.

"Chuck, TS has to start, we went over this," Gemma says, her eyebrows knitted.

"Gems, we can't have an American play. They know nothing about footie. They don't even call it *football*." Charlie scrunches up his nose. "'Soccer,'" he says with a scoff.

That's it. TS will not be talked down to on a soccer field. She's so sick of this.

"Okay, first," TS begins, "the American can hear you. Second, the term *soccer* comes from here. You all stopped using it in the 1970s because it *seemed* Americanized, even though *you* were the ones who coined the word." Again, TS has done her research, and wow, does it feel good to drop some knowledge on these snobs. "But most importantly, I can tell you that I'm good. Very good. If you want to lose because you've got something stuck up your—" She clears her throat. "Well, that'll be on you."

The group is quiet, probably not used to a loud Yank putting them in their place. Even though TS hopes she isn't ruining things with Gemma's family by being . . . TS. And totally right. For the first time since she landed in England, TS stands tall. She feels confident because she knows she's good. She got to where she is on the team back home because of hard work. It has nothing to do with titles or money.

There's also a growing part of TS that sort of doesn't care about making a good impression on Gemma's family anymore. If they don't like her, that's on them.

"Charlie, she can have my spot, you know Mummy is forcing me to play," a tall, thin ginger guy says. He looks about twenty years too old to be using the term *Mummy*, but whatever.

Charlie sighs. "Fine. But do try to keep up."

"Funny," TS says as she does a few quick kicks of the ball, "that's exactly what I was going to say to you."

Charlie's mouth drops open for a moment before he goes back to his boring plays. Gemma nudges TS and they have an unspoken conversation about the game, which boils down to them both realizing that they're just going to have to dominate and score because the rest of the team is useless.

Okay, sure, it's for charity and all, but that doesn't mean TS doesn't want to win.

TS and Gemma take to the field and TS can't help but smile. *This* is how she envisioned her summer, hitting the field with her girlfriend. It shouldn't be too much to ask. The icing on the cake will be when they win and she shows all the pretentious people watching that she belongs here with Gemma.

TS lines up for the start and spies Zara in a Lions jersey. TS gives her a nod and a cocky smile spreads on Zara's face.

"Just so you know," Zara begins, "Gems said I'm the best she's ever seen."

TS nods along. "Well, that was before she met me."

Zara's big brown eyes go wide, and there's a flash of respect on her face before it shifts into game mode: focused eyes, gritted teeth, and a don't-mess-with-me attitude.

The match starts and TS is surprised by how fast and competent most of the players are. There's a guy on the opposite team who looks like he belongs on an American football field—tall, muscular, built like a tank.

TS gets the ball and sprints toward the goal, when the giant comes and bumps into her so hard she goes skidding on the grass. She waits for a flag from the ref, but nothing.

"Oi, watch it, meathead!" Gemma screams at the guy before holding her hand out to help TS up. "You okay?"

"Guess I'll just have to be faster," TS replies, but grimaces at the sting on her knee.

"Yeah, well, the ref is blind!" Gemma lets her voice echo on the field.

They rush back on defense as Zara has the ball. She's good. Annoyingly so. Her feet are fast. TS tries to get the ball away from her, but she's too quick and kicks the ball to a teammate, who easily scores.

"Told ya." Zara bumps TS's shoulder harshly as she passes.

While TS is irritated that the Lions have scored—with an assist from Zara, no less—it's exactly what she needs to shift to another gear. She gets into her zone. The one where she pushes everything else out of her mind except the ball. It all fades away. The family drama. The shouting from the other players. The judgmental looks from the spectators.

TS is able to get in possession of the ball again and breaks away. She spies Gemma up ahead, near the goal, in position to score.

TS goes to—SLAM!

TS blinks for a moment. She realizes she's back on the grass. She's been knocked down. Again. Zara smiles from above TS for a split second before taking off with the ball. She can hear Gemma protesting that there isn't a flag, but it's becoming clear to TS that the referee isn't playing fair. Neither are the Lions.

Don't let it get to you, she reminds herself.

Then again, two can play that way.

TS gets up, her white uniform now grass stained and covered in dirt. Zara is up ahead in position to score. TS takes off. Zara shows off a few dribbling skills, then pulls her leg back to kick and TS gets the ball away from her, making the slightest bit of contact with Zara, who falls back on the ground in such an exaggerated manner she should be given an Oscar for her performance.

The ref blows a whistle. Oh, so *now* he's paying attention. Of all the things TS can anticipate on the field, what happens next isn't one of them.

The ref gives TS a red card.

"Are you kidding me?" TS says, getting in the ref's face. "I barely touched her, but you're more than fine for me to be pushed around?"

Gemma runs up behind TS. "Come on, Phils, what are you on about?"

The ref—without deigning to look at TS—motions for her to leave the game.

So that's how it's going to be. It's so unfair. TS wants to protest some more, but the field is quiet. Nobody else on her team is standing up for her. The spectators all look horrified that someone is being asked to leave the field. Where were they when TS got knocked down? *Twice.*

"It's fine," TS relents, not wanting to make a scene. Well, more than she already has. She walks to the side of the field and makes eye contact with Zara, who gives her a smug wink.

TS takes a long sip of water before spraying some of it on her blood-stained knee.

She can feel anger bubbling up inside her, but she tries to push it down. She doesn't want anybody—Zara, the other players, Cressida, Freddie—to know that they have gotten to her. *That* is a battle she will not lose.

As if she hasn't had to put up with enough, Freddie approaches her. He's wearing a blue-and-white-checkered suit, a cocktail in his hand. "Good thing I didn't put money on your team. I do so hate to lose."

So does TS, but she simply nods. She doesn't trust what will come out of her mouth if she speaks. Especially to Freddie.

Freddie sighs dramatically. "In the storied history of this weekend, nobody has ever been asked to leave a match. It's unsportsmanlike. To put it frankly, it's the type of behavior that's beneath this family."

TS clenches her water bottle tightly.

Do not let him win. Do not give him what he wants.

She goes off to the side to refill her water bottle. It's an excuse to distance herself from Freddie. But that doesn't stop the questions that start swirling around in her head.

Why is she here?

Is she really going to be able to put up with this for two more weeks?

Does she even want to make this effort for Gemma anymore?

If TS is so important to Gemma, wouldn't *she* be making more of an effort?

Why didn't Gemma warn her about her family?

Is Gemma embarrassed by her?

TS watches Zara, with her speed, looks, and money—maybe Gemma is better off with Zara. Is TS just second best? Is Gemma only with TS because Zara lives in England?

There are moments with Gemma, like when they're dancing, just the two of them, or when Gemma cuddles up to TS on the couch, that TS wonders how she got so lucky to be with such an amazing, talented, gorgeous girl.

It's not as if TS doesn't have confidence, she knows she's an outstanding soccer player. *However*, being in a relationship is new to her. So of course she has those insecure feelings. Sometimes when she looks at Gemma, *Why me?* will whisper in the back of TS's mind. But since being in England, that whisper has turned into a shout. Especially since TS feels like she doesn't really know Gemma at all. What with the gowns, and events, and . . . this life.

A whistle blows, causing TS to snap her attention back to the field. The match ends and, no surprise, the Lions win, 3–2.

Gemma comes over with a frown on her face. "That was ridiculous and so unfair. Are you okay? How's your knee?"

"I'm fine," TS lies. It's something she's been doing more and more lately. Obviously, she is not fine.

"You sure? Can I get you anything?" Gemma looks down at TS's bloody knee.

"A plane ticket home." It just slips out. But when TS thinks about it, all she wants is to go home and be with the people who accept her for who she is.

"Shaw . . ." Gemma's eyes dart around the spectators who have come out on the field to congratulate the teams. She drops her voice. "Can you please not start right now?"

"Are you kidding me?" TS replies loudly. TS also doesn't want to "start," but she's sort of done putting up with this crap. "Or are you just worried about me embarrassing you? Again."

"I'm not . . ." Gemma's face falls. She takes a step closer to TS. "I'm so sorry. I am, but I also feel like all I'm doing is apologizing to you.

I really thought it would be better with my parents here. I know you don't want to . . . Shaw, I want you here."

"Really? Because you could've fooled me. All I've been doing since I arrived is question why I'm here. So I'm going to need you to start acting like you want me with you and stop running the second one of your cousins snaps their fingers." TS's voice feels tight. She likes to be in control of herself on a soccer field, but she can't hold it in anymore. "I came here to be with *you*."

Gemma opens her mouth for a second, then closes it. TS can see how torn she is. Yeah, families can be complicated, but Gemma's feelings for TS should be clear.

"Okay, I see your point," Gemma starts, but her face remains hard. "However, you could've also made an effort. You choose to do pretty much anything else but come with us to events. I wanted you there with me, but you decided to go off on your own."

TS wants to protest but also knows Gemma is right. TS didn't want to go to the museums and art exhibits. It didn't occur to her that by saying no to Gemma's aunt and cousins, she was also saying no to Gemma.

What now? TS doesn't like to give in easily, but she also doesn't have home field advantage.

TS guesses it comes down to whether being with Gemma is more important than her pride.

And she does want to be with Gemma. This is just a little bump. They'll get through it.

"So . . ." TS kicks the grass. "Is this when we, like, shake hands and agree to a draw?"

Gemma's face opens back up. Her eyes are focused on a very dirty and sweaty TS. "I can think of something better than a handshake."

Then Gemma cups TS's face in her hands. She pulls TS in for a kiss, in front of the swarm of British high society.

TS tries to relax into it. She tries to push out all the questions and doubts that this trip has brought up.

There's a lot TS can do on a soccer field. Try as she might, even with the feel of Gemma's lips on hers, there's no convincing TS that things will be magically better now.

Our Chat (The Taylors Version)

TAYLOR🐝: Wish me and my team luck, we've got our first games today

TAY🎉: TEAM RED, ALWAYS AND FOREVER

TS ⚽: You got some fighters on your team

TAYLOR🐝: They were OBSESSED with you after your pep talk

TAYLOR🐝: They also think you're a princess with that CASTLE in the background!!!

TS ⚽: Princess? I prefer Her Royal Awesomeness

TEFFY📚: Queen of the Pitch.

TS ⚽: Look at Teffy breaking out the British terms

TEFFY📚: Want to make sure you'll still understand us, mate.

TAY🎉: DO I ASK?

TAY🎉: I GOTTA ASK, TAYLOR!!! HOW ARE THINGS WITH . . . the smallest man who ever lived?

TS ⚽: I'll be on the first plane home if he even thinks of messing with you

TAYLOR🐝: Who? 😉

TAYLOR🐝: Doing my best to ignore him

TAYLOR🐝: Which really, really annoys him

TAYLOR🐝: I've learned my lesson, I am never dating again

TS ⚽: While I agree boys are so ick, I don't know, Taylor, never say never

EIGHT

We Are Never Ever Getting Back Together

This means war.

"Are we ready?" Taylor asks the ten girls in her bunk Sunday morning at breakfast. They all nod, and a few rub their tired eyes. Not the overenthusiastic response Taylor was hoping for. "Okay, make sure you eat a good breakfast. We're going to need all our energy to win—GO, RED!" Taylor puts her fist in the air as ten pairs of eyes stare blankly up at her.

Would it be *that* wrong to spike their orange juice with coffee?

"Is TS coming today?" Tiana asks, her blond hair sticking up in every direction.

"She's in En-ga-land," Aria replies with a yawn.

There was no way Taylor was not going to tell her campers all about the Taylors. Like she could go a day, let alone a week, without mentioning her amazing best friends. TS even gave them a pre–Color War pep talk yesterday over video.

"Taylor?" Hazel shoots her hand up. "I need to go to the bathroom."

"Okay, we've gone over this, Hazel, you don't need to ask

permission. You know where the bathrooms are, so you can go. I'm going to fuel up and then we're going to take on the day!" Taylor claps her hands a few times, hoping it'll wake up her team.

It doesn't.

Taylor makes her way to the food line. Mia wasn't wrong about the food at Whispering Pines. The dining hall is in a large wooden cabin the size of the gym back at Harrison High. On one end is the line for hot food. Then, there are tables with baked goods and fresh fruit. There's a table with infused water and juices. It's absolutely ridiculous.

And Taylor is loving every bite.

Plus, Taylor knows she's going to need a lot of energy for today. She grabs two bagels, carbo-loading and all that. She sits down next to Mia, whose energy is matching their team's. She's yawning as she stirs her tea.

"What is going on with everybody today?" Taylor asks. "Am I the only competitive person on the Red Team? Because these other teams are going down."

Mia takes a long sip of tea. "Yeah, it's just this weather . . ."

It's been gray, miserable, and storming the last couple days, so the campers have been a bit stir-crazy, even though they've done arts and crafts, had a lip-sync contest, and made their own music video. They've been kept entertained, but they haven't been able to run around outside during a thunderstorm. While Taylor isn't very sporty, she's in charge of all the outside activities for the Red Team. She's excited to finally have something to do today. To be in charge.

Plus, it makes ignoring Hunter a lot easier if she's occupied.

Besides the whole being around her toxic ex thing, Taylor loves working at Whispering Pines. She excels at organizing events and people. The campers are all sweet. She adores Mia, who is funny and an amazing artist and becoming a good friend.

"What's up, Team Red?" Noah sits down with Caleb. "Re-eh-eh-eh-ed, Re-eh-eh-ed," they sing. Noah is a fellow Swiftie, so they and Taylor have spent each night after dinner doing performances for their bunks. Needless to say, the Red Team is already winning in terms of talent and taste.

How could they *not*, with her leading them?

"Please tell me *you're* at least excited about today?" Taylor asks Noah.

"Define the word *excited* when it comes to physical activity." Noah's lips curl in displeasure.

"I'm excited!" Caleb replies as he drops his tray down. This isn't a surprise. Caleb gets excited about pretty much everything, especially in the cafeteria. Taylor has never seen a human being eat as much as Caleb, and she's got three older brothers. "I got you a roll, Taylor, since they were fresh out of the oven." Caleb hands Taylor the most delicious-looking cinnamon roll to ever exist—it's practically the size of her head and is oozing icing.

"Oh, yum!!!" Taylor takes a bite and her eyes nearly roll back in her head. "This is *exactly* what I need. Carbs and sugar. Thanks, Caleb."

"That's so sweet of you, Caleb." Mia bats her eyelashes at Caleb, whose cheeks are getting even redder, practically matching his auburn hair.

"Well, they weren't vegan, which is why I didn't get you one," Caleb says into his glass of apple juice.

"Uh-huh, suuuure." Mia gives Taylor a wink.

Ah, what is up with Mia? Is she making it seem like Caleb likes Taylor? Because he's nice and sweet, but it's just a cinnamon roll. And Taylor wasn't kidding. She's got much more important things to think about than boys. She's learned her lesson.

"Hey, Taylor!" Jae, Liam's little sister, comes over to give her a hug.

"Morning, squirt." Even though Jae is on the Green Team, Taylor promised Teffy she'd look out for her. She only sees her at mealtimes since Jae's staying in the twelve-and-up lodges. "You come for your daily joke?"

"And here we go . . ." Noah shakes their head. "It was bad enough when it was this one doing the jokes, and now . . ."

"Gotta give the people what they want!" Taylor says.

"Exactly!" Caleb reaches across the table to give Taylor a fist bump. "Do you want to go first?"

"My dad sent me a good one this morning." Taylor made the mistake of texting her dad Caleb's joke that first day and now he's trying to one-up him in terms of dad joke cringe.

And honestly, it's a tie on who is winning. But is that *really* winning?

"Hit me!" Caleb claps his hands together as Jae giggles in anticipation, her eyes, the same dark color she shares with Liam, wide.

"Where do sheep go on vacation?" Taylor begins.

Caleb's entire face is lit up. He gestures to Jae, who replies, "I don't know, *where do sheep go on vacation?*"

Taylor leans forward, trying to not laugh. It's not like it's funny, but she likes how excited both Caleb and Jae are. Caleb really is a big kid. "The *Baaaaa*-hamas."

Okay, it is sort of funny.

Jae lets out a snort while Caleb starts laughing. *A lot*. Mia and Noah both have their heads in their hands.

"*Baaaaa*-hamas!" Jae repeats with a giggle. "I'm going to tell my table! Bye, Taylor!" Jae skips over to the other side of the hall, her slicked-back ponytail swishing in her wake.

Caleb gives Taylor a round of applause and she gives a little bow.

"Come on, Noah, it's funny!" Caleb jostles Noah by the shoulder.

"Seriously? You have shocking low expectations on what counts as humor, Caleb. Taylor, on the other hand, I expected far better." Noah shakes their head.

"Hey! I'm just the messenger!" Taylor defends herself, even though she looks forward to their morning routine of swapping jokes. Plus, the campers are loving it. She sort of gets why her dad likes telling them. Not that she'd ever admit that to him.

"Make fun all you want, but you'll thank my amazing and witty sense of humor when you hear the team names I've come up with." Caleb takes a huge bite of cinnamon roll, a smile on his face.

"Oh, I didn't realize we needed team names." Taylor just assumed they were the Red Team.

"We don't," Noah says with a dramatic sigh. "But are you shocked this one uses any excuse to be punny?"

"*Excuse me* for wanting to up the excitement!" Caleb throws a napkin at Noah. "We already know the Hot Tamales are gonna win!"

"Hot Tamales?" Mia replies with a snort. "Seriously?"

Caleb frowns for a second, before lighting back up. "Okay, what about the Spicy Peppers? Or the Ginger Snaps? Or the Firecrackers? Or the Scarlet Scamps?"

"Where do you even get these names from?" Noah steals a strawberry off Caleb's plate.

"Hey, you grow up a ginger, you get a lot of nicknames, whether you want them or not." Caleb ruffles his hair. "*Blaze McHotty* has decided to embrace the red."

"Blaze Mc—" Noah starts to say, but they're laughing too hard to finish.

Caleb ignores Noah and turns to Taylor, a hopeful expression on his face. "What do you think, Taylor?"

Taylor doesn't want to disappoint him, but they should be discussing strategy, not nicknames.

"Um, can we focus, please? It doesn't really matter what we call ourselves if our team isn't in the fighting spirit!" Taylor doesn't like to lose. She got that from TS. Why bother doing something if you aren't going to do your best? "We need to get them ready to take on the day!"

"That's what I like to hear." Hunter approaches the table. Taylor keeps her eyes glued to her plate. "Checking in that we're all set for today, but I see Taylor has it covered. Right, Taylor?"

Hunter has been doing this all week. Asking her a direct question so she's forced to speak to him. Because that's the only way she would deign to acknowledge his existence.

She gives a single nod.

"Are we really supposed to do the race and tug-of-war in the wet grass? It's sooooo muddy out there." Mia looks out the window with a frown.

"Well, I see one of you is prepared." Even though she's not looking, Taylor can tell Hunter's gaze has settled on her legs, where she's wearing her rain boots. "I like the confidence of the white shorts, Tay."

"It's Taylor," she replies, then winces. He did that to get her to talk. And it worked.

Again, Taylor doesn't like to lose, and she's sure not going to let Hunter Brown get to her. Any more than he already has. That was so last week.

Taylor stands, her focus on Mia, even though she can feel Hunter's gaze. "I'm going to get the team ready. See you all outside in ten?"

"I'll go with you." Mia gets up and takes her tray as the two walk to the other side of the dining hall. "You okay?" she whispers as they put their trays away.

"Yeah, he just gives me the creeps." Taylor shudders for a second. She had told Mia all about the disaster that was dating Hunter.

After dropping off their trays, Taylor and Mia head outside to the large field out front, where the first round of games will take place for the Color War. Today is pretty standard: sack races and tug-of-war.

"Ugh." Mia picks her feet up, which are covered in mud. "This is gross."

"Winning is never easy," Taylor replies in such a TS fashion, she's sort of impressed with herself.

The campers start filing out of the dining hall and get into their groups. Taylor gives her team another pep talk before they start with tug-of-war. "Remember, plant your feet and lean back," she repeats the pointers TS gave them. "It's all in the legs."

"Hey!" Caleb comes over with his and Noah's group of boys. "Okay, everybody, listen to Taylor."

"That's great advice. Evergreen, really." Taylor smiles at the rows of campers hanging on her every word as she demonstrates by taking the rope and digging her feet deep in the mud. She bends down a bit.

"Yeah, see how she's keeping her center of gravity low?" Caleb squats down. He gives her a nod.

The campers get low with them. They are so going to win.

"Looks like you got them ready to go, Taylor." Hunter approaches with that cocky smirk that makes Taylor want to scream.

"And Caleb," Taylor adds, not wanting Hunter's attention on her ever again.

"Just following Taylor's lead!" Caleb replies with a smile.

Unfortunately, Hunter's gaze stays on Taylor. "Well, I think we should have a quick practice with our team, make sure we've got their form down."

Taylor doesn't want to admit that it's not a horrible suggestion. Instead, she shrugs as Hunter divides the team into two separate groups. He starts giving them directions while Taylor studies her chipped red nails.

"I think it's best for you and me to be in the front for this practice round, Taylor." Hunter grabs the middle of the rope and hands it to her. "Show them how it's done."

Which means she'll be forced to be face-to-face with Hunter.

It used to be a face she couldn't wait to see, and now . . . Well, what a difference a few months can make.

"Fine." She gestures to the kids to get behind her, and they all giggle as they pick up the rope.

Hunter's group does the same. "I'd say let's see what you're made of, Taylor, but we already know, don't we?"

Ugh. Hunter is the worst. Taylor can't believe she ever fell for a single word that came out of his mouth. That she let those lips . . .

She wraps her fists around the rope. He is so going down.

There's more giggling from behind her. "Focus, team."

"Caleb, will you do the honors?" Hunter asks.

"Of course!" Caleb happily bounces to the center of the rope, which has a flag on it. There are two posts on either side of him. Taylor and her team just need to get the flag on their side and they'll win.

"One . . ." Caleb starts.

Taylor digs her rain boots into the mud and bends her knees.

"Two . . ."

She starts to lean back in anticipation of Hunter's team trying to pull her team forward.

"Three!"

Taylor yanks the rope hard, but she feels off-balance and before she realizes it, she's fallen back into the mud.

She blinks for a moment as she lies on her back on the cold, wet ground. Her mind starts racing as she puts together the pieces of what just happened. Hunter's team dropped the rope the second Caleb said three, and her team simply stood there. Letting her fall.

She looks around to see every single one of the Red Team campers giggling uncontrollably. At her. Like this is *so* funny. Only Mia, Noah, and Caleb are as confused as Taylor.

"Hunter made us!" Hazel says with a laugh. Covering her face.

"What?" Taylor attempts to stand up but slips. Her white jean shorts are caked in mud. Her legs and hands are muddy. She's a complete mess and it's all Hunter's fault. "Are you serious?"

Taylor is furious and she can't stand up because her boots have dug down so deep in the mud. It might be easier for her to take her feet out.

Well, that's it. There *is* something more humiliating than having fallen for Hunter Brown. Taylor is literally crawling around in the mud while being laughed at by a bunch of ten-year-olds.

"Here, let me help." Caleb holds out his hand, but Taylor ignores him. She can get up on her own. Besides, she's already a dirty disaster, so she kneels—her knees squishing in the wet soil—to finally get her balance on one foot and then slowly the other.

The Red Team campers are finding all of this *hilarious.* Hunter looks so smug, she wants to wipe the smile off his face.

Once she's securely on both feet, Taylor stomps over to Hunter. "Do you think this is funny? Humiliating a counselor is real mature, Hunter. I can't wait to tell Mr. Mason about how you treat your subordinates, even though it's not shocking to me, you total son of a—"

"Okay!" Mia interrupts, standing between Taylor and Hunter. "The children," she says under her breath.

"Well, I've got to go clean up now." Taylor turns on her heel and almost slips again, but steadies herself. Taylor walks to her cabin with her shoulders pulled back. She will not let anybody know how utterly humiliated she feels. Instead, she waits until she's alone in a shower.

Then, as the hot water starts to come down, she lets the tears fall.

Taylor had thought she was done crying over Hunter Brown.

She was wrong.

Taylor missed the first few games. She used cleaning up as an excuse, but she also didn't want to face her team. Face Hunter. She's still fuming. Although, Taylor can't imagine having any feeling other than anger when it comes to Hunter Brown.

"Hey." Mia knocks on the front door before coming in. "We came in second overall, so it's a good start. How are you doing?"

"Fine," Taylor says, keeping her voice calm. "Although, I threw out my shorts. That's what I get for being confident and wearing white." She tries to play it off lightly.

"Well, I need you to come outside for a second." Mia gestures to the front door of the cabin. "Please."

Taylor realizes she has to eventually face the world, and the longer she takes, the worse it'll be. She knows she'll have to smile and laugh and pretend that it was *just so funny*.

She walks out to find the entire Red Team—all a bit dirty from the day's activities—holding up handmade signs: WE'RE SORRY, WE LOVE TAYLOR, TAYLOR IS THE BEST.

"One, two, three," Noah begins, and then in unison the campers say, "We're sorry, Taylor. We love you."

Taylor can't help but be touched. She knows it's not their fault. They're just kids who were following orders. They were just doing what Hunter told them to do. She'd made that mistake before.

"Aww, thanks, everyone." Her cabin is the first in the rush to hug her, but before Taylor knows it, all twenty kids have come in for an epic group hug.

Which does make it a bit better. Knowing that the team appreciates her. That *they* didn't mean to embarrass her.

Then they part and she sees Hunter standing there with flowers. He looks down at the ground, like he's so ashamed of what he's done, but Taylor knows it's all for show.

"Hey, Taylor," Hunter says in a quiet voice. "That wasn't nice of me and I'm so sorry."

Taylor spies Mr. Mason off to the side. It figures. Hunter was probably forced to apologize.

No way is Taylor going to let Hunter off that easily.

"I don't think a senior counselor should be encouraging bullying," Taylor says loudly, because that's what that was. It was Hunter's way of putting Taylor in her place.

Hunter leans in while Taylor takes a huge step back. "Can we please talk?"

Taylor stays frozen. No way does she want to talk to him. To be forced to listen to more of his lies.

"Just . . ." Hunter starts, but it seems like he's at a loss for words, which would be a first.

The kids start to head back into the cabin to clean up before lunch, which leaves Taylor and Hunter alone.

"Okay, Tay," Hunter starts.

"It's Taylor," she snaps. He never called her Tay when they were together. Babe, sure, but not Tay. She doesn't know why he's doing it now. Probably to get a rise out of her. Which works. "Actually, it's Miss Perez, because you're nasty."

"Taylor." Hunter's face scrunches up like he really is sorry and for a moment, her treacherous heart flutters.

No. She is not going back there. Yeah, Hunter is gorgeous and he's looking at her in a way that she used to covet, but not any longer.

Hunter holds his hands up in surrender. "I'm really sorry, truly. I crossed a line."

"Well, that's certainly something you know a lot about."

Hunter hangs his head. "I deserve that."

"You do." Taylor is not going to let him weasel his way out of this.

"Taylor, I miss you. Don't you miss me?" Hunter's light hazel eyes blaze into her.

"Yeah . . . I miss feeling like crap for wanting to do things that don't revolve around you and making myself smaller for you."

"But, Taylor—"

"Stop! This is exhausting, Hunter, *you* are exhausting." Taylor didn't realize how much being around him had weighed on her until now. She can't imagine having to deal with this for two more weeks. "You were awful to me. You hurt me. I was just a game to you, why on earth would I ever trust another word that comes out of your mouth?"

"I made a mistake, I get that, Taylor, I do. I never met a girl like you and I've changed, you have to believe me." There's a begging tone in his voice that Taylor's never heard before.

She hates to admit it, but if he would've said this to her at the Homecoming dance, she might have listened. She had liked him so much.

So much.

"I guess it's true what they say, you don't know what you've got until it's gone." Hunter runs his fingers through his hair. It's a gesture that once made Taylor's knees weak.

"Oh, Hunter . . ." Taylor begins.

"Yeah, babe?" His face breaks into the smile that used to make Taylor's stomach toss and turn.

"You and I . . . are never, ever, *ever* getting back together." Taylor turns on her heel to walk away.

Yes, Hunter had meant the world to Taylor. But she grew up. One of them had to.

Then she turns back around to see a stunned Hunter, and flips her hair. *"Like, ever."*

Okay, perhaps Taylor still has some growing up to do, but she really, *really* enjoyed that.

Our Chat (The Taylors Version)

TAY🎉: TAYLOR!!!! QUEEN OF THE 🔥🔥🔥

TS ⚽: DYING! You're a LEGEND

TEFFY📚: Looks like he's going to think twice before messing with you again.

TAYLOR🐝: Honestly, he should've known better than to mess with a Taylor

TAY🎉: Especially THIS Taylor!

TS ⚽: I've got some snooty Brits I'd like you to have a word with 🙄

TAYLOR🐝: LET ME AT EM

TEFFY📚: Can you come back and help me with Liam's friends?

TAYLOR🐝: YOU MEAN YOUR BOYFRIEND LIAM

TAY🎉: YES, TEFFY'S BOYFRIEND!

TS ⚽: Teffy, you're going to have fun, Liam has excellent taste, obvs, his friends will love you

TAY🎉: And you look SO GORG in the outfit I picked out

TS ⚽: Oh, she called in the big guns

TAY🎉: THE BIGGEST!!!

TS ⚽: And loudest

TAYLOR🐝: Hey! I'm STILL HERE.

TS ⚽: Sorry. You are all impossibly loud, except Teffy. You are the quiet in the Taylors storm, have FUN tonight

TEFFY📚: Thanks, all! 🥰

NINE
Should've Said No

It's not like Teffy enjoyed keeping her relationship with Liam a secret. It was stressful. It was a lot of sneaking around. It was keeping her feelings in. While Teffy *is* the quiet in the storm that is the Taylors, she does like sharing bits and pieces . . . especially when she's as happy as she's been with Liam.

So it's a good thing that they're now out in the open.

It really is.

But . . . that means she now has to share Liam.

And she's nervous. Sure, it's just Liam having some friends over at his house. It's not like it's a big party or dance, but still. Teffy fiddles with the fluttered short sleeves of the blush sundress Tay helped her pick out. She braids her blond hair in a crown around her head. She's feeling very romantic and whimsical and *folklore*-ish. And somewhat terrified.

There's a knock on the door as Teffy's brother, Charlie, sticks his head in. "Well, look at you. Do you want me to come with, Teffy?"

"I don't need a babysitter," Teffy replies, even though she sort of does.

Charlie is good friends with Liam's brother, so he's spent about as much time over at the Yoons' as Teffy, but this feels different. It feels bigger.

"I know you don't." Charlie plops down on her bed. "But you're my little sis and I'm gonna look out for you, okay? I already told Liam I'd hunt him down if he ever did anything to hurt you."

Teffy twirls away from the mirror. "You did *what*? Please tell me you're joking."

"Hey, I want to make sure he treats you well." Charlie shrugs in that carefree way he's always had about him while Teffy hides her face in her hands.

"Thank you, I guess?" But for the record, she's horrified. Absolutely horrified.

"That's what big bros are for!" He laughs, but then he stops, carefully studying her. "Okay, what's going on?"

Teffy sits on the bed next to Charlie. "I don't know, it's just . . . Don't laugh." She shoots him a pointed look.

"Who, me?" Charlie bats his eyes in a totally innocent manner.

Oh, brother.

Teffy is embarrassed to even ask this, but Charlie's a jock. He's got lots of friends. He's popular. Teffy's about to walk into a world that's more familiar to him.

"Am I . . ." Teffy closes her eyes so she doesn't have to witness Charlie's reaction. "Cool?"

Silence. It's torture. Maybe if Teffy keeps her eyes closed, she can pretend she never asked such a cringey question.

But she can't help but wonder what people are going to think when they see gorgeous, popular football star Liam Yoon with . . . her.

Teffy slowly opens one eye to see Charlie's head tilt, his messy hair standing in every direction. "Teffy, are you being serious? Do you think any little sister of *mine* would be anything *but* cool? I mean, *come on*." Charlie leans back on Teffy's bed in that casual, confident way he has. Oh, how Teffy wishes *that* were hereditary.

Charlie studies Teffy for a beat before he sits up, his face set in a serious manner. "Okay, what's really going on? Because, Teffy, you're, like, this amazing musician and songwriter, and smart, and, like, *Taylor Swift* picked you out of how many people to get that hat? Doesn't that give you a zillion cool kid points for life?"

Charlie does have a point.

"It's just . . ."

The thing is, Teffy has always been able to be herself around Liam. It's one of the many reasons why she likes him. Liam doesn't expect Teffy to be anything more than who she is. And he *likes* her just as she is.

"Liam's friends are just . . . not . . . the kind of . . ." Teffy tries to find a polite way to say *loud and immature*.

Luckily, Charlie is never at a loss for words. "Teffy, some of Liam's friends are total tools, and that's saying something because you know the people *I* hang out with!" Charlie lets out a loud laugh, which makes Teffy relax ever so slightly. It's good to know it's not just her, but it still doesn't stop her from worrying about being with them tonight.

"And, well, there was the whole hat thing that happened with a few of them." While she should forgive John and his friends *for stealing Taylor Swift's hat* from her during a party last year, she sort of doesn't want to. It's not like Liam's friends knew what it was, they just saw Teffy wearing a hat and took it from her.

Jerks.

"And then there's Cat."

John is now dating Cat, so Teffy also has to hang out with Liam's former girlfriend as well. His cool, stylish, popular, beautiful ex.

Charlie's eyes get wide. "Oh, I forgot about that. Yeah, awk-ward!"

"That's not helping, Charlie." Teffy grimaces.

"You know I'm just kidding. And you are cool, but not the coolest member of the family. Second coolest." Charlie runs his hands through his hair.

Teffy narrows her eyes at her brother. "Yeah, it's so embarrassing for me to be second to Mom. What's it like being in last place, Charlie . . . *after* Uncle Bennie?"

Charlie puts his hand over his heart and falls to the floor with a thump. "Ouch! I've been hit! Medic! MEDIC!" He sits back up with a grin on his face. "Low blow, but I respect it." He holds out his fist to be bumped.

Teffy looks at the clock instead. It's fifteen minutes after she told Liam she'd be there. She finds herself sort of frozen.

"It's gonna be okay, Teffy. Go. Have fun. You need anything, give me a call."

"Why are you being so nice?" Teffy asks. It's not like she and Charlie have a bad relationship, he just has never been overly protective of her.

"Well . . ." Charlie starts playing with his watchband. "I'm heading to college in a few weeks. And, like . . . I might miss you."

"Aw, Charlie!" Teffy hugs her brother. She hadn't really thought what it'll mean when he goes away. Maybe because she doesn't want to think about it. It's more change.

Just like how hanging with Liam's friends is going to change her dynamic with Liam.

Teffy's phone pings and it's a message from Liam wondering where she is.

"Better not keep Loverboy waiting." Charlie rubs his fist against Teffy's hair, messing up her braid.

"Stop it!" She swats at him.

On second thought, maybe being an only child won't be so bad.

Teffy tames a few of her flyaway hairs and heads over to Liam's house, saying a quick goodbye to her parents on the way, who give her a "mm-hm." It's become their standard reply anytime she mentions seeing Liam.

As she arrives at the front door, Teffy notices there are already a few cars parked out in front. She'll be walking into a crowded basement.

"Teffy!" Mrs. Yoon answers the door. "I was wondering where you were. So happy you're here. I made the buffalo chicken dip that you like."

Teffy's stomach rumbles in happiness. "Oh, thank you!"

"Of course! Now, go! Liam's been waiting for you." Mrs. Yoon gives her a kind smile. "And you look beautiful, Teffy."

"Thanks!" Teffy blushes at the compliment. As she gets closer to the noise from the basement—shouting, cheering—she wishes she could curl up in bed with a book instead of making this effort. And it does feel like an effort.

When Teffy arrives at the bottom of the stairs, there's already a group seated around the large sectional couch. A few people are playing a racing game on the TV while the rest are busy staring at their phones. Liam looks up and jumps from the couch when he sees her.

"Tefs!" He comes over and wraps his arms around her, then gives her a quick kiss on the lips. "I was worried you weren't going to come. I had to fight off these dudes so they didn't eat all of my mom's chicken dip. Come on, I'll introduce you, even though you know everybody, but, like, now I get to introduce you as my *girlfriend*." His eyes sparkle when he says it and Teffy realizes she was silly for being so worried about tonight.

Liam takes her by the hand and has someone move over so there's room next to him on the couch. He piles up a plate of food for her as he introduces her to everybody.

"I knew something was going on!" John, the hat-stealer, says as his eyes stay glued on the TV. "Dude, you were being so secretive, and, like, now we know why."

"Yeah, well, with how you all behave, do you blame me?" Liam nudges Nick, a fellow member of the football team.

"Bro, are you embarrassed by us? *Rude.*" Nick shoves a handful of pretzels in his mouth and chews with his mouth open in an exaggerated fashion. The guys start groaning and egging him on.

While Teffy can't help but laugh. "You do realize I've seen Liam eat many times, and that's an infant's portion compared to what he normally fits in his big mouth."

Everybody in the room looks at her. "Dude, you didn't say she was funny. Nice!" John holds his hand up for Teffy to high-five, which she does.

"I see how it's going to be." Liam puts his arm around Teffy and she relaxes slightly. He then takes his finger and runs it through the dip.

"Hey!" Teffy swats his hand. "I mean, seriously, Liam."

He laughs as the group settles in. It's a lot of watching video games. Or being on their phones.

It's not that bad. Teffy was worked up for nothing. In fact, it's sort of . . . boring. Nobody is really talking. Although, she'll take boring over stressful and uncomfortable any day.

"Hello, hello!" comes a voice from the stairs.

And cue the uncomfortable.

Teffy plasters a smile on her face as Cat comes down with her friend Tiffany . . . and Hannah.

Well, there we go. Now it's also become stressful. *Fun.*

"Oh," Liam says, looking at Teffy. He then puts on a smile that matches Teffy's—in terms of being extremely strained and fake. "Hey!"

Teffy didn't realize Hannah Reed was friends with Cat and Tiffany.

Hannah is in Teffy's grade and has been nothing but a bully to her and the Taylors since fifth grade.

"Hey, Teffy!" Cat says with a wave. "Oh, I love your hair." She smiles at Teffy. A little too brightly. It's like she's making up for how awkward this is.

"Thanks, Cat. I like your outfit," Teffy replies. It's not a lie as Cat is always fashionable. She's wearing a blue tank top with blue-and-white-striped shorts. Her blond hair is in a high ponytail and she looks flawless as always.

"Hey, babe!" Cat sits on the arm of the sofa next to John. He looks away from the TV long enough to give her a kiss.

"Ah, so, um . . . do you want something to drink?" Liam offers the newcomers. "There's soda in the fridge."

"No need to get up! I know where everything is," Cat replies as she walks over to the refrigerator in the corner with Tiffany and Hannah. Of course Cat knows where everything is, since she used to be the one here sitting next to Liam instead of Teffy.

Hannah struts over like she owns the place. She's dressed almost identical to Cat but with a green satin jacket. Hannah whispers something to Tiffany that makes them both laugh. It's not really laughter, it's more like mean cackles.

"Oh, Teffy!" Cat exclaims. "The girls and I all have a group chat so we can arrange girl stuff, you know, when we need to get away from the boys." She gives Teffy a playful wink. "We also do locker decorating before the big football games and plan the dances and of course coordinate outfits. I need to get your number to add you!"

"Um, sure . . ." Teffy tries to sound excited, but she doesn't want to get away from *her* boy. And she has the Taylors for "girl stuff."

"And I'm obsessed, *obsessed* with Tay's new band," Cat adds. "It's such a vibe. Are you going to their next show? Because I have to be there."

"Yeah, they're really good." Teffy is so proud of Tay for finding her voice in Reece's band. She did have a slight pang of jealousy at how much fun Tay was having onstage, but Teffy knows she's not a performer like Tay.

"You should hear the songs Teffy writes, they're amazing," Liam states proudly. "Tay sings them sometimes."

"Oh!" Cat claps excitedly, ever the cheerleader. "Are you going to perform them with the band?"

Hannah lets out a snort. "Not likely, especially after our seventh-grade talent show, right, Teffy?"

Teffy wishes the couch could swallow her up right then and there.

"What's that?" Cat asks, blinking her impossibly long eyelashes.

"You don't remember?" Hannah begins, a calculating smile spreading on her face. She's so enjoying this moment.

"Hannah." Liam gives her a warning look, which Hannah ignores because she's the worst.

Hannah lets out a loud laugh, all the attention on her. "It was my seventh grade, but your eighth, and Teffy totally choked onstage. It was so tragic."

"I remember that!" John turns to Teffy. "That was *you*? Yikes."

"It was years ago." Liam puts his arm protectively around Teffy. "Who even cares anymore? Way to be the walking definition of a mean girl, Hannah."

"Me?" Hannah pretends to be shocked. "Did I say something wrong? I'm only filling them in on what happened. It's not like it was a secret, the *entire* school witnessed it."

"Well . . ." Cat looks at Teffy and bites her lip. "Tay's covers are killer, and I've been working on some ideas to use them in cheerleading routines for next year."

"That's so cool," Tiffany replies as she types into her phone.

"Yeah, *so cool*." Hannah smirks at Teffy.

"I'm sure Tay will love that," Teffy replies, her voice barely audible. Her throat has tightened up. Liam pulls her in closer and goes to say something to her, but she shakes her head. She's so close to crying right now, one kind word from Liam and she'll completely unravel.

"Oh!" Hannah jumps up and down. "Oh my goodness, everybody! *Everybody!*" Hannah demands the attention of the room. Heaven forbid she's not the center of everything. "My dad just texted that he got an advance copy of the new Marvel movie and is going to show it in our screening room. He's ordering pizza. Who's in?"

"Dude, yes!" John stands up.

"Whoa. Seriously?" Liam asks, his jaw practically on the floor. He's been talking about that movie since the trailer first dropped.

Guess he's no longer annoyed at Hannah.

Hannah puts her hand on her hip. “Yeah, the effects guy went to college with my dad and he’s always doing favors for him. You’ve *got* to come, it’s supposed to be sick.”

“Wow.” Liam glances at Teffy. “That’s . . . um . . .”

Teffy knows how much Liam wants to see that movie. But there’s no way Teffy is going over to Hannah’s, especially after she humiliated her. Not like Teffy has ever been invited to Hannah’s—she always makes sure to invite everybody except the Taylors.

Hannah looks on ecstatically as the basement starts to empty. Liam’s friends are racing over to her house. “You coming, Liam?” Hannah bats her eyelashes in an exaggerated fashion. “Teffy? Of course you’re invited, too.”

“Bro, let’s go!” John sprints upstairs. Leaving Liam, Teffy, and Hannah in the basement.

Hannah makes her eyes wide in this total innocent manner. “Teffy, I’m so sorry I mentioned the talent show. Liam is right, who cares about it?” She gives her a smile, but Teffy can tell it’s all a show for Liam.

“It’s okay.” Teffy returns an even bigger and faker smile. Two can play this game. “The past is in the past.” While that’s technically true, it doesn’t mean it doesn’t still sting and that Hannah didn’t know exactly what she was doing.

“Amazing! See you there!” Hannah joins the exodus to her house.

Liam rubs Teffy’s back. “Well, I’m glad that’s done because I have to see that movie!” He stands up excitedly.

Teffy remains seated. “I’m not going.”

Hannah could have an early copy of a new Taylor Swift album and she still wouldn't go to her house. She folds her arms. Teffy is staying just where she is, thank you very much.

"Oh, but I thought . . ." Liam looks genuinely confused.

"You thought what?" Teffy's voice comes out harsher than she expected. "That Hannah is actually sorry? Liam, you know she's been nothing but vile to me and the Taylors *for years*. I am *not* going over to her house." Teffy's cheeks are flushed. She can't believe she's letting Hannah Reed get to her. Again.

"Oh." Liam looks at the stairs, a grimace on his face. "Okay. Um, I guess I . . ." Liam's eyes keep darting to the stairs.

"You can go," Teffy replies, trying to keep her voice even.

But Teffy is mad. She's mad at Hannah for being Hannah. She's mad at Liam for wanting to go over to her house after everything Hannah's done. She's mad at herself for wanting to go home and get into bed and forget this evening ever happened.

"Tefs." Liam sits down next to her and places his hand on her knee. "Listen, I don't have to go. If you tell me no, then I won't."

Thing is, Teffy shouldn't *have* to tell Liam no. He should know the right thing to do. But he wants to go. He wants to see that movie. He wants to be with his friends.

"If you want to go, go. I'm really tired, Liam."

And it's true. Teffy is tired of being shy around most people. She's tired of questioning everything. She's tired of being forced to join Liam's world of loud jocks and mean girls.

“Really?” Liam looks so happy, it infuriates Teffy even more. “Are you sure?”

No.

“Yes.”

Liam jumps up from the couch. He looks so giddy. “You’re the best! I promise, no spoilers!” With that he runs up the stairs, calling after his friends.

Teffy looks at the mess in the basement and starts cleaning up. It’s too late in England to call TS. Taylor’s reception at camp is spotty, even when she has her phone. Tay is with Reece.

Teffy sits down in defeat. This is her fault. She should’ve told Liam to stay, but the fact that he wanted to go, that he wanted to be with his friends, well . . . What does that say about them?

It’s just one night, she tries to reason with herself.

But this was supposed to be the start of a new chapter for her and Liam. And if this is how it’s going to go . . . this is a story Teffy might not want to finish.

Our Chat (The Taylors Version)

TS ⚽: I hereby declare that Teffy should permanently wear the hat this summer if Hannah will be around

TAY🎉: YES!! NOT TO BE PETTY . . .

TAYLOR🐝: Please, HANNAH is the definition of petty

TEFFY📚: Liam said the movie was really bad, so . . .

TAY🎉: AND he brought Teffy flowers!

TS ⚽: Aww, so there ARE good guys out there. Who knew?

TAY🎉: ME!!! REECE!! 🥰

TAY🎉: LET'S HAVE SOME APPLAUSE FOR THE GOOD ONES!

TEFFY📚: 👏👏👏👏

TAYLOR🐝: As someone who has dealt with a really bad one, I'm going to be Team TS on this one. Sorry, dudes, you all need to stand in the corner and think about what you've done

TEN
Better Than Revenge

"So . . ." Mia says to Taylor at dinner Thursday night. She's got a mischievous look in her brown eyes as she pushes a cookie toward Taylor. "Are you really *that* full?"

Taylor leans forward. "Let me make something clear to you, Mia, I am never, ever turning down a cookie. *Like, ever!*"

The Red counselors erupt in laughter. Taylor has rightfully earned legendary status for her handling of the whole mud situation. And to Hunter's credit, something Taylor is very hesitant to give, he's kept his distance the last few days. As much distance as he can have and still be her supervisor. But he's left her alone when it comes to her activities. And it has made her even closer with her fellow counselors, who are all Team Taylor.

"Nothing but respect for *this* Taylor!" Noah double-taps their chest with a fist. "You were named well."

"Call me Mother!" Taylor says with her signature hair toss.

"So, when are we going to get another performance?" Caleb asks. He flips his Whispering Pines baseball cap backward, his auburn hair sticking out. "Since you're all about giving the people what they want."

Taylor leans forward. "Do *you* want to be taken down a peg?" She cocks her eyebrow.

Caleb holds his hands up. "Um, no, I just want to see you and Noah dance more. The strutting alone . . ." Caleb's cheeks get blotchy. He's in a constant state of flush the longer they sit at the table.

"Don't need to ask *me* twice!" Noah stands up and does a quick strut down the aisle before returning.

"I need energy first." Taylor takes a cookie—as she will always make room for dessert.

"Hey, Taylor!" Ms. Marlette, who oversees the art and music departments, approaches, her brown curly hair pulled back in a sequined headband that was one of the arts and crafts projects yesterday.

"Just the person we wanted to see," Noah starts. "Caleb was just begging us—"

"I wouldn't really call it—" Caleb begins, but Noah talks over him.

"*Begging* Taylor and me to perform. Mia can do the posters, all we need is a stage and decent lighting. I was born to be followed around by a spotlight." Noah puts on their red heart-shaped sunglasses.

"I'm also partial to a spotlight," Taylor admits with a shimmy of her shoulders. She doesn't necessarily want to perform on a stage like Tay, but she does like attention. Who doesn't? Well, besides Teffy.

"Thank you so much for the kind, generous offer, Noah. I'll see if we have a venue big enough," Ms. Marlette says with the patience one gets from having to deal with kids all day. "However, I'm here to tell

Taylor that Mr. Mason would like to have a word with you in his office."

"Ooooh, do you think you're getting a plaque for being a legend?" Noah asks.

Taylor stands and does another hair flip. "Obviously." Although, it's probably more to do with the book club she proposed. She wants to start a weekly "Chat and Chew" lunch where they'd read and discuss banned books, since unlike some antiquated school boards, she believes every person should see themselves represented on the page.

As Taylor walks to Mr. Mason's office, a bead of sweat runs down her back. It's one of those uncomfortably hot late June evenings. She's grateful to sleep in air-conditioning. And to have the dining hall and all the other buildings air-conditioned. Okay, so yeah, life at Whispering Pines is pretty cushy.

When she arrives, Taylor notices Erin, one of the Yellow Team counselors, wiping away tears outside Mr. Mason's office. Taylor met all the other counselors on the first day, but the Red Team has sort of kept to themselves. Erin's also a first-time counselor, probably the same age as Taylor, even though she's a lot shorter and petite, with curly strawberry-blond hair. Taylor remembered being surprised she was a fellow counselor as she looks way younger.

"Hey, it's Erin, right?" Taylor sits down on the chair next to her, but Erin keeps her head down, refusing to make eye contact. "Oh, um, I'm Taylor, from the Red Team. Are you okay? Do you need anything?"

Taylor's heart breaks for Erin. Maybe she's homesick. Taylor can relate. She feels the occasional pangs of missing her family and the Taylors.

Erin still hasn't acknowledged Taylor, so she gets up. "Well, I'm around if you need anything."

Taylor knocks on Mr. Mason's open door. He's typing on his computer but gestures for her to come in. He looks tired, with bags under his eyes. A frazzled state that wasn't there the first day of camp.

He finally looks up from his computer. "Thanks for coming, Taylor. Can you please close the door?"

"Of course." Taylor sneaks another look at Erin before shutting the door. "Is Erin okay? Does she need anything?"

Mr. Mason's brow furrows. "That's why you're here."

"Oh. Of course!" Taylor is somewhat honored that Mr. Mason would come to her to help him with an issue. She likes to think she's proved to be a good employee: enthusiastic, reliable, and organized. "What happened?"

Mr. Mason opens his mouth, then closes it again. He tilts his head before he replies, "You."

Taylor waits for him to continue, but it seems that he's done. "What do you mean *me*? I think we only spoke once, and that was me complimenting these cute rainbow socks she had." Taylor tries to remember any other time she and Erin have interacted.

Sure, the Red and Yellow Teams are against each other in the Color War, but Taylor has been sure to be a gracious winner as she wants to set a good example for the kids. Plus, trash-talking just isn't her style. Okay, except for Hunter. Trash deserves to be treated as such.

Mr. Mason pinches the bridge of his nose. "Erin has come in with some pretty serious allegations about your treatment of her."

Taylor can only blink in response, because none of this is making sense.

Mr. Mason continues, "She says you've been bullying her. Calling her names. Pushing her."

"I—I—" Taylor shakes her head, wondering what is happening. "Mr. Mason, there has to be some mistake. I'm really sorry for whatever Erin is going through, but it has nothing to do with me. I'm happy to help her, because nobody should be bullied." Taylor gets angry even thinking about bullies. Taylor can be tough, she can be confident, but she is *not* a bully.

Mr. Mason grimaces. "I'm going to ask Erin to come in here so we can get to the bottom of this upsetting matter."

"Yes, I'd like that." Taylor wants to make this right. She wants to help Erin. And more importantly, she wants to figure out who this bully is.

Mr. Mason goes out into the hallway and brings in Erin. She's shaking, and Taylor's heart breaks even more for her. Taylor can't believe they're the same age. Erin looks so vulnerable with those big blue eyes.

Taylor gives her a comforting smile. "Hi, Erin, I'm sorry for what you're going through, but I think there's some kind of mistake as I—"

"Please." Erin's voice comes out hard. It surprises Taylor. "Don't pretend like you don't know what you've done."

"I'm—" Taylor starts thinking about the other counselors, wondering who Erin may be confusing her with. "We've never had a proper conversation."

Erin grits her teeth, her gaze glued to the floor. "Well, that's true."

See! Taylor knew this was just a simple misunderstanding.

Erin continues, "You can't really call it a conversation, since you were too busy insulting me, calling me a Karen instead of Erin. Or stupid. Or ugly."

"What?" Taylor's head is spinning. She never in her life would ever call anybody those names. She starts to defend herself, "I would—"

"Taylor, please let Erin talk," Mr. Mason says in a stern voice before turning back to Erin. "This is a safe space, Erin."

Taylor feels helpless. There's no proof that Taylor has done anything wrong, yet here she is. Taylor supports women. Taylor believes women. She knows how hard it is to come forward, which is why she didn't say anything to Mr. Mason about Hunter. Now it's going to be Taylor's word against Erin's.

Erin sniffs into a tissue. "Mr. Mason, I've been coming to this camp since I was eight. I love it here. I've made so many great friends. I was so excited to be a counselor, but now . . . I don't think I can stay another night with *her* here."

Erin lets out a huge cry, causing Mr. Mason to bolt up from his chair. He rushes over to pat Erin on the back.

Taylor can only think that there has to be some kind of explanation. Maybe . . . Taylor has started sleepwalking and doing things to this poor girl, who is obviously very upset. Or Taylor has an evil clone. Honestly, those are the only scenarios that make sense because Taylor *hasn't done anything wrong.*

"Erin, I'm so sorry if—" Then Taylor notices something around Erin's wrist. "Where did you get that bracelet?"

It's the bracelet Taylor made Hunter.

For a split second, Erin looks panicked, before fixing her face back into anguish.

Twenty bucks Erin is a counselor for the theatre program.

Erin sniffs for a few seconds before she answers, "When I told one of the senior counselors about you bullying me, he was so kind and supportive and gave me a friendship bracelet."

"Hunter Brown, was it?" Taylor's voice is tight.

Of course. Taylor is being set up. She let her guard down, assuming Hunter was going to let her have the last word.

Well, Taylor was wrong.

Between sobs, Erin asks to be excused to call home.

Taylor does her best to not roll her eyes at this performance. Erin is lying. Taylor knows she probably won't be believed, but she has to at least try.

"Mr. Mason, I never—and I mean *never*—did anything to Erin. And, well, I should've said something to you on that first day, but I didn't. Hunter Brown and I have a history. I should've come forward when he played that mean prank that left me in the mud, but again, I didn't."

Mr. Mason leans back in his chair. "You should know that Hunter came to me right after the tug-of-war incident and owned up to it. He apologized, and I know he did the same to you. In fact, Hunter said he'd understand if I reassigned him, but I appreciated him stepping up."

Taylor knows all too well that Hunter Brown has this charm that lets him get away with whatever he wants. And it seems to have worked on Mr. Mason.

Mr. Mason rubs his tired eyes as he continues, "And, well, Taylor, Hunter said he saw you push Erin."

"I didn't push her, I've only ever complimented her." Taylor tries to keep her voice even, but her temper is fighting a losing battle. "So, what? You're going to fire me because someone is throwing around baseless accusations?"

"Of course not." Mr. Mason wipes sweat off his brow. "Look, I've spoken to your campers and the other supervisors, and they only have glowing things to say about you, but I can't ignore this. Erin's parents have been very generous to the camp."

Ah, it's all starting to make sense. It annoys Taylor that Hunter picked the right mark.

Mr. Mason shifts uncomfortably in his seat. "So you're being put on probation. You'll have someone assigned to you for all tasks going forward."

Taylor wants to protest, to complain, because this is so unfair, but she also knows she's been outmaneuvered.

For now.

Taylor takes a deep breath as she stands up, making sure she doesn't flip over Mr. Mason's desk, because that's exactly what she wants to do right now. "Of course. I appreciate the opportunity to prove that this is all an unfortunate misunderstanding, and I can assure you that I've done nothing wrong."

As Taylor walks back to her cabin—with the Yellow Team's senior supervisor—she starts to come up with a plan. This is not the first time Taylor has been underestimated. Maybe it's because she's the youngest of five that people assume she doesn't know how to stand on her own two feet.

Taylor is really good at a lot of things: debate, school, organizing, and being a friend.

And she's about to excel at revenge.

Our Chat (The Taylors Version)

TS ⚽: I stand by what I said about men. What. A. Jerk.

TEFFY📚: Oh no, Taylor. I'm so sorry!

TAY🎉: THAT'S IT. I'M ENTERING MY VENGEANCE ERA

TEFFY📚: SAME.

TS ⚽: We gotta squad up like the crew in the Bad Blood video, start practicing our ninja moves

TAYLOR🐝: I don't think he realizes I've got a specific set of skills

TAY🎉: AND FRIENDS WHO YOU DO NOT MESS WITH

TAYLOR🐝: Heaven help a boy—and I mean BOY—who thinks they can mess with a Taylor

ELEVEN
I Can Fix Him (No Really I Can)

Tay feels like everything in her life is exploding. Mostly in a good way.

Yes, there's her rage from what Hunter is putting Taylor through.

But there's also a lot of good. A LOT.

The band—totally blowing up! Her profile numbers have doubled since their performance at the Hancock County Fair. The band's following has tripled. They're getting booked for more gigs.

Reece—so sweet! Yeah, her dad doesn't get it, most people don't, but they don't see this side of Reece. The amazing, generous one.

"Come here." Reece pulls Tay into his arms before their band rehearsal on Monday. "Have I mentioned in the last two minutes how incredible you are? How you are the best thing to happen to this band . . . and to me?" He traces his callused finger around Tay's jaw. She likes that his fingers are rough from all his guitar playing.

"Hmm, I think it's impossible for you to say that enough." She plants a kiss on his cheek. "But it was *your* excellent taste in girlfriends and singers that got us to this point." She does a twirl around his basement, not wanting to contain this joy she's feeling.

Tay can't remember the last time she was this excited about anything, and Tay gets excited *a lot*. But this is different. This is what she's wanted to do for so long. And to think, it was *her* idea to do Taylor Swift covers that got them here!

Of course, Tay can't help but let her imagination get away from her. Maybe they'll blow up so big Taylor Swift herself will see them perform and then ask the Archers to open for her and then she and Tay will become best friends! Of course, Tay will make sure the Taylors go on the road so they can be one big happy family. No matter how high her star rises, she won't forget the people who truly matter to her.

Okay, maybe she's getting ahead of herself, but it's okay to dream big. It's exactly what Tay should be doing. Tay already knows what she's going to wish for when she blows out her birthday candles on Saturday.

Sweet sixteen, indeed.

"Yo!" Owen comes running into the basement, out of breath. "You aren't going to believe this, but my cousin is a promoter of this killer all-girl punk band that is getting radio play, and she's coming to our gig at the Crawford County Fair next weekend, and if we kill it, we're gonna open for them when they play Hi-Fi Annex next month." Owen finally comes up for air.

"Wait, dude, what?" is all Kai can come up with in response. Which is more than Tay can do as she's trying to catch up to what this all means. "Hi-Fi Annex is, like, what, over a thousand people?"

"I know, right?" Owen has his hands above his head. He looks at Tay. "So?"

"So!" Tay can't believe it. She's going to need bigger candles on that cake. She can't help it, and she jumps into a split. If she thought she had energy before . . . "Um, yes! YES! OBVIOUSLY! Okay! Okay! We can do this! Reece?" Tay turns to Reece, who is still.

Reece starts nodding slowly. "We are going to do this."

OH MY GOODNESS! THIS IS REALLY HAPPENING!!

"Okay, we need to come up with the most killer setlist for next week. And outfits." Kai pops the collar on his blue-and-white-checkered polo shirt.

"Yeah, and that was something I was going to bring up." Reece's eyes dart to Tay. "I want to do a solo set. Just me, my guitar, and my songs. I've been getting a lot of requests in my DMs from my fans for more me."

"What?" Kai replies. "You're kidding, right? We got this gig because we killed doing the covers, which Tay sang. Not like . . . your stuff."

"What's wrong with my *stuff*?" Reece's cheeks start getting flushed. "If I remember correctly, it was my *stuff* that got you interested in joining *my band*."

"Yeah, and *we* are a band. The Archers, not the *Reece Matthews Experience*," Owen fires back. "Look, I get you started this band to play your music, which is good, but it's just not what people want from us right now. You saw the response we had after we did those covers. You've seen our numbers. It would be a huge step back to play sad boy music when people want us to rock out to music they actually know."

Tay can hardly breathe. That excitement she had just a moment ago has vanished. Now she's worried this amazing opportunity could slip through their fingers.

"Come on, Reece," Corey adds with a frustrated sigh. "Don't you want to play Hi-Fi Annex?"

Reece folds his arms. "Not if it means compromising my art." He turns on his heel and stomps up the stairs.

Kai, Owen, and Corey stare at Tay. She's become used to being a mediator between Reece and the rest of the band. Between Reece and her dad.

But this time . . . Tay isn't really on Reece's side. While she understands where Reece is coming from—he started the band to play his original songs—she also knows that they'll lose their momentum if they don't play what people want to hear. And, yeah, what *Tay* wants to sing. This is the band that *Tay* wants to be in. And Reece isn't the only member of this band.

"Tay, your man is turning into a diva," Kai says, his jaw tense. "And he's not the one people want, it's you."

"Oh, well . . ." Tay doesn't know about that. She couldn't help but notice that Reece's followers have also grown and they're mostly girls. After all, he won her heart by singing. "Maybe we can find a song of Reece's that's more up-tempo, that matches the covers we do."

Corey lets out a snort. "Um, Tay, you know Reece's originals. Which one would you suggest, 'Tears on My Face' or 'Never Ending Heartbreak'? Or the one where it ends with two minutes of him scream-singing, '*I'm crying . . . I'm dying.*' There's a reason people left when we started off with his songs."

Okay, Corey does have a point, but Tay needs to find some sort of compromise.

"I've got a suggestion for an original song," Kai says. Tay gives him a grateful smile, knowing that being in a group means that she's not in this alone. "The one Teffy played the other day. It's a bop."

Never mind. Guess it is up to her.

"Yes, dude, so good!" Corey gives Kai a high five. "Love Teffy's stuff. It would totally fit in with our new vibe."

While Tay agrees and would love nothing more than to share Teffy's music, she knows Reece would have a problem with it. He gets really sensitive about Teffy's songs. Because they're *that* good.

Tay tries to think of something to get Reece on board. "Maybe there's a song of Reece's that we can . . . I don't know, maybe make a bit more, um . . ."

"Seriously!" Owen exclaims, throwing his head back with a groan. "We are *so close* to getting bigger gigs. We can't keep tiptoeing around Mr. Pretentious. We also have to stop pretending we're in two bands. I don't know about you, but *I* want to be in the fun band. The one people *want* to listen to."

Tay nods along as she totally agrees, *but* she knows how much this will hurt Reece. He built this band. He put everything into it. It would destroy him if he knew the band wasn't interested in playing his songs. Worse, if they started playing Teffy's.

"Okay, I get it," Tay relents. "I'll talk to Reece. Because I can fix this."

No, really, she can.

Tay hates to admit it, but she's pretty good at getting what she wants. She's become an expert at sweet-talking her father. She's been known to butter up a teacher or two. She's learned a few tricks over the years.

"This is so good, Tay." Reece pats his stomach.

And one way to win someone over is with food.

"You want more pasta?" Tay's dad had a work dinner, so she invited Reece over after rehearsal to make him her special pasta with feta and olives.

"I'm good. Actually, I'm great now that it's just you and me." Reece takes Tay's hand and puts it in his.

It's moments like this that Tay wishes she could capture when people ask her why she's with Reece. Whenever she watched rom-coms, she would dream of having someone say such sweet things to her. That day is now.

"I'm going to write an epic song about this right here." He kisses her hand. "It's moments like these that need to be captured, the sweet, everyday ones. These are the ones that matter."

See! Tay wants to scream at those whose eyes get wide when they see the bright and peppy cheerleader is with the tortured poet.

Reece stands up. "Let me clean up."

"No, sit!" Tay starts clearing the plates. "I don't want you to lift a finger. I know how stressful practice was . . ." Tay dips her toe into the stress-inducing waters.

"Yeah, I feel like a broken record." Reece's shoulders slump. "Look, I get what everybody wants, it's been bashed into me the last few months. *We want fun, Reece, not your music* . . . but I feel like I'm giving up on my dream." He places his forehead on the kitchen table.

Poor Reece. Tay wraps her arms around him. "I don't want you to give up on your dream. Nobody wants that. This is just one performance. Which could mean big things. We start getting more gigs and more exposure. I've seen your numbers, I know you're getting more fans. You even said that they want to hear more from *you*."

Reece looks up and his gaze is one of admiration, and it makes Tay melt. "Do *you* still want to hear from me?"

"Always. Think of this as a small sacrifice for the greater good."

Reece looks off into the distance, and then gives the tiniest of nods. "Okay."

"Really? We can do the covers next week?" Tay tries not to get too excited, since she knows by agreeing to this Reece is pushing a small part of himself aside.

"Yeah, but I want you to know, Tay, that I'm only doing this for you."

If that isn't love, then Tay doesn't know what is.

Our Chat (The Taylors Version)

TAYLOR🐝: Don't forget us when you're a huge superstar, Tay!

TAY🎉: NEVER!!!

TS ⚽: AFAIK UR a ☆

TAYLOR🐝: Um, you okay, TS?

TS ⚽: SRY @ fancy event

TAYLOR🐝: Looks like it won't be Tay abandoning us

TS ⚽: ILY

TEFFY📚: Um, what's going on?

TAY🎉: ICYMI, TS BZ 🐝

TEFFY📚: OK

TAYLOR🐝: Ugh. BRB. Duty calls!

TAY🎉: NP!

TEFFY📚: ILY, BFFs!

TWELVE
loml

Teffy has never been into drama. Even the thought of confrontation makes her break out in hives. So she accepted Liam's flowers after he went over to Hannah's on Sunday. They haven't spoken about hanging with his friends since. Which suits Teffy just fine.

"Okay, Tefs, I've got good news and bad news," Liam says when he picks her up after work on Tuesday. Teffy braces herself as he continues, "I've got a hankering for some frozen custard at Ritter's and would like to treat you, but when I walked by, I saw Charlie was working, so . . ."

Teffy relaxes her shoulders. "Ah, well, in that scenario, a cherry ice is worth having to deal with my brother." Even though Charlie has been really supportive of Teffy lately.

Liam takes Teffy by the hand as they walk along Main Street downtown. It's something Teffy never thought would happen, but here they are, out in the open. Liam even gives Teffy's hand an extra squeeze when they walk by the now-empty storefront that once housed Harrison by Design. Teffy usually walks around that block when she goes to work. It's unsettling to see something that represented her parents' hopes and dreams and hard work reduced to a FOR LEASE sign.

As they enter Ritter's, Teffy smiles as she sees Charlie behind the counter, wearing a bright blue apron and hat. He's busy serving another customer so it takes him a moment to notice Teffy and Liam waiting in line. This time it's Teffy who gives Liam's hand a squeeze, remembering that Charlie had threatened him.

"Welcome to . . ." Charlie starts before he sees them. "Oh, hey, what's up? Cherry ice, Teffy?"

"Yes, please." It's been her standard order since she was little. Every once in a while she thinks she should change it up, but there's too much change already happening in her life, so she'll stick with what she likes.

"And I'll have a white chocolate raspberry truffle custard in a waffle cone, Charlie," Liam orders, his arm snaking around Teffy's waist.

Charlie grimaces at Liam before ringing up their order. "Teffy gets the family discount, but you're gonna have to pay, man."

Teffy is now thinking that confiding in Charlie about how annoyed she was the other night was a bad idea.

"Yeah, of course!" Liam smiles at Charlie as he hands him a ten. "You excited for college? I know—" Liam stops when he sees Charlie's attention is on the door.

Teffy turns around and her stomach drops. In walk Cat and John. And then Nick and a few of Liam's other friends.

"Did you tell them we were here?" Teffy whispers to Liam.

"Huh?" Liam says before going over to greet his friends via their usual high fives, fist bumps, chest bumps, and just all-around bro-ish behavior.

While Liam looks genuinely surprised (and happy) that his friends are here, Teffy can't help but feel like this is some sort of setup.

"Teffy!" Cat comes over and gives Teffy a hug. "Oh my goodness, I wanted to let you know that some of us girls are going to go get our nails done on Friday. We like to pamper ourselves every once in a while. You totally have to come so we can gossip."

"Oh, um, I . . ." Teffy looks at her short nails, which currently have chipped pink polish. She never grows her nails out long because it gets in the way of playing guitar. "I have to work on Friday," Teffy replies. She doesn't, but she feels like that's a better excuse than saying she's not interested, because while Cat is nice and all, she doesn't know if that means Hannah will be there.

"Teffy, order's up!" Charlie calls out. As he slides her cherry ice to her, he asks quietly, "You good?"

She gives a silent nod, but it's like her moment with Liam has been taken over by his friends. Before she knows it, they've been guided out onto the patio and are seated at a large table. Everybody is talking over one another and Liam has been swept up in some conversation about the Indiana Colts preseason.

"Teffy!" Cat calls out from across the table. "Before I forget, Tiffany's birthday is coming up and we were thinking of putting together a video or something and would love to have you be part of it. Nothing big, just telling a funny story about Tiffany and then we're doing a scrapbook. If you don't have a pic with her, we'll get one this weekend at Tay's birthday."

"Um, okay," Teffy replies. Even though she doesn't really have a story about Tiffany, since she's only talked to her maybe once. And it was about Tay. She'll have to ask Tay for a Tiffany story since they're on the cheerleading squad together.

"Oh! And maybe we'll do our nails before then, so you can join us!" Cat claps excitedly.

Liam's face lights up. "Hey, Cat, thanks for including Teffy." He then turns to her. "I know without Taylor and TS around, and Tay busy with the band, you might like to have something to do."

Wait. Did Liam tell Cat to invite her along? While, yeah, it's thoughtful of Cat to include her, she doesn't want to get her nails done. She doesn't want to spend less time with Liam so she can be somewhere with people having conversations around her.

Unless, this is what Liam expects of Teffy. To be more polished like Cat? She'd probably fit in better with his world if she was.

Teffy thinks back to the beginning of the school year. Taylor changed herself for Hunter, she made herself smaller for him. Tay began wearing muted colors to appeal to Reece. And now TS is in England having to get dressed up and go to fancy events for Gemma. So maybe it's inevitable that you have to change to be in a relationship.

But if that's true, does Liam truly like Teffy for who she is?

Liam isn't perfect. He's messy. He's a bit of a pushover. But Teffy loves him just as he is. And she does love him.

"Hannah!" Cat calls out with an excited clap. "Ah, you're here!"

Teffy pushes her ice away. She no longer has an appetite. Instead, her stomach is filled with dread. How has her quiet afternoon with her boyfriend turned into *this*?

"Hey, all!" Hannah comes over to the table, carrying a tray with three different sundaes. She's wearing an emerald-green satin romper with wedges. "I couldn't decide what to order so I got enough to share!"

The group take spoons and start diving in. Hannah slides in next to Cat, who has to scoot over to make room, which then makes Teffy move so she's half sitting on the bench. Now she's as uncomfortable physically as she is emotionally.

"Oh, hey, Teffy. You on your work break?" Hannah glances at Teffy's light blue BY THE BOOK T-shirt. Then in a softer voice so only Cat and Teffy can hear, "Or did you run out of clothes? Not like you have a lot. Certainly not the kind of clothes *I'd* wear." She snorts.

Cat bumps Hannah with a scowl while Teffy folds her arms around herself. Yeah, she's got chipped nails and is wearing a T-shirt and jean shorts and canvas shoes. Maybe it's not cool and fashionable like Hannah's outfit, maybe Teffy isn't cool or fashionable, but if Hannah is what's considered cool, Teffy prefers being a nerd any day.

"Oh no," Hannah says loudly. "Looks like the guy who waited on me didn't put enough fudge on my sundae." She shoots a look at Teffy. "It's so hard to find decent help these days."

Okay, yes, Teffy doesn't like confrontation, but she's not going to be silent while Hannah belittles her brother.

"It's called *work*, Hannah," Teffy says in a loud voice, and it stops the different conversations around the table. "It's about earning something instead of having it handed to you. Maybe you should try it sometime, although even when you ran unopposed for class president, more people would rather write in Taylor's name than put a tick on a box with yours."

Teffy slides off the bench and stomps off. And you know what, it feels pretty good.

"Tefs!" Liam calls after her. "Hey, Tefs! Wait!"

Teffy goes around the corner before she stops, not wanting Liam's friends to watch them.

"Hey." Liam's forehead is creased. "What's going on?"

"What's going on?" Does she really need to spell it out for him? Again?

"Yeah, that was a bit of a low blow."

"Yes, it was," Teffy replies in a cold voice, but at least Liam seems to get it.

"Okay, so yeah, I'm sure if we just go back to the table and you apologize to Hannah—"

"What?" Teffy cries out. "Are you serious? You think *Hannah* is the one who deserves an apology?"

Liam runs a hand through his hair as he shifts uncomfortably from one foot to the other. "I mean, she's still really upset about the whole president thing."

"Oh, so it's okay for her to belittle my clothes, and the fact that Charlie and I have to work . . ." Teffy throws her hands up in the air. She cannot believe she has to have this conversation.

"Wait, when did she—" Liam starts, but Teffy isn't done.

"I'm not going to apologize to Hannah and I'm not going back there."

Liam lets out a frustrated sigh. "Okay, okay, I just . . ." Liam looks over to where they came from.

"Let me guess, you want to hang out with your crew." There's such a bad taste in her mouth.

"I mean, yeah, they're my friends. But it's okay, we can . . ."

A wave of exhaustion overtakes Teffy. "You know what, Liam, I'm tired, because unlike some people who were born with a silver spoon shoved up their—" She takes a deep breath. "I had to work today. And I'm tired. I'm going home."

"Tefs." Liam reaches out to take Teffy's hand, but she pulls it back. "We were supposed to spend the afternoon together."

Yes, they were.

"Yo, Liam!" John comes jogging over. "We're gonna go to the park and throw the ball around, you in?"

Liam studies Teffy. "No, man—"

"Go," Teffy replies. She's afraid of what will happen if he stays. What will be said.

"Tefs." Liam takes a step forward. "Are you sure?"

"I want to go home." It's the truth.

Liam takes her hand, and this time Teffy lets him have it. "Okay, tomorrow night. You and me. I'll do something special. Promise."

Teffy just gives him a forced smile before she turns around and starts walking home.

Today was supposed to be just the two of them.

Maybe Teffy should no longer believe Liam's promises.

I will not let Hannah Reed get in the way of my relationship with Liam. I will not let Hannah Reed get in the way of my relationship with Liam, Teffy keeps repeating to herself as she gets ready for their date on Wednesday.

"Why, you look lovely," her mom says as Teffy arrives downstairs. She's wearing a plum-colored sundress with long boho-ish sleeves. Her hair is back in her braided crown. It's quickly becoming her signature look. Plus, it's easy to do and keeps her hair off her neck when it's hot.

"Thanks." Teffy smiles at her mother as the doorbell rings.

Teffy opens the door to see Liam standing there in a light gray suit and blue tie. He's holding lilacs from his mother's garden. Even though she's frustrated about what happened both yesterday and on Sunday, her heart still beats in overtime at the sight of him.

"You look beautiful, as always." Liam leans in to give her a kiss on the cheek. He then holds up a canvas bag. "You're not the only person I'm going to try to make peace with tonight. I don't like there to be any tension between us and your family."

Before Teffy can ask what he's planning, Liam walks into the living room. "Hi, Mr. and Mrs. Bennett!"

"Hi, Liam," her mom says with a sad smile. "Oh, those flowers are lovely. Let me get a vase."

"I've got it, honey," her dad says before he excuses himself.

Her dad has mentioned how Liam looks more and more like his dad as he's gotten older. Teffy wonders if that's why he finds reasons to leave on the rare occasions when Liam comes over.

"Mrs. Bennett, my mom was cleaning out her closet and found these." He pulls out a cloth napkin embroidered with a lavender flower.

"Oh, wow." Her mom puts her hand to her heart. "We did these on that machine years ago."

Teffy's mom and Mrs. Yoon had gotten an embroidery machine and used it as an excuse to embroider everything: shirts, bags, napkins . . . It's what gave her parents the idea for the store.

Her mom inspects the flower with a smile.

"Yeah, so, I know she'd love to have you over," Liam throws out.

Teffy blinks in surprise. He's trying to mend the rift between their parents. It's a sweet gesture. Anytime Teffy tries to talk to her parents about the Yoons, she generally gets shut down. It doesn't really feel like summer without their annual camping trip.

Teffy's mom remains quiet. She hasn't stormed out or gotten mad, so Teffy is going to count that as a win.

"Well, we should go!" Teffy takes Liam by the hand, figuring it's best to escape while things seem somewhat hopeful.

"That was good, right?" Liam asks as they walk toward his mom's car. "I saw the napkin and it reminded me of a white flag. There's part of me that knows it's not my business, but I'm just over the drama, you know?"

Oh, Teffy does know. She's trying to push all that Hannah and

Liam's friends drama from her mind. It's just the two of them tonight.

Liam embraces Teffy and gives her a proper kiss. "I know I already told you, but you are absolutely stunning."

"You don't look so bad yourself." She straightens his tie. "So, are you going to tell me where were going?"

"We are going for a lovely meal in which I will be using utensils."

"Oh, that *is* fancy. Will you also be using a napkin?" The best way to describe Liam as he eats is very energetic and messy. And that's being polite.

"I will, my lady." Liam does a deep bow.

"I see. Such a gentleman. And will you be able to keep food off your clothes?"

Liam pulls her in and starts slow-dancing with her in the driveway. "Oh, Tefs, you know I can't promise that. But you'll still love me even though I'm a slob, right?"

Teffy melts into Liam, letting herself relax and putting yesterday behind her. Because when all is said and done, she does love Liam with all her soul.

Liam is a boy of his word. Mostly.

"Is it obvious?" Liam dabs his cloth napkin at the grease stain on his tie.

"It sort of blends in," Teffy admits with an amused smile.

Liam shakes his head. "I swear you can take me out in public. Sometimes."

Teffy can't help but laugh. So far their date has been amazing. He took her to Fiore's, her favorite Italian place. Her belly is full of lasagna and cheesy breadsticks. It's been only the two of them. It's all she needs. It's all she wants.

"Hey." Liam takes her hand from across the candlelit table. "I sort of wanted to talk to you about something important."

"Okay." Teffy swallows the butterflies making their way up her throat.

She and Liam haven't exchanged "I love yous" yet, but as she looks around the romantic restaurant, she feels it in her bones that Liam is going to say those words.

"Yeah, I just sort of wanted to . . ." He clears his throat and takes another sip of water. It's adorable how nervous he is. Maybe Teffy should just say it first, but she wants to hear it from Liam. "Yeah, I know the last couple times we've hung out with them, it's been a bit awkward, but I'd really like you to give my friends a chance."

Teffy blinks for a moment. She wasn't expecting this plot twist.

"Because they really like you," Liam continues. "I mean, how could they not? John even said you were chill, which is, like, a huge compliment from him, and Cat wants to hear your songs. My friends aren't that bad. They're harmless. It's like with our parents. I just don't want there to be this *thing*. I want us to all get along."

"I don't *not* like them," Teffy starts, but her stomach now feels like a ton of bricks. She doesn't want to talk about Liam's friends. She wants it to be like it used to be between them. Just her and Liam. "I just don't really feel like I fit in."

"Cat's been making an effort."

"Yes, she has." Teffy measures her words, because it's pretty clear Liam is pointing out that Teffy has *not*. "And I appreciate her wanting to include me, but I don't want to get my nails done and make videos and be turned into some clone. And then there's Hannah."

"Yeah, about that . . ." Liam starts to play with his cloth napkin. "I think that, maybe, it would be good for you to, like . . . forgive Hannah and be friends with her."

"Hannah?" Teffy's mouth hangs open. "Are you serious?"

Liam clenches his jaw. "I mean, I know you've had issues with her in the past—and I get that—but she was really cool the other night and apologized to me again when we were at her house."

"Liam, she only apologized to me about bringing up the talent show *because* of you. She has never once apologized for how she's treated me for *years*. Or to Tay. Or Taylor. Or TS." Teffy tries to steady her breath, but people like Hannah make Teffy so upset. It's easier to be kind than mean, but why is it that Teffy is expected to be the bigger person? "Or the countless people Hannah has bullied. Even *you* called her a mean girl!"

"Yeah, but that wasn't nice of me to do." Liam slouches in his seat.

"It was accurate because Hannah *is* a mean girl!" Teffy's voice gets loud, causing a few heads to turn. She takes a calming breath. "You know how devastated I was after the seventh-grade talent show, and yet Hannah loves picking at that scab. She's cruel. Then she had to make a dig at my clothes. My job. You know I don't like to be loud and to confront people, but if even *I* can stand up to Hannah, why can't you?"

Liam looks up at her, a hurt look on his face. "What?"

"You just want things to be easy, to not make anybody uncomfortable."

Liam tilts his head. "You say that like it's a bad thing. Can you just be . . . cool?"

"Cool?" Teffy feels the heat rising in her cheeks. So, yeah, she's the opposite of cool right now. She's fuming. "I'm sorry that I'm not popular or a cool kid, Liam. I'm so sorry that I'm not this pretty, perfect girl like Cat. You want to know why I don't like hanging out with your friends? Because I don't feel like I can be myself. I'm uncomfortable. I'm not loud. I'm not interested in what they are interested in, which is what, by the way? Video games and football? I'm not going to change myself for your friends. And you shouldn't ask me to."

"I'm not asking you to change, Tefs," Liam says.

"You're asking me to be okay with a bully. You're taking their side instead of sticking up for me because you want to be *cool*. You care more about what your friends think, what Hannah thinks, than me." Teffy knows she's being a bit harsh, but she's hurt. It seems like Liam wants Teffy to suck it up and be friends with people who have been unkind to her. "You can stare down a defensive line, but you don't have the guts to stand up to your friends."

Okay, now it's Teffy being cruel.

Liam is quiet, looking down at the candle. "I told John off for taking your hat that one time."

Yes, that one time. When they weren't even together.

"Liam," Teffy says softer, not wanting to be in a fight. She wants things to be back to normal. The problem is, now that they're out in the open, there's a new normal, and Teffy doesn't like what that means. "I'm sorry, but I'm hurt. I'm not going to pretend to be someone I'm not to fit in with the jocks and cheerleaders."

"But I'm a jock." Liam's cheeks are flushed, his jaw tightened. Teffy has never seen him this upset. "So that's it, then? You're just giving up."

"I'm not—" But is that what she's doing? No, she just doesn't want to play nice with bullies. She doesn't understand why he's continuing to push her to do something that makes her uncomfortable just to placate his friends.

"Yeah, you are, Tefs." His eyes darken. "You're giving up when there's a little bump in the road. Just like your parents."

Oh no he did not.

Yes, Teffy's frustrated that her parents haven't forgiven the Yoons, but their family business went bust. They also lost money on an investment that the Yoons talked her parents into. The Yoons aren't completely innocent in all this.

Teffy stands up and throws her napkin on the table. "Well, if this is how hurt and betrayed my parents feel, I don't blame them for walking away."

She storms out of the restaurant, not even bothering to look behind her. She knows Liam isn't going to chase after her. He didn't when she first told him about her feelings. Why would he now? No, he doesn't want to cause waves. He wants things to be easy.

Yeah, well, love isn't always easy.

Teffy has written countless songs about falling in love and wanting. She's had some experience in heartache. But she's never experienced this kind of void in her heart before.

Our Chat (The Taylors Version)

TS ⚽: HAPPY BIRTHDAY FROM LONDON, TAY! WISH I WAS THERE

TS ⚽: IN YOUR HONOUR (THAT'S HOW THEY SPELL THAT HERE) I WILL ONLY TYPE IN ALL CAPS AND USE A ZILLION !!!!!!!

TAYLOR🐝: HAPPY SWEET SIXTEEN TO OUR SWEETEST TAY!!!!!!!!!!

TEFFY📚: HAPPY BIRTHDAY!!!

TAY🎉: AWWWWWWW, TAYLORS!!! 🥰🥰🥰

TAYLOR🐝: SORRY I'M MISSING YOUR BIG PARTY!!!!

TS ⚽: BUT NEXT YEAR WE'LL BE CELEBRATING AT YOUR GIG AT MADISON SQUARE GARDEN, SUPERSTAR!!!!!

TAY🎉: AHHHH!!! I'M GOING TO MISS YOU BOTH, TS AND TAYLOR!!!!!!

TAY🎉: TEFFY IS GOING TO HAVE TO EAT EXTRA CAKE

TEFFY📚: THE THINGS I DO FOR MY FRIENDS.

THIRTEEN

The Lucky One

Tay is so excited!

Okay, she gets excited *a lot*, so that's nothing new, but she loves birthdays—presents, food, and friends!—and this year it's a big one. Sweet sixteen!

No surprise, her dad has gone all out. There's a rainbow balloon arch in the backyard for photos, her name spelled in lights along the side of the house, a ridiculous amount of food (including a three-tiered pink birthday cake), *and* a makeshift stage on one side of the pool for the Archers to perform on later.

"This is so cool," Kai says as he finishes setting up his drum kit. "I need to tell my folks they've got to step up their party game."

Tay claps excitedly. Okay, basically everything she's going to do today is going to be excitable, but she only turns sixteen once! She can*not* wait for it to be noon already so her friends will start showing up. She likes to spend the whole day—oh, who is she kidding, weekend! Week! Month!—celebrating her birthday.

Okay, a smidge of her energy comes from the fact that she feels a little bit of pressure. There are going to be a lot of people coming over. Tay knows Teffy feels uncomfortable around the cheerleaders after her fight with Liam, and now he's not even coming! *Gah!* And then there's Reece and the other guys in the band. It's been . . . a bit tense. Reece has agreed to the setlist, but he's even more mopey during rehearsal.

But no! Today will be amazing and positive and she just needs it all to go well.

"You good, Tay?" Kai asks as he tightens the screws on his hi-hats. He arrived early since his drum kit requires more time to set up.

"Yes! Great!" Tay fiddles with the party favors—hats, streamers, silly props for pictures—spread out on the tables set up alongside the pool. Making sure everything is perfect.

"Okay." Kai approaches her with his hands behind his back. "I know it's early, but I'd like to give you my present now. I think you'll know why when you open it." Kai reveals that he's holding a rectangular wrapped present with *Happy Birthday* written in rainbow colors.

"Oh!" Tay does a high kick. Okay, she probably needs to calm down or she's going to explode. "You didn't have to get me anything," Tay says, grabbing the present and tearing the wrapping paper in two. She's glad her dad is inside the house, or he'd lecture her about manners, but it's her birthday!

She opens the box to find a pink sequined headband and matching hair clips. It's *so* Tay: Pink! Sparkles!

"Thank you, Kai!" Tay throws her arms around Kai. He's a bigger guy, and Tay's surprised at how he's both soft and sturdy, but that makes sense as he's the calm center of the band. The consistent one. The one they all look at to keep them in sync.

"Yeah, well, I saw them when I was shopping with my little sister the other day and it practically screamed your name, and then when I walked in and saw your outfit, I knew I was right." Kai smiles so broadly, his dimples deepen.

"Oh, yes!" Tay spins around in her hot pink one-shouldered minidress with a ruffled neckline. "And I see you understood the assignment."

Kai copies Tay with a spin, showing off his light pink collared button-down shirt and pink-and-white-checkered shorts. "Anything for the birthday girl."

Tay may have put a recommendation to dress in pink on the invites. Her dad insisted she say it was a *recommendation* and not a *requirement.*

Dads.

Tay takes the two barrettes and uses them to pull back her hair from one side. She didn't even think about what she was going to do with her hair today since she knew she'd be wearing the hat. It's a Taylors tradition, after all!

The doorbell rings and Tay rushes up the stairs, knowing it's going to be Teffy. She promised to come early to set up, even though her dad had already done everything before Tay had even woken up. So yeah, Tay's not the only one in the house that's excited.

"I'm so—" Tay starts as she opens the door to the house, but pulls up short.

Because there in the middle of her living room next to a beaming Teffy is Taylor Perez, wearing the hat.

"SWEET SIXTEEN SURPRISE!" Taylor puts her arms above her head to strike a killer pose.

"TAYLOR!" Tay runs over to her friend and basically tackles her in a hug. "Wait. What? You said you couldn't make it? I didn't think I was going to see you until your Friends and Family Day! How did you get away from camp? How long are you here? It's not because of that jerk, is it, because I swear—"

"Tay-Tay!" Her dad laughs, still the only one allowed to call her by her middle school nickname. "Deep breath. Let Taylor speak."

"It's okay, Mr. Johnson. To be honest, this is the kind of reception I *should* get when people see me." Taylor puts the hat on Tay. "And, Tay, are you kidding me? You thought I was going to miss *this*? I get one day off a week and worked two weeks in a row and moved a few things so I could be here for your sweet sixteen. Because that's what best friends do. Happy birthday!"

"It's my birthday!" Tay can't help it, she does a back handspring. The party hasn't even started yet, but it's already the best birthday *ever*. "Hi, Teffy!"

"Happy birthday!" Teffy laughs.

"I didn't forget you, I just got distracted by Taylor, who's here!" Tay still can't believe it. She's missed her so much.

"It's fine. I'm also excited, but I don't want to know what I'd pull if I even tried to do a high kick." Teffy then does the saddest kick

Tay has ever seen, but it doesn't matter since it's HER BIRTHDAY.

"Aww, Teffy." Tay gives her a big hug. "How are you? Because if you don't want to see—"

"It's okay," Teffy cuts her off. "I know practically the entire school is going to be here, plus, I've got this one." Teffy gestures at Taylor.

"Oh, you know I've got your back." Taylor puts her arm around Teffy. "Although, I can't believe Liam turned out to be such a jerk."

Tay's leg starts shaking because Tay has a *secret*. And it is absolutely killing her to not tell Teffy that everything is going to be okay!

At least she hopes it will.

Maybe it won't.

Gah! Why are parties so much pressure!

"Listen, Teffy, you do not need to change for any guy, take it from me." Taylor gives her an extra squeeze. "And we all know I'm speaking from experience."

"Did you see the pic TS sent us?" Teffy abruptly changes the subject.

"Oh my goodness, she looks amazing!" Tay screams. "I can't believe she's going to a ball! A BALL!!!"

Okay, deep breaths. Tay really is going to explode. Yeah, she hopes everything goes well, but she's also so happy. Tay loves her friends! She's in a band! And she has Reece!

She's so lucky!

The doorbell starts ringing, and before Tay knows it, her house is being flooded with friends from school, the cheer squad, and her gymnastics class. All decked out in different shades of pink. Her heart is so full.

But then she spies Reece on the balcony and her heart bursts! He's looking out at everybody dancing and eating around the pool, and when he spies Tay, his face lights up. He's holding the most gorgeous bouquet of pink roses. Tay can forgive him for wearing all black.

Reece rushes down the stairs and wraps his arms around her. "Happy birthday, Tay." He hands her the roses. "You are the brightness in my heart and life."

Seriously? COME ON. He's just THE BEST.

This is what it's like to date a guy who writes music. *Swoon!*

"Sorry I didn't wear anything pink, but it's your birthday so I will happily put on anything you'd like. The more sparkles, the better."

"You *are* so going to regret that!" Tay exclaims. She rushes over to the photo area and pulls out a bright pink boa and wraps it around Reece.

"That's all you got?" He laughs as he flings the boa around his neck.

"Don't threaten me with a good time, babes." Tay grabs the pink sparkly headband that Kai got her and puts it on Reece's head, pulling back his hair so his beautiful face and eyes are on display.

Happiest of birthdays to her!

"Well, that's not my only present." He gives her a tender kiss on the lips.

Okay, Tay has already said it fourteen thousand times, but this is the Best. Birthday. Ever! It might even be the Best. Day. Ever! It is competing with the Eras Tour and getting the hat, but still. It's THE BEST to have so many favorite days.

"Picture!" Tay wants to remember every single detail about today. She pulls in Reece for a selfie and plants a kiss on his cheek. She studies the photo, how happy they both are. "Totally got to post this, hashtag rock 'n' roll royalty!"

"Tay." Reece bites his lip in that totally cute way he does when he's nervous. "Maybe don't post one of us kissing? I want to protect our private lives and not let the fans get into our business."

Fans? Tay sometimes forgets that she has fans!

"Let's do another one." Reece takes her phone and presses his cheek against Tay's. She can't help but beam, being so close to him. "How's this one for our fans?"

The photo is almost as good as the original and Reece does have a point, even though he didn't mind posting about them being a music power couple a couple of weeks ago. But so much has changed since then. If Tay wants to be a huge superstar like Taylor Swift, she has to learn how to manage a fanbase. She needs to keep some things to herself, which is hard for her to do since she likes Reece so much! And keeping secrets is *so hard*. She glances over at Teffy, who is seated in a corner with Taylor.

"It's perfect," she replies to Reece. Besides, this means the one of her kissing Reece is just for her.

"*You* are perfect." He gently cups her head in his hands. "I gotta make sure everything is set up for later, but I'll be right back." He kisses her on the lips before he heads over to the stage.

"Oh, Tay." Cat comes over with Tiffany. "I didn't realize how cute Reece is, well done."

"Thanks!" Tay didn't want to remind them that they felt sorry for Tay when she was assigned to be biology partners with Reece. But look how everything turned out! She got a B-plus and a boyfriend who is A-plus-plus-plus-plus-plus!

"Excuse me!" her dad's voice booms from the stage. "Thank you all for coming to celebrate my baby girl's sweet sixteen. I'm so incredibly proud of the young lady she's become and I hope you join me in singing . . . *Happy birthday . . .*"

The crowd starts singing along as Teffy and Taylor approach Tay with her cake that has sixteen candles lit around the border. Tay takes in all these people in her life who are there for her, wearing pink and having a good time.

As the song ends and Tay blows out the candles, she feels like most of her wishes have already come true.

"Speech!" Taylor calls out, and a few others follow.

Tay is handed a microphone. You don't need to ask her twice.

"Thank you!" Tay's face hurts from smiling so wide. "I love you all so much. First, Daddy . . ." Her throat gets caught for a moment. "Thank you for everything, Daddy, you're the best. And my friends, especially the Taylors." Taylor gives out a loud yell. "And, of course, Reece and the band. When I moved here from Florida right before fifth grade, I wasn't sure if I'd make any friends, if I would find a place here in Indiana. And now . . . Well, my heart is incredibly full."

There's a strumming of an acoustic guitar, and all eyes go from Tay to the stage, where Reece is standing—with the boa and headband still on. "I have a new song that I wanted to play today for Tay . . . since I wrote it about her. It's called 'Brighter Than the Sun.'"

A rush of bodies go toward the stage, and Tay can't help but notice it's girls that have lined the front, blinking up at Reece as he begins singing, *"I've been holding onto so much for so long, then I met you . . ."* Reece's gaze meets Tay as he continues. *"I've been scared of so much, for so long, then I met you . . ."*

Tay feels as if her body is floating over the pool as she takes in this love song that Reece wrote about her. How she's his *"shining star, who owns my tender heart."* Tay's entire body is buzzing. She glances over to her father, who looks impressed.

See! This is the greatest day in the history of the world!

Teffy and Taylor come over and put their arms around Tay as they sway to the song. Tay closes her eyes, taking in this moment so she can replay it and replay it.

Tay has no idea why she was so stressed out. Everything is turning out better than she could ever hope.

Our Chat (The Taylors Version)

TAY🎉: TS! THAT PIC!!! YOU LOOK AMAZING!!!! THAT DRESS!!! YOUR HAIR!!! AND YOU'RE WEARING MAKEUP!!!! ARE THOSE FAKE EYELASHES?!?!?!

TS ⚽: So we're still doing all caps then

TEFFY📚: You look like the queen you are! 👑

TAYLOR🐝: 🔥🔥🔥🔥🔥

TAY🎉: EVEN THOUGH I WISH YOU WERE HERE! HAVE SO MUCH FUN AT YOUR BALL!!! GAHHHH!!! WHAT A DAY!!!!!

TS ⚽: And down the rabbit hole I go

FOURTEEN
Wonderland

TS has never experienced imposter syndrome before. She's heard her teammates talk about that feeling like you don't really deserve to be where you are.

One of TS's favorite USWNT moments is when Megan Rapinoe held their World Cup trophy and shouted, "I deserve this! I deserve this! Everything!" And, you know what? She did. She *worked* for that. Of course, there were people—mostly men—who said Megan was being egotistical. What's so egotistical about knowing you got what you fought so hard for? That win wasn't handed to her, it was earned.

No, on the field, TS knows she belongs there. Every accolade, every win, is earned.

Going to a ball, however . . .

It's yet another thing that TS has said yes to. Since the match, she's been going to every event. In return, Gemma has made more time for TS.

As much as TS wants to believe everything is back to normal and great, she still doesn't feel like she belongs. She's doing it for Gemma. This is TS trying.

"Have I told you how absolutely radiant you look?" Gemma takes

TS's hands as the hair and makeup team—it took a small army to make this happen—puts on finishing touches.

"Oh, this old thing," TS jokes as she studies herself in the mirror. Her red hair has been smoothed down in large ringlets that cascade down her back. The sides of her hair have been pulled back with pearl combs that come from Gemma's "family jewel collection." Let that sink in: They have a jewel collection! TS has, like, seven earrings, and only two complete pairs. Do the math on that one.

Gemma's grandmother insisted that both Gemma and TS have specially made gowns. TS is wearing a floor-length emerald-green satin dress with a cowl neck and fitted waist. While Gemma looks like an actual princess with her brown hair swept up in an actual diamond tiara and a strapless lavender gown with layers of tulle, very reminiscent of Taylor's "Enchanted" dress from the Eras Tour.

For the record, TS is very enchanted.

Gemma gently places her hands on TS's face. "Thank you for doing this."

"What? Get dolled up? Go to a ball? Hang out with my gorgeous girlfriend?" TS jokes, but honestly, TS is exhausted by all the smiling and tongue biting she's had to do at these boring and stuffy events.

On the bright side, all that frustration has meant TS has hit a running pace of just under a seven-minute mile.

"Well, nothing will tear me from your side this evening, and that's a threat." Gemma goes to give TS a kiss, but then remembers her lips are covered in lip liner, lipstick, and gloss.

TS wasn't kidding when she said it took a small army—and a countertop of products—to get them ready.

"Knock, knock!" Cressida calls out as she glides into Gemma's suite. "Oh, don't you both look smashing!"

TS hates to admit that Cressida looks like she belongs on the cover of some high-fashion magazine, in a cream-colored gown decorated with feathers.

"Gems, Grandmama wants to make sure your tiara is properly secured, can't have that go missing!"

Gemma gives TS one of her *here we go again* looks. "I'll be right back."

"No need!" Cressida claps impatiently. "Guests have started arriving. We shall meet you there. I'll help TS get finished so she'll be . . . appropriate."

Is she kidding? TS has been plucked and prodded at for hours. And she's not exaggerating. The team arrived at four o'clock for a ball that starts at eight.

"See you down there." Gemma gives TS an apologetic smile before she leaves.

TS turns to the floor-length mirror and runs her hands down the soft satin of her dress. Cressida comes from behind and pulls TS's shoulders back.

"Don't slouch, darling. And chin up." Cressida flicks her finger at TS's chin.

TS bites the insides of her cheeks. It'll be easier to get through this evening if she smiles and keeps quiet. Although, that hasn't helped so far.

"There's one thing missing and Grandmama insisted you have it." Before TS realizes what's happening, Cressida takes an antique brooch and begins to fasten it to TS's gown. TS tenses at the hole that's been poked into her extremely expensive dress. When Cressida steps away, TS is able to get a good look at it. "Is that a . . ."

"Yes, it's a bug, but darling, it's art deco with diamonds and emeralds. It's a very important and valuable piece, but you're a part of this family and Grandmama felt it appropriate for you to wear it tonight. Be sure to take special care of it."

TS swallows hard. This is a lot of pressure. While she sort of can't believe she's being trusted with yet another item from the family jewel collection, she knows it's a big deal.

"I'll protect it with my life," TS says with a wavering voice.

Cressida gives TS a Cheshire Cat smile. "Fabulous. Well, let's go downstairs to the ballroom. We can't keep our guests waiting. Now, I'm sure you were given a rundown of the important people coming, but let's be real, they're *all* important. When in doubt, bow, but please do remember your place. There will be some of the most distinguished families here who may not, well, be a fan of . . ." Cressida then mouths, "America." She continues out loud, "And best for you to say that you and Gemma are really good mates."

There it is. Sure, TS knows some people aren't fans of Americans—and she doesn't really blame them—but she can't help but wonder if the issue people have with her being here is that she's Gemma's girlfriend.

But they also don't seem to have a problem with Zara, so . . .

TS lets out a sigh.

"I said don't slouch!" Cressida is aghast as she exaggeratedly pulls her own shoulders back. "Now, for our entrance, best for you to let me go first. There will be photographers capturing this for the society papers and, well, I like to make an entrance."

TS follows Cressida down the staircase that overlooks the main entrance and sees the hall swarming with people dressed in gowns and suits. She notices the average age seems to be seven hundred.

"Cress, darling!" an elderly woman dripping in diamonds gives Cressida air-kisses while TS stands awkwardly behind her.

Cressida takes the woman by the hand as they follow the crowd into the ballroom, because yes, in the east wing of the castle, there's a ballroom. The walls are painted light blue with white columns and intricate plasterwork while the ceiling features three huge chandeliers. There are bouquets of blue, white, and yellow flowers throughout the room. On either side of the entrance are food stations with towering fruit and cheese platters that are works of art. In the far corner, on a small stage, a string quartet is playing.

TS weaves between the crowd as she tries to find Gemma, the heels she's wearing already pinching her toes. TS's feet were meant for running, for kicking, for dribbling, not to be squeezed into four-inch heels. But at least the extra height lets her peer over most of the crowd.

There's a series of flashes up ahead. TS finally spies Gemma being lined up with her family for photos in front of a painting of some really old white guy. When TS was given a tour her first day, she was told who all the portraits were of, but she got lost in all the "Earls" and "Dukes." While this new world should be exciting, she finds it stuffy. This room is huge, but it's the first time TS has experienced claustrophobia.

TS makes her way toward Gemma, waiting patiently for the photos to be over. Gemma and her relatives appear to be the perfect family: polished, prim, all smiles.

Even though TS looks the part right now, in her gown and makeup, TS doesn't belong here.

But it's for Gemma, she reminds herself.

As if Gemma could read her mind, she lights up when she sees TS. "Get in here, Shaw!" Gemma motions for TS to come next to her.

"This is for family only." Her grandmother sniffs but keeps her smile steady for the cameras.

"I'd like for her to be included," Gemma presses.

"Yes, Mother, at least for our personal photos." Gemma's mom gives TS a kind smile.

"Get in here, kiddo!" her dad says as he holds his arm out for TS.

Her grandmother's icy glare suddenly defrosts. "Well, Zara, sweetheart, you are a vision. Come next to me for a photo." She opens her arms and TS can only watch as Zara glides in, wearing a red column dress decorated in roses. Her skin is luminous, and her short hair has rose petals strung throughout.

So it's confirmed: The coldness isn't because TS is gay. It's because TS is TS.

It's almost easier to accept people not liking you because they're small-minded and homophobic. But the fact that Gemma's family doesn't like TS because she's . . . her, *that* stings.

TS takes a step back and lets herself get swallowed up in the crowd. She smiles politely at the passing people and pretends like this is just a typical Saturday night for her, even though she wishes she could magically transport herself to Tay's birthday party.

The quartet starts up and the dance floor clears as people start doing some dance that looks like it belongs in one of those old stuffy historical movies that her mom loves. There's bowing and gliding. TS makes her way to the food. When in doubt, eat. Although, there are several decorative globs of food she doesn't recognize, so she sticks to eating cheese. You can never go wrong with cheese.

"There you are," comes Freddie's bored voice.

"Hello," TS replies cooly. She's not deluded enough to believe that Freddie looking for her could ever be a good thing.

"Enjoying the evening?" He takes a cracker and runs it through some gray mush that makes TS's stomach recoil. Although, it could also be her present company. "I'm sure you're not used to things like this in the States."

"Yes." Short but sweet is going to be TS's philosophy for dealing with him.

"Well, it's important to do things for *charity*."

TS can't help but notice how he looks pointedly at her when he says "charity." Okay, yes, this event is for charity, which is lovely and all, but TS thinks about all the money that has been spent on the food, drinks, entertainment, and dresses. Money that could also do good.

All TS knows is when she makes her millions from being a soccer player, she's going to give back. Start a foundation. Make a difference. Never make someone feel like they don't belong.

"Did my cousin teach you any of the—"

Freddie is cut off as TS is slammed by a tall, muscular blond dressed in a tux. He loses his balance and falls on TS for a moment. By some luck—she figures she's due—TS remains on her feet and doesn't knock over any of the food.

"Sorry! So sorry! Didn't realize where I was going!" he stammers as he walks away.

TS moves her shoulder, making sure it's still in its socket. "Have you seen Gemma?"

Freddie glances at her and gives her a smug smile. "Can't say that I have."

TS nods, but then feels a hand on the small of her back and all her tension releases. She knows that touch anywhere.

"Hey." Gemma puts her chin on TS's shoulder. "I'm so sorry about all that. I'm not leaving your side for the rest of the night."

It's a promise Gemma has made a lot on this trip. TS takes Gemma's hand and hopes this will be the time she doesn't break it. Gemma leads her to the middle of the dance floor.

"I don't know this dance," TS admits.

Gemma smiles. "Neither do I, but I don't care. I want everybody to see me with you. And besides, that dance is *so* seventeen hundreds."

Gemma spins, her dress fanning out, and then comes back to TS. "What matters to me is you."

And that's all that should matter to TS. Not the glances she's getting from the people nearby.

"Once tonight is over, I'm going to see if we can go with my parents somewhere, maybe the Lake District, just to get away from . . ." Gemma doesn't need to finish that thought.

"That sounds perfect." Some might be impressed by the castle and fancy meals and people, but TS can't wait to leave it all behind.

"Maybe we can go there now?" TS asks hopefully.

"I know it may seem that my family doesn't like you, but they do, they just . . . are very British and don't know how to show emotion." Gemma looks down and frowns. "What happened to your gown?"

"What?" TS looks down and notices a small tear near her right strap. Where Cressida had put the antique brooch, which is missing. TS's stomach bottoms out. An unfamiliar energy courses through her body. It's sheer panic. "Oh no! The brooch. No!"

Gemma looks confused. "What brooch?"

TS lets go of Gemma as she scans the floor, moving and bumping into a couple dancing next to them.

"Pardon me!" the woman protests.

"Sorry!" TS pats down her dress, hoping it may have fallen inside it, but she feels her breath start to quicken. This can't be happening. She has to find the brooch. It has to be here somewhere, but with the mass of bodies moving around the ballroom, she's worried it'll be trampled.

"What's going on, Shaw?" Gemma asks, but TS is busy retracing her steps to the food table. Wait! She was bumped! Yes! She bets the brooch tore off when that guy slammed into her. It's probably near the food.

There's a group of people enjoying the cheese platter. There's no discreet way to do this, but she also knows she can't afford to replace a priceless family heirloom, so TS gets on her hands and knees to scan the area. She should feel humiliated rummaging around the floor, but all that matters to her is finding the brooch. To prove to Gemma's family that she can be trusted.

"AH!" a woman cries out as she trips over TS.

"Shaw!" Gemma hisses. "What are you doing? Get up!"

TS is so focused—and freaking out—that she ignores Gemma. Sure, Gemma may be embarrassed by TS now, but it will be much worse for them both if she can't find the brooch.

"What in heaven is this all about?" Freddie comes over with Cressida on his heels. They both seem to be enjoying the sight of TS on her hands and knees.

TS pops up and brushes her dress out, even though she knows there's not a spot of dust on that hardwood floor. "Nothing, I just . . ."

"Oh dear!" Cressida's mouth goes open. "Where's the brooch?"

"Not the antique brooch from the Countess of Hartshorn!" Freddie puts his hand dramatically to his chest.

"What brooch?" Gemma looks between her cousins.

"Freddie!" TS exclaims, a little too loudly, causing heads to turn, not like she didn't already have an audience. But she doesn't care. She knows she's desperate if she's looking to Freddie for help. "Do you know the guy that bumped into me earlier? I think maybe when he did that, the brooch tore off."

"You wouldn't be accusing Richard Conyngham the Fourth of stealing, would you? My dear, he does *not* need the money." Freddie looks around the room, bored. "In fact, the only person here who would have anything to gain by stealing the brooch is . . . well, you." Freddie blinks back at her.

"What?" TS's stomach has dropped. She feels like she's going to be sick. She doesn't know how this evening—let's be honest, this whole trip—could get any worse. First, she loses the brooch and now Freddie is accusing her of *stealing*. "I didn't . . ." TS's breath is becoming strained. She tries to calm herself, but she's so lost right now. The attention from the spectators isn't helping.

"What on earth are you up to, Freddie?" Gemma's dad joins them, with Gemma's mom.

"Probably only trouble," Gemma's mom says with a shake of her head.

"Mr. and Mrs. Walker, I'm so sorry," TS starts, her heart beating fast. "I don't know what happened. I was wearing a bug brooch that was lent to me and now it's . . . gone." TS gestures at the tear in her dress. "I didn't mean to lose it, I just—" TS's throat catches.

She didn't just lose a piece of jewelry. TS has failed. She tried, she really did, but she just can't make herself fit in with Gemma's family.

What does that mean for her and Gemma?

"Bug brooch?" Mrs. Walker folds her arms and turns to Freddie and Cressida, her face unamused. "Bug brooch, *really*?"

Then Freddie and Cressida's shocked faces slowly morph. It starts with the pinching of lips before they both let out a loud cackle.

"Sorry, Auntie, we just couldn't resist a wee prank." Cressida blinks in an innocent way nobody is buying. "You have to admit it is rather hilarious. Imagine thinking that wretched thing was priceless! I can't believe she even let me put it on her."

Wait. WHAT? TS's mind is busy racing. What does that mean? This was all some sort of sick *joke*? A *prank*?

Gemma reaches out to hold TS's hand, but she pulls it away.

No, TS has never had imposter syndrome. True, she doesn't *deserve* to be here. Because TS is better than this load of pretentious crap dressed up in diamonds and pearls.

"And I can't believe you," TS says as she pokes Freddie in the chest. He takes a step back, surprise on his face. "Do you feel good? Do you? For humiliating me? Making me feel like crap?"

"Shaw . . ." Gemma tries to take TS by the hand, but TS pulls her hand back.

"No!" TS exclaims loudly. The dancing around her has stopped, and the music has, too. Freddie and Cressida exchange infuriatingly satisfied looks. "I can't believe I tried to get you to like me. Why? Why would I want to be anything like you? You may be offended by me being an American or middle-class or gay, but at least I'm not some stuck-up, useless piece of—"

"Shaw!" Gemma scolds her. Gemma's eyes are glassy, her face tight. She looks around to the other people. "I'm so sorry, I am . . ."

It's then that TS realizes that Gemma isn't apologizing to her. She's apologizing to the societal spectators. She's embarrassed by TS.

"No, Gemma." There's an unfamiliar burn behind TS's eyes. "I'm the one who is sorry. For ever thinking I was on an even playing field."

TS storms out of the ballroom, on the verge of tears. She's tough, but this world of Gemma's isn't fair.

And TS doesn't want to have any part of it.

"Shaw!" Gemma calls after TS as she sprints up the stairs. She decides to skip a step and her ankle twists. TS hits the ground, grabbing her ankle.

"Are you okay?" Gemma sits on the step and tries to touch TS's ankle, but she pulls it away.

"Don't!" TS snaps.

Gemma's parents have followed them up the staircase, with a crowd gathered below. Cressida and Freddie have made sure to be in the front. TS knows they must be enjoying every second of this.

"I'm so sorry, TS," Gemma's mom says. "My sister raised a bunch of entitled brats."

"I'm sure they—" Gemma starts, but TS stops her.

"Do *not* defend them." She can feel a tear trickle down her face.

TS doesn't give up easily. But she knows when she's had enough. When she's lost.

"I wasn't going to," Gemma replies in a small voice. "I just don't want there to be a scene . . ." But Gemma has to realize it's too late. The majority of the guests have gathered to watch the drama unfolding on the staircase.

TS looks around at the oil paintings, the marble statues, the gold leaf, the people who look down on her. She's done with it all.

"I want to go home." As soon as those words leave her, she lets out an actual sob. She didn't realize how much she needs to be home until she said those words. "I *need* to go home. I can't stay here one more night, sleeping with one eye open. Your family doesn't like me, and to be honest, Gemma, I don't like them. No offense, Mr. and Mrs. Walker. I don't mean you."

Gemma's dad sits down on the stairs. "I know you don't, and I'll get you on a flight home. Why don't you pack, and you and I can head to London tonight. Get away from all this."

TS sniffs. "Thanks." She stands up and there's a sting in her ankle that she ignores as she goes into her room. She takes off the heels. She strips off her dress. TS feels a sense of lightness with the removal of each item. She puts her hair up in a ponytail and pulls on a pair of shorts and a T-shirt.

There you are, TS says to herself in the mirror.

Gemma comes into the bedroom cautiously. "I can't believe you're doing this."

"Really? What aren't you getting?" TS slams her suitcase on the bed. "Your family hates me for no reason. They are cruel. And you . . ."

Gemma takes a hesitant step forward. "What about me?" Her green eyes are wet.

"I don't know! I feel like I don't know you anymore. The Gemma

I know wouldn't spend all her time trying to impress vapid people. She wouldn't be horrified by my inability to be some Socialite Barbie. She would've stood up for me. She wouldn't have abandoned me."

Gemma lets out a long breath. "This has been hard on me, too."

"Oh, has it?" TS says roughly. "Because this entire trip has been a nightmare for me. I went into it waiting for the right moment to tell you how much I love you, but then at every chance, your family got in the way. And you went along with it. It's like I didn't even matter to you."

"Wait." Gemma takes a step forward. "You love me?"

TS opens her mouth. She's not so sure now. Looking at Gemma hurts. And if it's really love, it shouldn't hurt this much. It shouldn't be this much work. TS isn't afraid of work, but not if she's expected to carry the weight by herself.

"Shaw?" Tears are falling down Gemma's face.

"I—I—I—" TS can't get the words out. Instead she tells the truth. "All I know is that I can't be with you if this is what comes with it."

Gemma's face darkens, her voice barely a whisper. "They're my family."

"Well, then, I guess we know where we stand." TS keeps her head down as she starts packing her bag. She leaves the dress and heels behind. It only takes her a few minutes to pack. After zipping up her bag, TS finally looks up to find Gemma is gone.

TS collapses on the bed.

She can't wait to go home.

Where she belongs.

Our Chat (The Taylors Version)

TAY🎉: This wasn't the birthday surprise I was hoping for, but still happy you're coming back, TS

TEFFY📚: We'll be here with open arms. Whatever you need.

TAYLOR🐝: Ditch those clowns

TS ⚽: 🫶

FIFTEEN
The Alchemy

If Teffy is doing the math correctly, TS is somewhere over the Atlantic Ocean right now.

Teffy is torn. Her heart aches for TS. That Gemma's family could be so cruel. But she's also happy to have her friend back home. She doesn't feel whole without the Taylors being together. And next Sunday, in a week, they'll properly reunite at Friends and Family Day at Whispering Pines.

TS isn't the only thing that's tearing Teffy up. It's the whole Liam mess. And it *is* a mess. Teffy hasn't spoken to him in four days. Four days. She pulls out her phone and studies their last exchange after she stormed out of the restaurant.

LIAM: Can we please talk?

TEFFY: I'm too upset right now.

LIAM: Let me know when you're ready

TEFFY: OK

The thing is, Teffy wants to talk to Liam, but she doesn't know what to say. Or how to fix this.

Can they really be a couple if what they want is so different? Liam likes to be in a big crew. Teffy wants it to be just the two of them. Or at least not with Hannah.

All Teffy knows is that she wants to be with Liam. But she shouldn't have to compromise who she is or be forced to be around someone who has been so awful to her. Liam should know that. She's not sure what the answer is. Teffy would never want to be the kind of person to stop someone from hanging with their friends. And that's not what she wants.

Teffy can't help but think about Reece and Tay. It's not like Reece hangs out with the Taylors a lot, which is fine with Teffy. She likes having her time with just Tay. Tay isn't forcing Reece on her friends. Sure, Teffy sometimes goes to their rehearsals, but she likes the music the Archers are playing now.

There are moments when Teffy sees how much joy Tay has onstage that she wishes she could be brave enough to perform. She loves music so much. It's in her bones. It's the performing part that she can't seem to get past.

There's a lot that Teffy can't seem to get past.

"These just came in. Can you stock them, please?" Cathy, the manager at By the Book, sets down a box of romances on the checkout counter.

"Of course." Teffy takes the box, happy to have something to do. It's been a fairly quiet Sunday afternoon. The sun is shining through the two large windows in the front, illuminating the rows and rows of bookshelves. There's a children's section in the corner, with a painted

Alice in Wonderland mural and fairy lights strung over the store. It's one of Teffy's favorite places.

Teffy goes over to the romance shelves and starts putting the books in their place. She hasn't been in the mood to read romance lately. As she looks at the pastel covers with the smiling heroine and her perfect mate, she feels a pang of want. She had that, for just a moment in time.

Is she ready to let that go?

She's not so sure.

Teffy sighs heavily as the overhead bell goes off, signaling someone's come into the store. She looks up and sees two girls from the cheerleading squad. They were also at Tay's party yesterday.

Teffy gets up from the floor to greet them. "Hi, Rachel and Cecilia! Anything I can help you find?" she says with a smile. It takes a lot of effort to smile.

They look at each other with their lips pursed. "Um, we're . . ." Rachel starts, and then giggles for a moment. "Just looking," she finally gets out. Then they do this weird shimmying of their shoulders as if they're about to burst. It reminds Teffy of Tay yesterday. She was *extra* Tay, which is saying a lot.

"Well, I'll be right over there if you need help finding anything." Teffy turns her back, but then the overhead bell rings again. Cat comes in with a guy from the cheerleading squad, who is wearing an Eras Tour T-shirt. Maybe the cheerleading squad is meeting here. "Hi, Cat."

"Just looking, Teffy!" Cat calls out quickly before she goes over to a corner.

"Ah, okay." Teffy can't really blame Cat for the fight with Liam. She was really welcoming and nice, but that doesn't mean it isn't awkward. Cat kept her distance from Teffy at Tay's party, which was appreciated. Seeing her and the cheerleaders reminds Teffy of Liam.

Basically, everything reminds Teffy of Liam.

Teffy glances at the four cheerleading customers, who are at opposite parts of the store, glancing at one another. Teffy's instincts kick in. They are acting very, very shady. She starts watching them closely, hoping they're not here to steal.

"I'll be in the back," Cathy says with a smile as she heads toward the office.

What? Teffy doesn't want to be left alone. What if they try to take a bunch of books? Not that she would think Cat would do such a thing, but she *is* acting weird.

The overhead door pings again and Teffy feels relief as Tay walks in. She's wearing the hat—she sort of insists on having a birthday month—and has a portable speaker in her hand. Before Teffy can say a single word to her, Tay presses play, and By the Book is filled with the familiar beginning of "Cruel Summer."

As if on cue, the four cheerleaders and Tay start dancing to the song. In the middle of the bookstore.

"Um . . . ?" Teffy says, looking for Cathy to come out and get angry about . . . whatever is happening right now. The five cheerleaders are all bright smiles as they dance in sync to what happens to be one of Teffy's favorite bops, but really, there is a time and place to dance along to Taylor Swift, and it's not at Teffy's work.

"Tay . . ." Teffy starts, panicked that she's going to get in trouble, but Tay winks at her as she shimmies along to the second verse. Teffy glances toward the back room and spies Cathy singing along, filming the dance. Maybe she planned this as some kind of promotion? But why wouldn't she tell Teffy?

Okay, if Cathy is cool with this, then Teffy is going to enjoy the performance. Not like she can help her hips from shaking. Her lips twitch. She's only human, after all, and this song always brings back the most amazing memories of being with her best friends at Lucas Oil Stadium for one of the greatest nights in her life. Her legs start shaking as she gets ready for the bridge—aka the most iconic bridge in the history of bridges. Is she really going to scream it in the middle of the store? Is it even humanly possible to *not* sing along to it?

Right as the bridge kicks in, Teffy is floored because storming through the door on cue is Liam.

"Oh, hi!" He throws his arms up and then begins strutting and singing along to the song like he studied the Eras Tour concert movie, the five cheerleaders in step with him.

Wait. Did they *practice* this?

What on earth is going on?

Liam is marching toward Teffy, screaming the bridge in an adorable off-key way, but as Teffy takes in the lyrics and meaning, it's so perfect right now. The song is about a secret summer romance and the pains and yearning that go with it. As he gets to the end, he drops down on his knees in front of Teffy, hand on his heart as he screams, "*I love you, ain't that the worst thing—*" and then his voice cracks, which causes him to nearly fall over laughing.

Teffy can't help but laugh, too. At all of this. At this . . . Oh my goodness, it finally hits Teffy what's going on. She's read enough romances to know. Liam is making a grand romantic gesture. In a bookstore. To a Taylor Swift song.

Teffy is going to write the most epic love song after this.

But first.

Teffy gets down on her knees so she's eye to eye with a smiling Liam. The dancers around him continue, and Tay has seemingly gone off choreography as she starts doing high kicks. Tay puts the hat on Teffy's head and gives her a hug before she leads the cheerleaders out of the store.

The store is quiet, save for the regular acoustic music playing in the background.

"Hey." Liam takes Teffy's hands.

"Hey." Teffy studies Liam's sweet face, wanting to remember every detail of this perfect moment.

"I know you said you needed some time, but it's been torture waiting for you." Liam bites his lip. "I've missed you, Tefs."

"Same."

Yes, it's only been four days, but it's clear to Teffy that she can't go this long ever again without being with Liam. If that means she has to deal with Hannah, well, she's going to have to do it.

Cathy clears her throat, reminding Teffy they're not alone. "Why don't you take a break, Teffy?" She chuckles to herself as she picks up a stack of books.

Even Cathy is in on it? The amount of planning, and the fact that Tay could keep this a secret! *That* is something.

Liam takes Teffy by the hand, and they stay quiet as they walk to a plaza off Main Street with a few benches. Liam gestures for Teffy to sit down.

"Okay," he begins. "I've been trying to figure out the best way to do this, and well, just bear with me. I did your thing, Tefs, and now it's time to do mine." Liam reaches into the back pocket of his jeans and pulls out a Harrison Eagles baseball hat. He places it on his head—his unruly hair sticking up around the cap—and then puts a whistle around his neck. "Okay, Bennett, we gotta talk about this team." Liam's voice is deeper, imitating his coach. "Our current defense isn't working, and we're gonna lose some dead weight." Liam puts his foot on the bench next to Teffy as he starts chewing on the whistle.

"You should know, Bennett, you're the MVP of this team." Liam taps his heart. "Anybody else, well, if they don't pass muster, they don't get a spot on this roster, you get what I mean?"

"Um, maybe?" Teffy finds Liam's serious tone hilarious, but she's not exactly sure what he means.

Liam drops the coach act. "I've told the crew that Hannah isn't invited to anything I'm at. And I'm going to put you first. You don't have to hang out with them if you don't want to. You don't have to do anything you don't want to. The most important thing to me is for you to be happy and comfortable. Besides, I like it best when it's just the two of us." Liam straightens up again and blows his whistle. "Okay, what do you think of this new game plan, Bennett?"

"You're not going to make me do sits-up or anything, are you, Coach?"

"Well, if you want to keep your MVP standing, I'm going to need at least five . . . kisses." Liam touches his lips.

Teffy stands up and takes the whistle from his hand. "Liam, I don't want you to stop—"

"Tefs, I'm not giving up anything. I'm prioritizing who I want to spend my time with. And those guys, Tefs, they're only my teammates. *You* are my trophy. I fought hard for this, and I'm not letting go." Liam wraps his hand around the back of Teffy's neck and pulls her in for the sweetest kiss. "I love you, Teffy Bennett."

Teffy has never been into sports, but she feels like she's just scored the biggest touchdown.

Our Chat (The Taylors Version)

TAYLOR🐝: I've heard rumors of an epic performance for our Teffy ♡ ♡ ♡

TEFFY📚: 🥰🥰🥰

TAY🎉: IT WAS SO HARD NOT TELLING YOU ON MY BIRTHDAY, BUT I HAD NO CHOICE! I NEARLY EXPLODED!!!!!

TAYLOR🐝: Jae told me that Liam FaceTimed her for pointers

TEFFY📚: 🥰🥰🥰

TAYLOR🐝: Aww, she's speechless

TAYLOR🐝: Please give TS the biggest hug from me!!!!

TAY🎉: IT WILL BE THE BIGGEST!!!

TEFFY📚: You up and ready for visitors yet, TS?

SIXTEEN
right where you left me

What a sad sight.

TS looks at herself in her bedroom mirror. Her hair is messier than normal. She's still wearing the cozy tracksuit she wore on the plane ride home. Her eyes are baggy. She's been up since four in the morning, staring at the ceiling. She could blame the jet lag, but her mind won't stop going back and forth, replaying her time in England. It was supposed to be a dream, and ended up a nightmare.

She's almost numb to it all. Even though she's in her bedroom, she doesn't feel like she's *home*. It was all she wanted, to be back here, but there's a big part of her that she left behind.

There's noise coming from downstairs, voices followed by stomping on the stairs. It's loud. It's chaotic. Which can only mean one thing.

"You're back!" Tay screams as she comes bursting into TS's room. She flings her arms around TS and rocks her back and forth. "We missed you so much and we want to hear everything and you need to tell us who are our enemies now. We are, forever and always, Team TS!"

"Hey, TS," Teffy calls from behind Tay with more of a reserved enthusiasm. She's wearing the hat. When Tay finally lets her grip go, Teffy comes in for a more comforting hug. When she pulls away, she places the hat gently on TS's head. "Figured you might need this."

"Thanks." TS closes her eyes and tries to transport herself to a happier time, when she first wore the hat. To let that feeling of joy take over her. For her to feel *something*.

Nope. She's got nothing.

"Okay!" Tay claps her hands. "We are taking you out!" Tay starts making herself busy by picking up some of the clothes that TS threw on the floor, which was her entire suitcase. "And we want to hear everything, the good, the bad, the very Brit-*ish*," she says the last part in an awful British accent that almost gets TS to crack a smile.

Almost.

"What are you in the mood for?" Teffy asks, reading the room and being her usual cautious self. "Pizza?"

TS shakes her head. Ugh. TS loves pizza, who doesn't? But that reminds her of Gemma. They'd usually go get pizza after a game. Who is TS kidding, everything is going to remind her of Gemma.

"Okay, well, there's the new café on Main Street that's supposed to make a really good tuna melt," Teffy offers.

"Oh, melty cheese, sign me up!" Tay claps.

TS sighs. While she appreciates her friends' help, she's just sort of . . . stuck. She feels nearly frozen, wondering how she got to this place. It's like there's a flurry around her, with Tay throwing her clothes and Teffy taking her gently by the hand, and before she really knows how it happens, she's seated cross-legged at a window booth at KT's Café, looking out at shoppers enjoying this sunny July Monday.

As they look over the menus, TS realizes it's too quiet. It doesn't feel right. She's with her best friends. This is what she was missing when she was in England. This was what she wanted, right? To come back to this.

But the *this* always included Gemma. TS focuses on the future a lot: making the national team, winning the World Cup, and in every scenario, Gemma was always a part of it somehow.

The waiter comes to take their order, and then Tay and Teffy start filling TS in on everything she's missed. She knows they mean well, but can't they sense that she needs time to process her thoughts, her feelings? Because TS still doesn't really know what to think except that she never wants to be put in that position again. To be made to feel like she doesn't belong. Like she's worthless. But that means . . .

TS blinks, trying to focus on her friends talking, but it's like they're off speed-reading a book while she's stuck on the same page.

"It's silly." TS didn't realize she said that aloud.

Tay stops talking and turns to her. She cautiously reaches her hand out as if TS were some kitten that could be scared away. "What's silly?"

"Me. This. My reaction." Right then, the waiter comes over to place their food in front of them. TS's focus is on her cheeseburger. "It's not like this is the first time in history this has happened. People break up all the time." TS's voice hitches.

"Is that . . . official?" Teffy asks with a frown. "You didn't really say for sure . . ."

She didn't, but that's what happened, right? TS told Gemma she couldn't be with her. Then TS fled the ball, but unlike Cinderella there was no fairy godmother, just Gemma's dad, who kept apologizing for his wife's family.

Gemma sent her two texts while TS was on the plane:

Let me know when you get home.

I really need to talk to you.

TS hasn't replied, maybe because she knows it'll be too hard to hear Gemma tell TS that they can't be together. That Gemma doesn't love her.

No, it's better to be the one to cut things off.

Then why does it hurt so much?

"We broke up."

TS has experienced hurt before: She's sprained her ankle, she's broken a finger, she's lost matches. But this . . . This is a different kind of pain.

TS remembers when she first developed feelings for Gemma, she thought about that broken finger. It healed. She foolishly thought a heart would be the same.

Now TS isn't so sure.

"You'll get through this." Teffy rubs her back. "Look at Taylor."

Yeah. Taylor bounced back after the whole Hunter situation. Even though they were only together for a month. Gemma and TS have been together . . . nine months? How is that possible? And Taylor has to deal with Hunter at her summer camp, so she's not rid of him.

While Gemma . . . she's TS's teammate.

Told you. See, this was why TS was hesitant to get involved with Gemma in the first place. How it would affect her head, her play . . . her heart.

"She left me no choice," TS says, her voice hoarse.

While she means having to leave Gemma behind, she's also referring to falling for her. How could she not? Her smile is as bright as the sun. Her face is an open book. She makes TS want to run faster, laugh louder, live bigger . . .

"Hey, TS, you're back!" TS snaps out of her internal crisis to find Shanti, her team's goalkeeper, walking toward them, holding hands with her younger sister. "Hi, Teffy and Tay."

"Hi!" Tay says in her very loud fashion, but TS knows she's just making up for TS being . . . well, TS isn't sure what she's being right now. "How's your summer been, Shanti? Have you been here before? The fries are so good!" Tay pops a fry in her mouth.

"Ah, no, not yet. Um, my summer has been good." Shanti gives TS a curious look. "You feeling okay, TS?"

"Jet-lagged," TS replies, wondering how long she'll be able to use that excuse. She pushes her plate away from her. She doesn't have much of an appetite.

"Yeah, I'm sure. I sort of can't believe it, though, about Gemma, you know? What's the team going to do?" Shanti lets out a breath.

Teffy looks between TS and Shanti. "What do you mean?"

"Oh!" Shanti's brown eyes get wide. "I thought you would've . . . um . . ." Shanti shifts nervously on her feet.

"What have you heard about Gemma?" Teffy asks.

TS knows it's bad when Teffy has to be her voice.

"Just that . . . I mean, I could be wrong, but she did text me this morning that, um . . ." Shanti looks toward the door, but she has to know that she can't outrun TS. Whatever it is has to be bad. "That Gemma might not come back. She might stay in England."

It's as if the lights inside TS's brain have been turned on all at once. So that's why Gemma wanted to talk to her. To tell TS that she's not coming back. That she's out of TS's life for good.

TS stands up so suddenly that her glass of water falls over and crashes onto the floor.

"Don't worry!" Tay says as she grabs napkins and starts carefully picking up the large broken shards. "It's okay, we can clean this up."

Yeah, it's easy enough to clean up after a broken glass, but a broken heart is a whole other matter.

Our Chat (The Taylors Version)

TAY🎉: We are only down one Taylor now!

TAYLOR🐝: And not just ANY Taylor

TAY🎉: OBVS

TAYLOR🐝: I'm setting off for our day trip with the kiddos

TEFFY📚: Have fun! Give Jae a hug from me!

TAY🎉: And glare at YOU KNOW WHO for me!

TAYLOR🐝: Done and done

SEVENTEEN
the lakes

Taylor always thought it would be glamorous to be famous: the fans, the clothes, the money, but after spending the last seven days basically being followed around, she realizes that perhaps living a quiet life is the way to go.

Okay, it's not like it's paparazzi stalking her, but her fellow counselors have been watching her, babysitting her. It's irritating since, for the zillionth time, *Taylor didn't do anything wrong.*

Well, that's not true. She trusted Hunter once upon a time. And now she's in this position because of his lies. His manipulations.

And Taylor is so over it.

"We're almost there!" Caleb calls out as the bus pulls into the parking lot at Worster Lake, a large lake in the middle of Potato Creek State Park.

Taylor is almost there as well because she's got a plan. She's spent the last few days putting it all into place. And it's going to be so sweet once she gets her revenge on Hunter.

The campers cheer as the large lake of dark blue water comes into view. Then a rumbling starts at the back of the bus, the kids overly giddy about their day out.

"What are they doing?" Taylor asks Caleb. He's been assigned to be Taylor's "bus buddy," aka her monitor. She and Caleb are taking the Red and Green Teams on a hike, along with two of the Green Team counselors. They're sharing supervising duties, so it should be a fun, chill day.

"Are they . . ." Taylor turns around to see the kids are clapping in unison, and a name starts ringing out.

"Ca-leb! Ca-leb! Ca-leb!"

Caleb's face lights up, although he's perpetually in a cheery mood. "Better give the people what they want." He stands up to cheers.

Before he even opens his mouth, the campers are already giggling.

Come to think of it, Taylor can't help but smile around Caleb. He's such a positive, funny person. Her dad has started asking more about Caleb than Taylor, their jokes a constant back-and-forth. And Caleb's generous. He's always bringing Taylor treats from the dining hall. And he's goofy. See . . . well, right now.

"Okay! Okay!" Caleb calls out, and the bus falls eerily quiet, the campers hanging on his every word. "What's a frog's favorite summertime treat?"

The campers reply by throwing out random answers like "Worms," "Ice Cream," and because there's always one troublemaker, "Butts."

Caleb shakes his head, then leans forward as the noise dies down, save a few giggles. "*Hop*-sicles."

Taylor hangs her head as she laughs. She can't help it. The jokes have become a bright spot in what has been an incredibly stressful week.

"Okay! Let's get ready to enjoy this gorgeous day!" Caleb says to a round of applause, like he's personally responsible for the sun. It's pretty adorable how much the kids love him.

As the kids start filing off the bus, Caleb turns to her. "Okay, on a scale of hilarity to perfection, how was that joke?"

"I honestly don't know who is worse, you or my dad," Taylor replies with a shake of her head.

"Why, thank you!" Caleb gives her a bow.

"And thank *you* for babysitting me," Taylor replies with a scowl. Even though she would've sat next to Caleb regardless, the fact that he was "assigned" to her stings.

Caleb lets out a long breath. "First, you're, like, way more mature than me, second, always a pleasure, and third, it's ridiculous. For real, Taylor. You're handling this so well."

Taylor isn't so sure about that. Sure, she smiles and goes along with being watched, but it's incredibly unfair.

"I just can't believe Mr. Mason." Caleb grits his teeth as they make their way off the bus. "That he took that jerk's word over ours."

Caleb, Mia, and Noah sat down with Mr. Mason to defend Taylor, but it didn't change anything. It seems that Hunter's word and Erin's parents' money won.

For now.

As they step off the bus, the weather really is perfect: sunny with a scattering of clouds. It's warm but not too hot.

"Be sure to put on extra sunscreen!" Taylor says as she hands the campers their bags with food, water, sunscreen, and an activity book to help identify the birds they'll spot on their hike.

"Thanks, Taylor!" Jae gives her a hug.

"You're welcome. And this is from Teffy." Taylor gives Jae an extra squeeze.

"I can't wait to see Teffy on Friends and Family Day." Jae juts her hip out. "Okay, *and* my brother. I guess."

"Same." Taylor doesn't believe in wishing time away, but she just can't wait to be with the Taylors. Plus, it marks the end of Color War. Red Team is down by only ten points. Then there's closing day and she'll be home, where she won't be treated like a criminal. "By the way, Jae, that brother of yours has some moves."

Jae starts giggling. "I'm going to make our parents play the video from the bookstore at his birthday party."

"You're a *cruuuuel sister*!" Taylor sings, knowing she's no Tay. "But I love it!" She gives her a high five before Jae goes over to her friends.

Taylor takes this quiet moment to stare out at the glistening lake before she has to wrangle the kids. She breathes in the fresh air, the smell of charcoal being barbecued nearby mixed with sunscreen.

"Pretty romantic, huh?"

And then it gets shattered as Hunter stands next to her.

"Remember when we went to a lake together?" He takes a picture with his phone.

Taylor's head starts throbbing. "Yes, I do recall. What with you not even caring that you were supposed to be my ride home and being a jerk about it. Pretty big red flag, but I was naïve back then. I've learned my lesson."

Hunter grimaces, like he regrets what he did to Taylor, what he's *currently* doing to Taylor. "Aw, Taylor, that's history." History that Taylor will not be repeating, thank you very much. "Well, I'll be joining you on the hike today."

"Why? Looking for a place to bury my body?" Taylor snaps. "There are witnesses." She gestures at the Whispering Pines campers and counselors, including Caleb, who is keeping an eye on Taylor. But she knows with Caleb it's for *Taylor's* protection. "You made sure of that."

Hunter places a hand over his heart like he's so innocent. That may play with Mr. Mason and some of the campers, but it stopped working on Taylor a long time ago.

She humphs as she stomps over to Caleb.

"You okay?" Caleb glares at Hunter. It's the only time his usual sunny disposition is clouded over. He puts his arm around her. "Don't let him get to you."

"I know." She does know, but there's something about Hunter that just burrows under her skin. She wants to scratch him away. For good.

"I've got another joke for you," Caleb starts, a mischievous smirk on his face. "Ready?"

Taylor nods. She needs something to make her smile.

Caleb tilts his head toward Hunter. "Hunter."

Taylor waits for a setup or a punch line.

"That's it, because *he* is the biggest joke there is."

Taylor gives him a grateful smile. She knows the Red Team is on her side. It just stings that Mr. Mason isn't.

"Okay, you fortunate campers going on a hike!" Hunter calls out and gives Taylor an infuriating wink. "Let's line up and get ready. Ty and Dylan, you two up front," Hunter instructs the Green counselors. "And, Caleb, why don't you go in the middle, while Taylor and I take the back."

And of course.

So much for today being a fun, chill day.

Although . . . this could be just the opportunity Taylor needs to help clear her name.

"Do you want me to talk to him and get us switched?" Caleb asks.

"No, I'll be okay." Taylor has been avoiding Hunter, but her plan does require her to get up close and personal.

Gag.

Caleb glares at Hunter. "Well, I'll be just ahead. If you need anything, and I mean anything, just call my name and I'll come running."

"Thanks, Caleb. Truly." Being around Caleb has been good for Taylor, a reminder that not all guys are jerks.

As the group enters the dirt path, Taylor keeps her focus on the kids in front of her. She steals the occasional glance at the trees towering over them, trying to soak in the peaceful views. The kids are walking so slowly, it's more of a crawl than a hike. Taylor stands in front of a scattering of red flowers and takes a picture. And begins step one of her revenge.

"So . . ." she throws out to Hunter.

Hunter's eyebrow shoots up. "So . . . you're going to talk to me, then?"

"Well, I was hoping we could have a chat."

Hunter nods along. "I'd like that. I don't like you being mad at me, Taylor. We had some good times, right?"

Taylor's mind betrays her by thinking of how comfortable she was in Hunter's arms. How much she relished the feeling of his lips on hers.

"Why did you lie?" Taylor asks, remembering all the bad times. "About me bullying Erin."

For a moment it's just the sound of leaves crackling under their feet and the conversations of the campers ahead. Then Hunter finally speaks. "I was looking out for you."

It takes everything in Taylor not to laugh aloud at that bald-faced lie.

"And how is that looking out for me? How is accusing me of something I didn't do helping me?" Taylor tries to keep her voice even, but she cannot get over the sheer gall of this guy.

Hunter nods to himself for a moment. "Well, you're on the radar now, right? And everybody is paying attention to you and hearing only amazing things. Because you are amazing, Taylor."

"Hold on." Taylor doesn't believe in violence, but she so wants to punch Hunter in the face right now. Instead, she takes a deep breath. "Let me make sure I have this correct. You think I'm *so amazing* that Mr. Mason and the other senior staff should be aware of it, so instead of telling them that, you had someone accuse me of bullying so I'd be put on probation and supervised, so they could see for themselves how I'm *so amazing*."

Honestly, who would be foolish enough to fall for that?

"I mean . . ." Hunter laughs for a moment. "I guess it's a lot, but I figure you sort of owe me now."

This freaking guy.

"And Erin, how did she get roped into all of this?" Taylor asks, even though Taylor knows exactly how manipulative Hunter can be.

"Hey, you gotta admit, Erin's a really good actress, right?" Hunter says with a laugh. "I only had to give her a little direction."

"You're pathetic," Taylor says in a low voice, even though the campers have been distracted by some birds. "You know I could go to Mr. Mason and tell him all of this."

Hunter lets out an actual scoff. "Now, why would you do that, Taylor? Besides, no way would he believe you. I've got that dude wrapped around my finger. You out of everybody should know the things I can make people do. So it's best for you to keep quiet, stay in line, and be a good little girl."

Taylor clenches her fists so tightly, her nails dig into her palms. "Oh, I do know." She swallows the bile that's creeping up her throat.

There's a scuffle up ahead as some campers have spotted a red-bellied woodpecker. Hunter moves forward to inspect while Taylor takes her phone out of her pocket and stops recording.

Yep. She's got him.

But that's only part of her plan.

"Hey, Jae!" Taylor calls out. "Got a second?"

Taylor is just getting started.

Our Chat (The Taylors Version)

TAYLOR🐝: Take ALL OF THE videos of our Tay's performance!!!

TAY🎉: MY DAD IS BRINGING THREE CAMERAS!!! 😂

TAY🎉: And Kai's sis is LIVE STREAMING!!! on our band account

TAYLOR🐝: Looks like my afternoon plans are settled, the campers will be THRILLED

TEFFY📚: TS and I were at the rehearsal yesterday and it was so good!

TS ⚽: I so need a reason to sing and dance

TAYLOR🐝: Sending you the biggest HUG, TS—can't wait to see you tomorrow!!!

TS ⚽: 🫶

TAYLOR🐝: And TAY! You're going to be SO famous, I'm going to put your picture on my wall next to my Eras Tour poster!!!!!

EIGHTEEN
Superstar

"Smile on three!" Tay's dad says to the band as he snaps a photo before their show at the Crawford County Fair on a sunny Saturday afternoon.

Like Tay needs to be told to smile. She gets to perform! In a band! And the Archers are no longer tucked away in a food court. They're on a stage in the middle of a plaza with a crowd already forming. Tay cannot—CANNOT—wait to get on that stage and sing and dance and be with Reece!

Tay wraps her arm just a little tighter around Reece. He leans his head toward her as they all smile for the camera.

Her dad snaps about a zillion pictures. He studies them with pride on his face. "I think we have a couple options for the inevitable album cover! Now let's get some with the Taylors, minus one."

"Yes!" Tay exclaims as Teffy and TS stand next to her. If only Taylor was here, but there will be plenty more gigs for Taylor to come to . . . like the Hi-Fi Annex! Tay hopes. *Gah!*

Reece goes off by himself to do his preshow ritual, which involves him literally standing in a corner, eyes closed, hands in a prayer pose, where he doesn't move for, like, ten minutes. Tay doesn't understand how that helps hype him up to perform, but everybody is different!

Tay strikes a few poses with her best friends. Teffy gets in on the fun while Tay can tell it's taking everything to get TS to even attempt a smile.

"Work it, own it!" Liam says as he snaps a few pics next to her dad.

"Thank you again for coming!" Tay holds on tight to her best friends.

"No way were we going to miss this." Teffy gives her an extra squeeze.

"Hey, Taylors!" Kai twirls his drumsticks. "What do you think of my new look?" He bats his brown eyes, which have some eyeliner on them, and shows the black nail polish on his nails. "My little sister couldn't resist."

"I like." Tay holds out her own hands, which are painted with black glitter polish. She is totally feeling her new rocker vibe: black fake-leather shorts, a *Rep* T-shirt that she has tied at her waist, and her hair tied up in ponytails down the center of her head, which has become her new performance trademark: a faux-hawk. She's even rocking a red lip and feeling very powerful. When she hits that stage, she's going to channel *the* Taylor when she strutted with purpose at the beginning of the *Reputation* set to the beat of ". . . Ready For It?"

"And this one!" Kai holds out his fist to Teffy. "Your song 'The Way I Feel' is such a bop, like, it's been stuck in my head since you shared it with us yesterday. I'm getting lyrically *Fearless*, but with a *1989* pop vibe."

Oh my goodness, Kai is so right! When they took a break yesterday, Teffy played the song—without Tay having to beg—and everybody loved it. They even played along at one point. It's sooooo good.

Teffy blushes at Kai's compliment. "Thanks," Teffy replies way too modestly. She gives Kai a fist bump.

"Girl is in her glitter gel phase." Kai nods with respect.

"Right?" Tay can't believe Kai knows about glitter gel! "Oh my goodness, Teffy, I love it, it might just be my favorite." Okay, Tay loves all of Teffy's songs because they are THAT good. But the ones that she's been writing lately have been super poppy and fun.

"Hmm, I wonder who she could be writing about?" Liam throws his arm around a smiling Teffy. "What's the line . . . something about 'he is the beat of my heart'? I mean, that dude sounds like a total keeper. And, like, really handsome and charming."

"Artistic license," Teffy fires back as she playfully nudges him.

Liam nods. "Yeah, my girlfriend is kind of a big deal." He plants a kiss on top of her head.

"Well, Tay is the one who is onstage and a total big deal." As always, Teffy deflects the attention off herself. "And you look amazing."

"Thank you!" Tay does a little walk, feeling powerful. "Should I have a stage name? Although, 'Tay' does look good in lights."

County fairs today . . . packed stadiums tomorrow. Tay is all about dreaming big!

"Yo!" Owen exclaims when he peeks at the audience. "My cousin Olive is here. She's in the front row in her reserved seat."

No pressure, just the person who is going to decide whether the band is going to open at an actual concert venue in Indianapolis. In front of hundreds of people.

"Told you reserving seats was a good idea!" Tay's dad pipes up. "In fact, I should make sure nobody else takes *our* seats." Tay's dad came super early and put signs up on every single seat in the front row.

"We should go, too." Teffy gives her a hug. "Have so much fun up there."

"It is fun," Tay admits. SO FUN. But she knows Teffy would never join her and that's okay.

TS steps forward. She's hardly spoken since she got back. "I don't know if I'm supposed to say 'break a leg,' but how about since you're a woman leading the boys . . . Smash the patriarchy."

Tay can't help but laugh as she embraces her. "Works for me!"

"Two minutes!" one of the fair techs calls out as the band forms a circle. Reece comes over from his corner and takes Tay's hand.

"Okay, we've got this," Tay says. "We have our setlist. We have our friends and family here."

"It's a full house," Owen adds.

"Wait, what?" Tay knew there were people, but she didn't realize it was full.

"Standing room only." Owen nods.

Tay's heart starts beating faster, adrenaline kicking in. "Okay, great! We are going to show them how the Archers rock. We'll get them singing and dancing in no time." They rehearsed through their set twice yesterday. Six songs for their allotted slot, and they practiced another one just in case they're asked for another encore.

"Yeah," Reece says quietly. "And maybe leave some room for a few surprises."

Surprises?

"What does that—" Tay starts, but then the MC begins his introduction, and Tay can't hear what he says because the crowd starts to cheer. *Before they've even hit the stage.* What a difference three weeks—and thousands of followers—makes.

Tay runs onstage last and takes in the crowd, who are already all on their feet. Before she can truly let it sink in, Kai drums the beginning of "Style" and Tay starts singing.

The crowd is amazing! They're singing along from the very first note. Even though there are seats, a swarm of girls go to the front of the stage and lean on it, mostly gathered over on the left side of the stage, where Reece is playing. He smiles that beautiful smile at the wide-eyed girls, giving them a playful wink. A few even call his name.

Tay doesn't blame them one bit. There's something special about Reece when he's onstage, that quiet confidence, his love of music. After all, she fell for him after hearing him play that first note back at that party freshman year.

The band kicks into "Bejeweled," and Tay jumps up and down. She feels so free. She knows within her heart that this is what she's meant to do.

When the song finishes up, the crowd is cheering. Tay takes a moment to soak it in, then pulls the microphone to her mouth, and the crowd cheers even more. She loves moments like these, when the band is waiting for her to start a song.

Tay raises her hand up and sings, *"Trouble! Trouble!"* The crowd goes wild as Reece's guitar kicks in, followed by Kai's drums.

Tay loves the attitude of "I Knew You Were Trouble," and their rock version ramps it up. Tay comes over and starts playfully singing the song to Reece. The girls in the front are loving it, screaming his name.

They can scream all they want, but Reece is hers. Tay puts her elbow on Reece's shoulder and leans into him . . . and he keeps his focus on his guitar and the girls down front. Tay does a huge roll of her eyes for the audience and dances over to the middle of the stage. A few people have their hands out, wanting Tay to touch them, like she's famous!

As Tay leans over and gives some high fives, the crowd's screams intensify.

This might be the greatest feeling in the world.

After "I Knew You Were Trouble," they do "Anti-Hero" followed by "Maroon." The crowd keeps growing in size and volume. As the band gears up to play their last song, "Cruel Summer," knowing it's going to bring the house down, Reece grabs Tay's microphone.

Tay blinks for a moment, wondering what's going on.

"Thank you, Crawford County!" Reece says with a confidence Tay has never seen in him before. Even though she wasn't prepared for this, she's so happy he's finally feeling comfortable enough to talk. Maybe a taste of success is what he needed. "We're the Archers and we're not just a cover band. I'm going to play an original song for you."

Tay smiles brightly, trying to not let on that she has no idea what Reece is doing. She looks behind her to see that Owen, Corey, and Kai are not that great of actors: They look confused and angry. Tay steps back to hear them over the crowd.

"What's he doing?" Owen hisses as he glances at his promoter cousin, who has spent most of the gig on her feet.

"He better not—" Corey starts, but it seems that Kai is one step ahead.

Before Reece can open his mouth, Kai starts drumming a beat, and it's not to one of Reece's songs. Or even Taylor Swift. But it's one Tay recognizes immediately.

Yes! This is exactly what they should be playing. Owen and Corey start in, leaving Reece staring at them with a betrayed look on his face. He then looks at Tay, practically pleading with his eyes for her not to sing. To take his side.

But the crowd is dancing along to the beat.

She walks over to Reece. "Make them stop," he says with a growl.

Instead, Tay does something she knows will not go over well with Reece. She takes her microphone back.

"Tay?" Reece asks, his forehead creased. "What are you doing?"

The thing is, Tay knows exactly what she wants. And in the moment, it's to sing this song, so she ignores Reece's glare, struts to the front of the stage, and sings.

Is that . . .

Teffy's eyes are wide as she watches the Archers perform her song, "The Way I Feel." She's in shock. That the band even remembers it. That they're performing it. And most of all, the crowd is loving it.

Sure, they don't know the words, but they're dancing. They're smiling. To a song she wrote.

"This is my girlfriend's song!" Liam screams as he points to a stunned Teffy.

TS has linked her arm with Teffy as she sings along.

To the lyrics Teffy wrote.

Teffy blinks, trying to figure out how this all happened and how she feels about it. Her hands are shaking, but she has no reason to be nervous, she's not the one performing it. And the band . . . is doing a great job.

Tay comes over from the stage and gives Teffy a look that seems to ask if this is okay. First, it's a little too late as they're already performing it. Better to ask for forgiveness than permission, she guesses. But if they would've asked Teffy before, she would've said no. And now, well, she . . . likes it. Teffy realizes the shaking isn't from nerves, it's from adrenaline.

She's always kept her songs to a small circle, which only recently included the Archers, and that was at Tay's insistence. Okay, at Tay's relentless begging. Teffy had assumed the guys were just being polite with their excitement, but now . . .

Olive, the promoter with long auburn hair, leans toward Tay's dad and shouts, "Which one of them wrote this song?"

Tay's dad points to Teffy, who replies with a small wave.

Olive gives her an appreciative nod. "Not bad, kid."

Oh my goodness.

A *music promoter* likes her song!

She'd been scared to have her music performed, assuming the worst. That seventh-grade talent show really did a number on her.

But now . . .

As Teffy watches the Archers finish, there's a foreign feeling growing inside her. It takes a second for her to realize it's envy. Teffy wishes *she* was up there. Playing the guitar. Dancing along with Tay.

Well, would you look at that? The song isn't the only surprise of the day.

The last note rings out from "The Way I Feel" and the crowd cheers.

"Thank you, Crawford County!" Tay takes a bow. She's been terrified to look over at Reece since they started the song. "That was an original song from Indiana's very own Teffy Bennett!" Tay points to Teffy in the audience. TS and Liam are losing their minds, screaming and jumping up and down, while Teffy gives Tay heart-hands.

Phew. Tay was worried Teffy would be mad she didn't ask first, but until four minutes ago Tay didn't know they were going to play it. But she loves that Teffy got to see that people enjoy her music. No, they LOVE it!

As the band takes their final bow, Tay reaches for Reece's hand, but he pulls away. *And here we go . . .* How can Reece be upset with her? *Reece* was the one who was going to play a song without consulting the band. *Reece* was the one who nearly sabotaged their performance in front of a music promoter.

The crowd is already asking for an encore before they even leave the stage.

"No surprises, we're doing 'Cruel Summer,' you know, a song people *want* to hear." Corey grimaces at Reece as they get back into place to perform.

Reece goes to say something to Corey, but Tay steps between the two, a forced smile on her face. "Not onstage. We'll talk after. Let's end on a high note."

"'Wreckage of My Heart' would've been a high note," Reece says between gritted teeth.

Tay gives him a squeeze on his shoulder, but he shrugs it away.

"Here's 'Cruel Summer' to close out," Tay quickly says to the crowd so Reece doesn't have the opportunity to go rogue. Again. By the audience's reaction, she knows she—*the band*—was right.

As Tay sings the bop, she can't believe that Reece would think this crowd, who came to a county fair on a Saturday afternoon with their families, would want to listen to one of his most depressing songs, which is saying a lot. Tay loves encouraging Reece, but "Wreckage of My Heart" is such a downer. When he plays it, Tay feels like she should be in a basement during a thunderstorm with the lights off and, like, super depressed.

That's not the kind of music Tay wants to sing. Sure, she loves a good sad song, but she has to come to terms with the fact that maybe she and Reece aren't musically compatible.

But as Reece stands in front of his growing legion of female fans,

Tay feels invisible to him, even though the spotlight is on her. Reece bends over and blows a kiss to a pretty blonde in the front row.

Tay can't believe that Reece nearly ruined what may be one of their greatest moments as a band. Now he's, what? Flirting? Tay doesn't think this is just playing to the crowd. This feels personal.

The song finishes and the band takes their final bow. Owen and Kai surround Tay, taking her by the hand, probably knowing what they're walking into once they get backstage.

And what a scene it'll be.

"Who do you think you are?" Reece starts, getting into Kai's face the second they are securely backstage and away from prying eyes.

The thing is, Reece is tall but skinny. While Kai is maybe an inch shorter, he's bigger. He has muscles from playing the drums. He has a presence. Kai doesn't shrink down. Tay knows he's a big teddy bear, but by the look on Kai's face right now, she knows he's not to be messed with.

"Dude, it was *you* who wanted to sabotage our setlist to make it about *you*," Kai says in a calm voice, but his cheeks are red, and there's sweat coming down his face.

"Then *you* went and played another original song, by someone who isn't even in the band!" Reece's face is pinched.

"Because Teffy's song fits better," Corey argues. "We just played it yesterday, and if we performed your mopey stuff, the crowd would've dispersed. So we improvised."

"But this is *my* band," Reece says, his fists squeezed tightly. "You don't get to—"

"Yo, chill!" Owen says as he gestures to the side of the stage, where Olive is making her way to them. Tay's dad follows Olive, talking her ear off.

No, Tay needs to fix this. They can't blow up before their big break.

"Smile," Tay says brightly, her heart hammering. "Hi, Olive!" Tay's body is buzzing from the performance and the tension.

Olive begins clapping. "That was amazing. I took some videos and know the girls will love you. And I want to hear more of those songs by . . ."

"Teffy Bennett, she's one of my best friends," Tay fills in proudly, knowing full well that Reece is going to have another fit over this.

Reece steps in front of Tay. "I also have some songs, they're more of a singer-songwriter vibe, not kiddie stuff."

Olive nods along. "Cool. Why don't you send me some songs, and the band and I will decide what will fit in best for their gig at Hi-Fi."

Wait. Does that mean . . . ?

The band look around at one another.

Olive laughs. "The Archers will be performing at Hi-Fi Annex in two weeks."

Tay lets out a scream that she knows isn't professional, but how is she supposed to keep this in? They did it! They're going to be performing on a stage that has hosted huge indie bands, like The Lumineers, Walk the Moon, and Edward Sharpe and The Magnetic Zeros. This is the Archers' start.

The band go into a big group hug, but when they pull apart, Tay realizes Reece is standing off to the side, his arms folded.

"Seriously, dude?" Owen spits at him.

"Reece." Tay approaches him cautiously. She knows it's up to her to calm Reece down, but honestly, she's annoyed. Why does he have to make this so difficult? Okay, yeah, she gets that he's upset that Teffy's songs got attention and his didn't, but still. He should be happy for the band. For what this means for the bigger picture. "I know you're upset, but look at where we are now. Take a deep breath and know we're going places, and that's because of something you started."

Reece nods along for a moment. He places his hand gently on Tay's cheek and she relaxes into it. See, she knew he'd realize he overreacted.

"Tay, you need to decide which band you want to be in, because this isn't me. If this is where we're headed, if we don't go back to playing my songs, I'm out." He gives her a quick kiss on the forehead before he walks away.

Tay blinks in his wake. Did he just give her an ultimatum? Does she have to pick between Reece and the rest of the band?

The thing is, Tay feels like herself when she's onstage singing fun songs, like Teffy's, that bring people joy. The songs people want to sing along to. That make people feel things, that aren't all doom and gloom.

So what will it mean for her and Reece if this version of the band *is* Tay?

Our Chat (The Taylors Version)

TAY🎉: SO EXCITED FOR US ALL TO BE TOGETHER AGAIN!!!!

TS ⚽: wow, Tay's excited 😉

TAY🎉: IT'S BEEN FOOOOOREEEEEEVEEEEER!

TS ⚽: um, four weeks

TAY🎉: TS!!!!!!

TAY🎉: Taylor, TS is kidding, she's next to me in the car and I CAN SEE she's excited

TEFFY📚: We are ALL excited to see you and cheer on Team Red!

TAYLOR🐝: ♡ ♡ ♡ ♡

NINETEEN
I Can See You

"Move fast and keep quiet," Taylor tells her team as they creep across the woods.

She bristles at every twig snap beneath their feet. The Red Team is in second place in the Whispering Pines Color War, and now that the Yellow, Blue, and Green Teams' flags have been captured, it's just Red and Orange left. If Red can capture Orange's flag first and bring it back to their area, their team will win the whole thing.

Taylor can practically taste the win. Their team had been scattered throughout the woods behind the open field, but now the team's sole survivors—Taylor, Noah, and four campers—have gathered to come up with a plan for victory.

Noah ducks behind a tree, motioning for Taylor and her crew to follow. Noah goes down on their belly, looking at the Orange flag flying just a few yards away, being guarded by six Orange team campers.

"What's the plan?" they whisper as all eyes are on Taylor.

She's itching for the win, and not just for the trophy—she can't wait to get to the picnic area to see the Taylors. And her family. Most of all, she wants to give TS the biggest hug.

But first, they need that flag.

So Taylor does what she does best: take command. "I think it's time for some self-sacrifice. I'll go and divert them, but I need a couple of brave souls to risk getting caught with me. We need two to sprint for the flag."

"I'll totally get caught," Noah offers. "Not like I'll make it easy."

"Good." Taylor gives them an appreciative nod. "Okay, Hazel and Alkesh, are you two good to grab the flag while the rest of us are being chased?"

Hazel and Alkesh nod, both determined.

"Okay, Noah and Aria, you go to the right while Tiana and I go to the left. If anybody remains guarding the flag, Alkesh runs to get their attention and Hazel grabs that flag, then sprints to our area. Got it?"

Hazel blinks up at Taylor with her big blue eyes. "You want *me* to grab the flag?"

"Of course it's you, who else?" Taylor puts her hand on her hip, trying to give Hazel the confidence she needs.

Hazel grits her teeth and Taylor does her best not to laugh since it's freaking adorable and not the least bit intimidating. "Okay, I got it."

"Yeah, you do." Taylor squats down, getting a good look at the guarding campers. "On three . . ." Taylor's lip twitches, thinking about the Taylors and their cheer. "One . . . Two . . . Three!"

With that, Taylor bursts from behind the foliage and screams, "Ahhhh!" Subtlety, thy name is *not* Taylor Perez.

She and Tiana pretend to go for the flag, but then veer to the left, hoping the flags attached to their belts stay on long enough for Hazel to grab the Orange Team's large flag.

"Go! Get them!" she hears different voices call out as it's a blur of Red and Orange Team members giving chase. Taylor sees Noah being pursued by two campers and getting tackled. Taylor zigs and zags, trying to channel TS as she runs down the soccer field. She weaves between the trees.

"I've been caught!" Tiana shouts behind her.

An Orange camper comes dangerously close to grabbing Taylor's flag from around her waist when she hears more voices.

"We got it!" Alkesh's voice rings out.

Yes! Taylor turns around, and it's now her turn to chase the Orange camper whose attention has now gone to Hazel, who needs to get to the Red Team's area on the opposite side of the open field. Taylor sprints her way across the clearing, panting and ignoring the stitch in her side. She can't see any of the other Red Team members, just the Orange team camper who is annoyingly fast. As she breaks through the trees, Taylor slams into the Orange camper who has stopped cold, causing them both to tumble to the ground.

Because there, in the safety of the Red Team area, is Hazel holding the Orange Team's flag in her hand. The Red Team are gathered around her, cheering.

"Go, Hazel!" Caleb yells as he picks up and twirls the tiny camper around. "Red Team wins!"

A whistle is blown as Mr. Mason hands Hazel the trophy.

“We did it!” Noah, Mia, and Caleb come over to Taylor.

Caleb holds out his hand to help Taylor up. “I heard this was all your plan. You have my vote for MVP.”

“I think that’s supposed to go to the campers,” Taylor replies, happy that her idea worked.

As the other team campers come over to their area to celebrate, Taylor glances at Jae, who gives her a nod. While Taylor is ready to celebrate, she has something else to do first.

Because Taylor has one more plan of attack for today.

Taylor takes a quick detour before she can settle in at the picnic being held on the open field in front of the dining hall.

She goes behind the building, where there’s a small walkway used to store the recycling and trash bins. Opposite the path are the woods. Voices drift over from the start of the picnic and Taylor swears she can hear Tay even from this distance. She just wants to get this over with so she can join everybody. But first, she needs to clear her name. Yeah, camp is over tomorrow, but it’s the principle.

Taylor quickly glances over at the trees that line the building.

She hopes this works.

“What’s this?” Hunter turns the corner and heads down the walkway. He’s holding the note Jae passed him asking to meet Taylor here.

“I wanted us to have a chance to talk before we leave tomorrow,” Taylor says. She keeps her voice from having any ounce of emotion. Be professional, be succinct, and be smart. She glances behind Hunter, wondering where the second part of her plan is. Erin is supposed to meet her as well. Taylor knows she needs to also get Erin on record admitting it was all fake.

"Just a chat?" Hunter raises his eyebrows in a playful way. "Because I see the way you look at me. You can admit it, you miss me, you miss this . . ." He traces his fingers up her arm and Taylor shrugs away.

How delusional can one guy be?

"Hardly." Taylor takes a step back. "And clearly, you don't know what *contempt* looks like." She gives him a glare.

Hunter pushes Taylor up against the wall, putting his hand over her mouth. "Don't make a sound."

No.

Panic envelops Taylor. This isn't part of her plan. This isn't supposed to be happening. Erin should be here. Taylor can only pray that Jae is where she's meant to be: recording on her phone from the trees.

But as Hunter's grip on her arm tightens, Taylor realizes that she should've had backup. She shouldn't have asked a camper to help. She should've asked Mia or Noah or Caleb. But she thought that it would be less suspicious if it came from a camper.

But no. This is all wrong.

"Are you going to behave?" Hunter asks with a sneer. Taylor gives a subtle nod, her mind working overtime. "No screaming." Hunter slowly takes his hand away from Taylor.

Taylor makes sure she's steady on her feet before she speaks. "I should suggest the same for you."

Hunter's face is confused for a moment and that's when Taylor, with every ounce of strength she has, drives her knee between Hunter's legs.

"Ah!" he cries out as he crumples onto the pavement.

"Jae, run!" Taylor screams as she takes off for the safety of the picnic and crowd. Once she gets out from behind the dining hall, she sees Jae dragging a confused Mr. Mason by the hand toward her.

"What's going on?" Mr. Mason asks.

Jae is out of breath. "I didn't get it all on video because I ran as soon as he grabbed you."

Mr. Mason looks between Jae and Taylor, panic settling on his face. "Wait. Who grabbed who?"

At that moment, a limping Hunter comes from behind the building. Taylor takes her phone out and starts playing the recording from the other day. Hunter's voice comes from her phone, "Hey, you gotta admit, Erin's a really good actress, right? I only had to give her a little direction."

Hunter stops when he realizes what's going on. "I—I—" he starts, that confident façade of his fading.

"There's more." Taylor continues the rest of the recording, watching Mr. Mason's expression change from confusion to shock to anger. His cheeks are red, his jaw clenched as he stares at Hunter.

"And I have this!" Jae shows Mr. Mason the video of Hunter grabbing Taylor, but it's only for a moment, as Jae went running as soon as she saw Taylor was in trouble.

"Hunter, my office, now." Mr. Mason points toward the administrative building. "And . . . Taylor . . ." He rubs the back of his neck. "I just . . ."

"I really liked being a counselor, Mr. Mason, but I think I'll be taking my talents elsewhere next summer." Taylor turns her back on Mr. Mason and Hunter, takes Jae by the hand, and goes to find her family, both real and chosen.

"There she is!" Tay screams so loudly it cuts through the noise of nearly a hundred campers being reunited with their families. Which is really something, but then again, so is Tay. And Taylor loves her for it.

"Hi!" Taylor goes running over and is engulfed in a hug with Tay, Teffy, and TS—who are all dressed in red. "This feels so right."

"I know! I don't want to let go!" Tay hugs even tighter.

"Okay, but I think my ribs may break," TS protests with a laugh. They finally pull away. "Jeez, Tay, I thought *I* was strong."

"Congrats on winning the Color War," Teffy says. "But none of us are shocked."

"That's my girl!" Taylor's dad comes over with her mom. "We missed you, kiddo."

"Hey, Mom and Dad!" She gives them both a hug. This is the longest she's been away from home and she really missed them. "Thanks for bringing the Taylors."

"We had an epic singalong during the drive." Her mom brushes Taylor's hair out of her face.

"Yeah, I think I'm deaf." Her dad puts his hand up to his ear. "What did you say?"

"ARE YOU IMPLYING THAT WE ARE LOUD, MR. PEREZ?" Tay screams before she does a cartwheel.

"*Implying*? Absolutely not. It's a *fact*." He laughs as her mom hits him playfully.

Mia approaches Taylor, with Caleb and Noah trailing behind. "I'm assuming these are the infamous Taylors."

"The ones and only!" Tay does a high kick. Taylor isn't surprised by Tay's pent-up energy—it was a two-hour drive.

"And which one of you is Caleb?" Taylor's dad asks as he looks between Noah and Caleb.

Caleb clears his throat. "Why do fish swim in salt water, sir?"

Her dad lifts his eyebrows, a smile spreading on his face. "Because pepper would make them sneeze."

As Caleb and her dad share a laugh, her dad extends his hand to Caleb, who happily shakes it.

Taylor can't figure out if this sort of cheesy-joke alliance is a good thing. But then she realizes that she's leaving tomorrow. As much as she can't wait to get back to the Taylors and away from the drama that has been being around Hunter, she's going to miss Caleb's jokes. Her talks with Mia. Her dances with Noah.

"Have you heard the one with—" Taylor's dad starts, but her mom grabs him by the elbow.

"Miguel, let's go grab some food and let Taylor catch up with her friends." She shakes her head as she leads him over to the grills that have been set up.

As Tay talks off Mia's and Noah's ears, Caleb stands in front of Taylor, his hands in his pockets. "Your dad is a legend."

"That's one way to describe him," Taylor replies with a chuckle.

Caleb's face turns serious for a moment. "Um, hey, are you okay? I heard there was some commotion over by the dining hall."

"Yeah, I'm fine."

His lips twitch. "Well, you know how news travels around here. Hunter's apparently in trouble. Rumor is that he's being asked to leave."

"Scratch what I said, I'm *fabulous*!" Taylor feels her back release. She didn't realize how tightly she'd been wound up having Hunter here. As she looks around at the campers, she wishes she would've gotten rid of him sooner, but better late than never.

She just wants to put him behind her, for good. Now she can concentrate on her friends and the rest of her summer.

"Yeah, um . . . have you, ah . . ." Caleb fumbles for a moment. "There's this . . ."

Taylor tilts her head, amused. Caleb is usually full of energy and not unsure of himself. "*You* okay there, Caleb?"

"Well . . ." Caleb's ears are turning bright red. "I didn't know if you, like, knew that I'm just the next town over from you . . ."

"Let me guess, you want to come over and hang with my dad." Taylor shakes her head.

Caleb shifts on his feet. "Oh, well, um—"

"And who is *this*?" Tay comes over and looks at Caleb with her eyebrows cocked. She studies him with a smile.

"Hey, I'm Caleb!" He gives Tay his bright smile, that uncertainty from before vanishing.

"Ah, dad joke guy!" Tay gives him a high five.

"And *you're* the amazing singer."

"Yes, I am!" Tay twirls around.

"Tay!" Jae calls as she drags Liam by the hand. "You have to meet my friends!" There are over a dozen girls behind Jae, all looking at Tay with wide eyes, in awe of her.

"Can I have a selfie with you?" A girl blinks up at Tay like she's a princess.

A "Me too!" chorus erupts.

Taylor can't help but laugh as she watches Tay get the star treatment she deserves.

"We all love that new song," says a girl who is having Tay sign her shirt.

And then they start singing the chorus of "The Way I Feel."

Teffy, who was talking to Liam's parents, turns around, her mouth open in shock.

"I'll be right back," Taylor says to Caleb as she takes Teffy by the arm to the fangirls. "Meet the songwriter of 'The Way I Feel.' The one and only Teffy Bennett!"

Well, that does it. The girls get even more excited. Their enthusiasm makes Tay look like a sloth.

"Can I take a picture with you?"

"Me too!"

"Do you know Taylor Swift?"

Teffy looks like a deer caught in headlights, but then begins to relax as she starts taking selfies and accepting hugs.

A sly smile spreads on Tay's face. "Would you like to hear even more songs written by Teffy?"

"Yes! Yes!" they all cheer.

Taylor's heart is so full. Her team won. Hunter's been fired. And now Tay and Teffy are becoming this little duo. She glances at TS, who has been quiet.

"Hey!" She goes over and hugs TS. "How are you doing? And be honest."

"I'm okay," TS answers quietly. Her eyes glance over to the field, where some kids are kicking around a soccer ball.

Taylor proceeds with caution, but she wants to know every single detail about what's been going on with her friends. "Have you talked to Gemma at all?"

TS shakes her head, her focus on the impromptu soccer match.

"So . . ." Taylor knows exactly what her friend needs right now. "I think that group could use some pointers on the field, don't you?"

TS's face lights up, not as bright as it usually would be when soccer is involved, but still. "Would you mind?"

"Of course not, go! Teach the youths a thing or two."

TS doesn't even wait for Taylor to finish as she's already rushing over to the field.

"Hey!" Tay wraps her arms around Taylor.

"Oh, hello, Miss Superstar."

"Who, me?" Tay fluffs her curls. "That Caleb is cute." Tay starts wiggling her eyebrows.

"Oh my God, he's almost as bad as my dad with the jokes." Taylor looks over to the picnic area, where Caleb is now chatting with her dad. They're both laughing. "But he's become a good friend. He's super sweet. And thoughtful."

Huh.

"And . . . ?" Tay prods her.

"What? Um, nothing." But it isn't really nothing, is it? And by the look Tay is giving her, Tay doesn't believe her, either.

After Hunter shattered Taylor's heart, she busied herself. She put all her energy into the presidency and being with the Taylors. She hadn't opened herself up to the possibility of dating again, and now . . .

She isn't sure. Maybe?

Teffy comes over to join Taylor and Tay. The three watch TS play, a joy they haven't seen for a while on her face.

"Is she going to be okay?" Taylor asks, knowing that soccer is only a Band-Aid.

Teffy and Tay exchange a look, and then Tay starts jumping up and down. "Oh my goodness, Taylor, it's been *killing* me keeping it in! Pure torture! I can't with all these secrets and schemes and GAH!"

Teffy shakes her head as Tay does a cartwheel.

"Keeping *what* in?" Taylor asks.

Teffy leans in and whispers, "There's a plan."

Tay jumps in the air. "AND IT'S SO GOOD!"

Our Chat (The Taylors Version)

TAYLOR🐝: Do you feel that magic in the air? I'M BACK!

TAY🎉: TAYLORS UNITE!!!

TEFFY📚: What time are we meeting at Tay's?

TAY🎉: 6

TEFFY📚: 🫶

TAYLOR🐝: 🫶

TAYLOR🐝: TS????????

TAY🎉: TS?!??! YOU HAVE TO BE THERE!!!!

TEFFY📚: It won't be the same without you!

TS ⚽: 🫶

TAY🎉: I AM SO EXCITED!!!!!!!!!!!!!!!!!!!!!!!!!!!!!!!!!!!!

TWENTY

Today Was A Fairytale

TS was never someone who believed in fairy tales.

Maybe it's the whole damsel in distress who needs a prince to be rescued thing. It's *so* outdated.

Even though TS felt those magical feelings with Gemma, they crumbled all around her. It's TS's heart that's in need of rescuing.

She drags her feet up to Tay's house and braces herself. She knows her friends are just trying to help, but Tay has been EXTRA lately. Which is saying a lot. She's practically bursting with energy and joy and . . .

It's not like TS isn't happy for her friends. Tay's music career is flourishing, Teffy's songs are being recognized, and Taylor is back home after serving some sweet revenge, but TS feels like she's somewhere else.

At least part of her.

TS lived fifteen years before knowing Gemma Walker, but after they started dating, it didn't feel like TS's day started or ended until she talked to Gemma.

Twelve days.

It's been twelve days since TS left London. Twelve days since she felt Gemma's touch. Twelve days since she looked into those big green eyes. Twelve days since she felt Gemma's lips on hers.

TS knows she should've replied to Gemma's text. She should've talked to her, but she just couldn't bear to hear Gemma tell her she's staying in England.

She takes a steady breath and tries to smile, to get ready to be around her friends.

TS doesn't even get a chance to ring the doorbell as Tay practically rips the door off its hinges to greet her. "TS! Hi! So glad you're here! And this is *so* cute!" Tay gestures at TS's dark gray T-shirt and jean shorts.

Wow, Tay is really laying it on thick.

Tay, of course, is wearing the cutest pink sundress, but TS just hasn't felt like making much of an effort since she got back from London.

Tay links her arm with TS's. "Teffy and Taylor are already here. And we have so much to talk about, like we think that cute, tall redhead counselor has a crush on Taylor, and Hunter got fired, and, um . . ." Tay drags TS through the den and directly to the backyard. Of course, TS knew all of that. She was at Whispering Pines and they had the drive back where they talked about it. Well, TS mostly listened.

She hasn't been in a talking mood, either.

Teffy and Taylor are lounging on the wicker chairs. There are fairy lights wrapped around the banisters and tea lights lit up around the ends of the pool. Flower petals are strewn around on the ground. Tay has really gone all out for Taylor's arrival, even though it seems a bit over-the-top and romantic, but whatever.

"TS is here!" Tay is bouncing up and down while TS is doing her best not to roll her eyes.

Then again, she has been in a *mood* lately, and the fact that her friends are excited to see her should brighten her up, but still.

Meh.

"Hi!" Taylor and Teffy both say in a normal way, probably trying to temper down Tay's excitement, which, let's be honest, takes a village.

"We were just talking about Tay's rehearsal tomorrow for next weekend's big show," Teffy says, darting a glare at Tay.

"Yes! That!" Tay plops down on the chair next to TS. Then she grimaces. "It would mean a lot if you were all there."

"You mean I get to see my favorite new band perform before their big Indianapolis debut?" Taylor stretches out her legs. "Obviously."

"I'll be there." Teffy gives her a smile.

TS looks at Teffy. "Do you think you're going to share more songs? With the Archers?"

"OH, YES, PLEASE!" Tay jumps up. Clearly there's no way she's going to be able to sit still. If TS could bottle up that energy, she would outrun every opponent on the soccer field, well, more than she already does. "Although, it'll be a *whole thing* with Reece, but honestly, lately everything is a *thing* with Reece. It's our first rehearsal since our last gig. Reece said we all needed a break to reassess the direction of the band." Tay sticks her tongue out and dramatically rolls her eyes. "So, yeah, I need backup for tomorrow."

"You got it," Teffy replies.

"Same!" Taylor kicks her foot out.

"Got you." It's not like TS has anything else to do for the rest of the summer.

"You all are the best." And with that Tay is back to bouncing around the pool area.

Teffy and Taylor give her a look, which causes Tay to slow down only slightly until her phone pings and Tay actually screams. "Ah! I'll be right back!" She tears off up the stairs into the house.

"Okay," TS starts. "What's going on with Tay? Is it just the band nerves or—"

"Yes!" Taylor interrupts. "She's, like, just excited, clearly, and stressed and, um . . ." Taylor gets up slowly. "Let me check on her." Taylor then practically sprints up the stairs.

TS looks over at Teffy, who is suddenly very interested in her chipped fingernail polish. "*Teffy.*"

"Mmm-hmm." Teffy won't look at her.

"What's going on? Why is everybody being so weird?" Is TS the one making people feel uncomfortable? Is her attitude turning her best friends against her?

"TS." Teffy finally meets her eyes and gives her a soft smile. "When are we ever normal?"

Well, Teffy's got her there.

"But you are right." Teffy glances up at the house. "Let me go check on those two, I'll be quick." She gets up and starts walking up the stairs to the house, but then turns around. "TS, it's going to be okay."

TS isn't so sure about that.

Left alone in the backyard, she stretches out on the lounger and closes her eyes.

It's going to be okay, it's going to be okay . . . She keeps repeating that to herself, but as her heart beats in time to her mantra, she doesn't know how it could be.

TS finally had love and now it's—

"Enchanted" starts playing over the outdoor speakers. It's the song she and Gemma screamed in the car when they first arrived in London. An ache overtakes her body, and she feels tears start to well up. A heaviness in her heart.

She opens her eyes and everything around her seems to blur except for the person standing on the top of the stairs.

Gemma.

Back in her lavender hair.

TS sits up and rubs her eyes.

That's it, she's officially lost it.

But no. It's really Gemma. She's smiling at TS as she walks down the steps.

"What . . . How . . ." TS shakes her head, trying to figure out what's going on. But it doesn't matter. Gemma is here. She came back to her.

Gemma reaches out her hand to a still-stunned TS. TS takes it and stands up.

"Hi." Gemma puts her forehead to TS's.

"Hi." TS takes in this moment, this girl, this feeling of hope, which seemed impossible just a minute ago.

“What are you doing here?” TS starts, although does it really matter?

In a way, it does. There’s a part of TS that realizes, as much as she missed Gemma, she can’t pretend that England didn’t happen. She can’t erase the hurt. The fights. The person Gemma became when they were there.

But she wants to. Desperately.

Gemma tucks a strand of TS’s messy hair behind her ear. “I had to come back to where I belong, and that’s with you.”

TS’s heart does a little skip, but she has to be practical. Does TS belong with Gemma? Sure, Gemma is here now, but it’s not like her family is going anywhere.

“Gemma, I know we—” TS starts, but Gemma puts a finger to her lips.

“We both know that this is on me, so please let me be the one to start.” Gemma takes a deep breath, the kind she does before she’s about to kick a penalty shot. “I’m so sorry. I know it’s only words. After you left, I had to take a step back and really look at what I put you through. And you were right, I had changed. I did what I could to make being around my family easier on me, but didn’t think about what that meant for you. So I ended up putting you last. Please believe me when I say how awful I feel. I hadn’t truly realized how bad my cousins and grandmother were with you. Once I put myself in your shoes, I’m surprised you stayed for as long as you did. And you didn’t punch Freddie. Please know I gave him, Cressida, and even my grandmother a talking-to.” There’s a mischievous glint in Gemma’s eyes and

TS now wishes she would've stayed. She would've loved to have seen that.

Gemma continues, "And for you to think, for even a minute, that you aren't important to me, well . . ."

TS's heart starts beating. She wants, with all of her being, to forgive Gemma, but there's still a part holding her back. "I have never felt so betrayed." TS's throat hitches.

"I know. I'd ask you to tell me what to do to make it up to you, but I don't deserve to be let off that easily. Instead, I'm going to prove it to you, every moment of every day. Because I know all the things I should've done. I can't change that. But I can be there for you now, if you'll have me."

As much as TS wants to believe Gemma with all her heart, she still hesitates. "You've broken a few promises to me already. Why would it be different now?"

A tear runs down Gemma's cheek. "I did break those promises. I won't excuse what I did. But, Shaw, you're my future. I will fight for you as if you were a gold medal. Because you are my prize. So if you'll have me, I will make it up to you. And if I don't, well, then I would understand, as I don't deserve you."

TS takes in the scene in front of her. This gorgeous girl with a big heart, owning up to what happened. Working with her friends to create this beautiful moment.

And just like that, TS has fallen in love with Gemma a little bit more.

"You came back to me," TS says, almost as if she needs to say it aloud to make it true.

"Of course. I love you, Shaw." Gemma wraps her arms around TS, which is a good thing because TS suddenly feels very swoony. "And I completely understand that it might take you more time to be able to—"

Now it's TS who gently places her finger to Gemma's lips. "I love you, too."

TS leans in and gives Gemma a kiss. She's missed those lips so much it made her heart ache. She runs her fingers through Gemma's hair. She relishes the feeling of Gemma pressed against her.

This is what home feels like.

TS wants to stay like this forever and—

A loud eruption of cheers comes from the balcony, causing TS and Gemma to break into laughter.

Gemma shakes her head. "I seriously thought there was no way your friends were going to keep this surprise."

"I think Tay was close to bursting a vein," TS replies with a laugh, feeling so grateful in this moment for her friends.

"I missed you." Gemma kisses her on the cheek. "You're so beautiful."

TS looks down at her ratty T-shirt. "I'm a mess and you know it."

"Well, you're *my* mess."

Gemma pulls TS in for another kiss. She smiles as the cheers from her best friends continue.

Scratch what TS thought before. She absolutely believes in fairy tales.

Our Chat (The Taylors Version)

TS ⚽: 🥰🥰🥰🥰

TAY🎉: I NEARLY PASSED OUT FROM THE EXCITEMENT!!! SERIOUSLY, I TOTALLY LOST CONTROL

TS ⚽: I can't believe you were able to keep it a secret

TAY🎉: IT WAS KILLING ME! PURE TORTURE!! FIRST LIAM! AND THEN GEMMA!!! YOU ALL ARE LIVING YOUR BEST ROM-COM LIVES!! GAAAAAAAH!!!!

TEFFY📚: Seriously, we almost had to lock Tay in her bedroom.

TAYLOR🐝: And you think I'M dramatic 🙄

TS ⚽: Well GEMMA and I can't wait to cheer you on and have your back and whatever you need today

TAY🎉: GAH! THIS SUMMER!!!!

TWENTY-ONE
Is It Over Now?

Tay is so glad she has backup. As she glances at the Taylors and Gemma sitting on the couch, watching the Archers rehearse on Friday afternoon, she gives them a grateful smile as Reece and her bandmates are in the middle of yet another fight.

And it's super uncomfortable.

"Dude," Owen starts. "I told you that Olive said the band wants us to do the covers and Teffy's song, just like last weekend. I'm sorry they didn't pick your song, but it's time for you to face facts."

"And I told you I'm not interested unless we play my songs. Besides, *they* aren't in charge." Reece's face is splotchy. He's fiddling with the lid of a takeout coffee cup.

"Yeah, Tay is," Kai pipes up from behind his kit.

Tay's eyes are wide. For months she's had to be Reece's voice, but it seems that he's finally comfortable enough to use it himself.

And Tay doesn't like what happens when he does.

"This is *my* band," Reece says, a hardness in his voice. "And *this* isn't what I signed up for." Reece gestures around at the group. "Actually, no, I take that back. Since I'm the one who started this band, you all knew what *you* signed up for." Then Reece turns to Tay, an annoyed look on his face that she's never seen before. "And, Tay, need I remind you that the Archers was a band you liked."

Tay sits for a moment on the word *liked*.

Because if she's being honest with herself, she liked *Reece*. She liked that *he* was in a band. She liked having someone who loved music and wanted to share it. She liked that he was different from most of the guys in school, because he explored these deep feelings. She liked that he was shy and didn't mind when Tay talked and talked *and talked*. She liked that he asked her to join the band and brought her into this world where she gets to be onstage and sing.

But Tay can't help but notice that she's also using the word *liked*. Past tense.

Tay *loves* the band as it is now. Playing fun Taylor Swift rock covers. Playing Teffy's songs, which she's letting them share! Having fun onstage. This is the version of the band she wants to be in.

Reece continues, and Tay is going to let him talk. "You all can't just change everything about the band now because we got some gig."

"Some gig?" Owen takes his hands and puts them through his thick brown hair. "Some gig? You call playing in front of *over a thousand people* at Hi-Fi Annex and opening for a band on a record label, where there will be people in the music industry, *some gig*. You used to be fine playing parties and anything we could get. *Now* you take some artistic stand?"

"While you all seem fine selling out." Reece sniffs.

"It's not selling out, it's being in a band and having fun." Kai stands up. "Let's take it to a vote, then, see what we all—"

"No!" Reece actually stomps his foot.

It causes Tay to take a step back, it's such a childish gesture. Okay, sure, Tay has done that a few times in the last year with her dad—and it's been arguments *about* Reece. But as she looks around the huge basement with a recording studio in his gigantic house, she thinks maybe Reece isn't used to being told no. Not getting what he wants.

"This is my band."

"It's *our* band," Corey replies calmly.

"Is it?" Reece's voice is high. "Is it? Is it?"

"Okay, let's just calm down." Kai comes out from behind his drum kit, hands out like he's dealing with a spoiled toddler. Which maybe isn't that far from the truth. Kai glances over at Tay. "Tay?"

Tay has been oddly quiet during this entire fight. Usually, she loves nothing more than to talk, but . . . she also knows the second she took the mic away from Reece at their last gig, she'd already made her choice.

She glances at her friends, who are probably wishing they were anywhere else. But having them here is giving Tay the confidence to do what she needs to do. Tay would never tell her friends to settle. To ignore their hearts.

And Tay Johnson certainly isn't going to do it.

"People love what we're doing now," Tay starts calmly, to which Reece actually scoffs. "And more importantly, *I* love it. It's what *I* want to do." She folds her arms to show that she means business, but also to disguise her trembling hands.

"So that's it, then." Reece shakes his head. "It's over."

Does he mean the band or their relationship or both?

Huh. It's then that Tay realizes that it's the band that she cares about more. When she thinks about what she wants for the future, it's exactly what they did the other night. Performing with joy. That's what it feels like to perform with Kai, Corey, and Owen. She feels free. She feels like herself.

And she's not going to let anybody hold her back.

"Well, Reece, I guess it is," Tay says, her voice strong and clear.

Reece laughs bitterly. "You know what, I don't know why I'm surprised. We were finished the second you played *her* song instead of mine." Reece points accusingly at Teffy, who looks down at the floor, her cheeks turning the color of TS's hair.

It hits Tay. That's all that matters to Reece. His music. Not Tay. Not his fellow band members. It's always been about Reece. Of course it has. Ugh, this means her dad was right. She can do so much better. And she will, because it *is* so over.

"Yeah, well, do you blame us? Teffy's songs are amazing." Kai gives Teffy a nod.

"Well, you can forget that gig, then. I'm out. Bunch of traitors . . ." Reece goes storming out of the basement.

It really is over.

And yet . . . Now that she's had that taste of performing to crowds and knowing in her bones that it's what she wants to do, she doesn't want to stop.

All can't be lost. Not when they're so close.

Tay is going to be positive, because that's the kind of person she is! And you know what? Without Reece around, Tay can relax. She doesn't have to tiptoe around him anymore. He often told her how special she was, but he's so quick to turn his back on her now. She searches her heart to try to feel a crack—her first relationship has ended—but right now all she wants to do is perform with this band, in this way: Corey, Owen, and Kai.

The room is uncomfortably silent. The remaining band members look at one another, wondering what they're going to do. It's as if nobody wants to be the first to talk.

Leave it to TS to ease the mood. "Um, so not to mention the obvious, but this is Reece's house, so should we leave . . . ?"

"Yeah." Corey unplugs his guitar.

"No, I mean, yeah," Kai says. "But we gotta figure out the band first. We still have to play that gig. I don't want to stop this." He looks at Tay.

Of course Tay doesn't want to stop.

"Well, we need another guitar player," Corey replies. "Someone who can learn this stuff fast. Gig's in seven days. Who do we know who plays? And, most importantly, is cool and not an egomaniac."

Corey, Owen, and Kai start throwing out names and begin arguing over who would fit in with them. Tay can't help but wonder if a new person would be a good or a bad thing.

It takes Tay a moment to realize that Teffy is standing.

Teffy doesn't know what she's doing, but she sees Tay's mouth open in a surprised O. TS has grabbed Gemma's hand. Taylor is nodding, like she's willing Teffy to speak.

Teffy opens her mouth, and before she can talk herself out of it, she says, "I'll do it."

It's gone still in the basement.

Tay takes a hesitant step forward, probably sensing that Teffy could bolt at any moment. "Are you sure?"

No. Teffy isn't sure at all. But she's inspired by her friends. She wants to take a risk. To put herself out there. To stand onstage.

Teffy gives the slightest nod.

Well, that does it. The room has gone completely chaotic.

Tay starts jumping up and down. "Oh my goodness! I've been waiting for this moment my entire life!" She launches herself onto Teffy.

Taylor, TS, and Gemma have stood up to cheer while the rest of the band start high-fiving one another.

"Welcome to the band, we've been waiting for you." Kai hands Teffy the guitar that Reece had thrown down.

She puts the strap around her and starts strumming the opening to "The Way I Feel." Kai jumps behind his drum kit and kicks in with the beat, and the rest of the band comes in.

It feels right.

Maybe what Teffy needed all this time was a bigger safety net. It's not just her playing. This time, there's a band. A team. A unit.

Teffy always felt more secure with the Taylors. Now she has a new group that can help her get the courage to play in front of an audience.

Tay starts singing the lyrics and Teffy closes her eyes, savoring this moment. The song finishes and TS, Taylor, and Gemma erupt in applause.

Owen comes over and pats Teffy on the back. "Not surprised at all. So, do we get to hear some more of these songs of yours?"

Teffy surprises herself again by saying, "Sure." She likes seeing her songs in a new way. Where it's not just her on guitar or piano. She can add more parts. It'll make the songs better. Then maybe she'll feel strong enough to stand onstage under the bright lights.

"Ah, everybody." Corey looks at his phone. "Reece just texted that we have ten minutes to leave or he's calling the cops."

Kai jumps up from the drum kit. "Yeah, let's go."

"We can practice in my backyard," Tay offers as she wraps her arms around Teffy. "Oh my goodness, Teffy. I can't believe that what I've been dreaming about for so long is coming true. And for the record, I'm talking about playing with you."

Teffy nods. She's not going to lie, she's nervous, but she's also excited.

Maybe Teffy can start dreaming a lot bigger now, too.

OUR CHAT (The Taylors Version)

TAYLOR🐝: OMG!!! STOP! Just saw the marquee with THE ARCHERS on it! BIG TIME!

TAY🎉: I KNOW! I TOOK LIKE A ZILLION PICTURES!!!

TS ⚽: How you doing, Teffy?

TEFFY📚: 😬

TWENTY-TWO
Timeless

Teffy isn't kidding. She thinks she's going to vomit.

Why did she think this was a good idea? Why did that voice in her head that always tells her to stay quiet go silent when she *volunteered to join a band*?

Deep breaths, she reminds herself as she stares in the mirror backstage at Hi-Fi Annex. She was fine all week during rehearsals. Okay, she can admit that she actually enjoyed it. The camaraderie. The fun of playing. She was even okay at their sound check a couple hours ago.

But now . . . she can hear the venue starting to fill up. With people. Lots of people. Who are here to listen to a real band. Not some high school kids who cover Taylor Swift. And let's not forget they'll be playing one of her songs.

"There's my rock star girlfriend." Liam comes backstage, wearing an I KNEW YOU WERE TROUBLE T-shirt. "You ready?" He gives Teffy an encouraging nod.

Nope.

Although, what's the worst thing that could happen?

You could throw up onstage.

Honestly . . .

"Hey." Liam takes Teffy by the shoulders and leans down so they're eye to eye. "You've got this. You're stronger than you know. You're braver than you know."

Teffy nods along, hoping—oh, how she hopes—that Liam is right.

♥♥♥♥

The last time Taylor was this excited for a concert was almost five years ago for the Eras Tour.

She can't help but think this is a new era for the Taylors. Teffy and Tay are in their Rocker era. TS is in her Lover era. While Taylor is in her Fearless era.

"Hey!" Mia calls out to Taylor outside Hi-Fi Annex, with Caleb and Noah behind her. "We're so excited. And, oh my goodness, classic Taylors, plural!" Mia gestures at Taylor's WE ARE NEVER EVER GETTING BACK TOGETHER, LIKE EVER T-shirt.

Noah spins around with a red boa wrapped around their shoulders. "And I've been telling everybody I know that I'm *on a list*. I'm *with the band*. *VIP*, baby."

"We're such big deals." Taylor flips her hair. She's glad to have these new friends, and she gets excited thinking about what sophomore year will bring.

Caleb steps forward. "Hi, Taylor, um, this may be silly, but, ahhh . . ."

"*You? Silly?* Never!" Taylor says with a laugh, but she finds that her stomach is swirling around at being near Caleb.

"I got you this." He hands her a small cardboard box. "My parents own an antiques store and I saw this and thought of you."

"Oh, wow, thanks." Taylor's heart does a familiar skip. She opens the box to find a silver bracelet with a bee charm.

"Yeah, I know a bee is your emoji on your chats, so . . ."

It's so sweet. And nice.

And Caleb is sweet. And nice. And cute. And age appropriate.

"I love it." Taylor puts the bracelet on as she guides her friends inside. She glances down at the bracelet and back at Caleb.

Her heart does another somersault, and Taylor likes it.

TS doesn't get nervous.

Sure, she'll have a rush of energy before a big match, but she finds herself fidgeting as they wait for the Archers to go on. She's excited for Teffy to finally step out into the spotlight—even though Teffy kept saying she's going to be as far away from the front of the stage as possible.

TS loves her friends. She'd fight a war for them. She'd do anything, but as she watches from the safety of the audience, there's not a thing she can do for them right now and it's killing her.

"Hey, I'd say penny for your thoughts, but . . ." Gemma nudges TS as she points down at her own T-shirt: I BET YOU THINK ABOUT ME.

TS can't help but laugh. "Yes, obviously." TS is wearing a THIS IS NOT TAYLOR'S VERSION tee. It was Gemma's idea for them to all wear matching Taylor Swift–inspired shirts to cheer on the Archers and their Taylors.

"Although, I know that look. You're scheming, you're planning."

Gemma puts her head on TS's shoulder. "It's why I'm glad we're on the same team, for now."

"For now?" TS raises her eyebrow. "What does that mean?"

Gemma wraps her arms around TS. "I mean it's only inevitable that you'll be drafted for the US Women's Team and I'll be on the England squad."

"Good thing I know your weak spots." TS reaches in and tickles Gemma on the side, where she erupts into laughter.

"And I know yours." Gemma then pulls TS in for a kiss that makes TS's knees buckle.

TS doesn't mind having this weakness.

Tay always dreamed about having one of those once-in-a-lifetime loves. She'd listen to songs and watch movies all about happily ever afters.

Maybe her great love isn't a guy.

Tay's great love is her music. Her friends. *Their* band.

Anything else at this point would just be a cherry on the most delicious sundae.

Plus, she just turned sixteen. She's got time. First get her driver's license, then deal with boys.

Well, first she has to get through this performance. Teffy looks extra pale. The red lip Tay put on Teffy stands out against her skin, along with her black faux-leather leggings and black tank top. Teffy looks like a rocker who is about to pass out.

"Hey, Teffy!" Tay starts. "I don't really know how to explain it, but I have this feeling like this was all meant to be, you know. You. Me. The Taylors. It wouldn't have mattered if we weren't named after the greatest artist of all time or we weren't in the same class that day in fifth grade. We would've come together somehow. You know? Like, it's fate."

This gets Teffy to smile ever so slightly.

The lights go down.

"That's our cue!" Kai calls out as he and the other guys take the stage.

Tay holds out her hand to Teffy, who looks at it for a moment. Tay isn't going lie, she's worried Teffy isn't going to take her hand and instead, she'll bolt out of the building.

"Yeah, I know what you mean." Teffy puts her hand in Tay's. "It's once-in-a-lifetime stuff."

♥♥♥♥

As Teffy walks onstage to very tepid applause from the audience that isn't in their friends and family section, she tries to block out flashes from the seventh-grade talent show.

Because, let's be honest, this is a zillion times more terrifying.

The crowd is mostly talking to one another or on their phones, not paying attention to the teenagers who have taken the stage.

Teffy puts the guitar around her as Tay walks up to the microphone and takes it off the stand. She looks to Teffy, who gives her a nod, even though Teffy's pretty positive she's going to hurl all over this stage.

"Indianapolis!" Tay calls out. "We are the Archers, and you all look like you're . . . *trouble, trouble, trouble*!"

Tay starts singing, which is Teffy's cue to start. She closes her eyes and starts strumming the guitar, letting muscle memory take over. She's practiced so much in the past week, she could play these songs in her sleep. Which is good, since she doesn't want to have to open her eyes.

Before she realizes, the song is over and she hears some applause. Teffy dares to open one eye, and she sees that there are some people gathered toward the front of the stage now.

But more importantly, she did it. She performed onstage without dropping a pick or running to the bathroom to cry.

Well, she's lasted one song. Four to go.

Tay starts singing the beginning of "Getaway Car," which is just Tay with Corey's bass for the first few lines. Teffy glances toward the back, seeing her family, along with Liam, Taylor, TS, and Gemma . . . She stands up a bit straighter.

Teffy wills herself to keep her eyes open. To not shut this out. She is facing one of her biggest fears head-on. When it comes to the chorus, where her part comes in, she strums with more confidence.

Tay comes over and dances next to Teffy and gives her a playful wink.

More people start gathering around the front of the stage and singing along. When they get to "Bad Blood," it's even more.

And it's possible that Teffy is enjoying herself. Her body has relaxed into the music. She even sings along a few times. She glances at her bandmates: Kai is smiling as he drums away, and Teffy can't help but notice he can't keep his eyes off Tay. Both Owen and Corey are moving around and playing to the audience.

This is . . . fun.

This is *fun*?

YES! THIS IS FUN!

"Thank you!" Tay says to the cheering crowd. "We are Indianapolis's very own the Archers, and we're going to take a break from performing songs by the one and only Taylor Swift to play an original by Teffy Bennett."

Never mind. Teffy is gonna barf after all.

Playing Taylor Swift songs is one thing. They're iconic. They're beloved. While she's just . . . Teffy.

Maybe they can do a different song, maybe they . . .

It's now quiet as everybody is waiting for Teffy to start playing. But she's frozen. it's just like seventh grade. She can't possibly—

"THAT'S MY GIRLFRIEND!" Liam calls out from the back, getting a few "whoops" from the audience.

"THAT'S MY BEST FRIEND!" TS screams, and Taylor quickly follows her.

"THAT'S MY DAUGHTER!" Teffy's mom shouts, and the crowd gives an appreciative chuckle, along with a few "awws."

Teffy loves her boyfriend and friends and parents so much in that moment. She also loves writing music, and if it's something she wants to do, she has to be brave enough to share it.

Teffy starts strumming the beginning of the song and the band joins in. Tay spends most of the song near Teffy, which prevents Teffy from slinking behind a curtain. But as Teffy dares to glance out in the audience, she sees more than a few heads bobbing along. And a lot of phones recording. She makes eye contact with a young woman who cheers for her.

When the song ends, there's growing applause. There's some whistles. It's the loudest they've been since the Archers set foot onstage.

For a song Teffy wrote.

Teffy lets out a long breath.

She did it.

"Give it up for Teffy Bennett!" Tay bows down to Teffy. "That's a name you're going to want to remember."

There's even more cheering now. Teffy looks out at a sea of smiling faces. Smiling at *her*.

She glances toward the back and can no longer see Liam. Or Taylor or TS. Or even Gemma.

"And now our final song—I know, I know." Tay juts out her lip as some people in the audience seem genuinely upset that they're almost done. "But be sure to follow us so you can come to our next show, where we'll play even more Teffy Bennett songs." The thought doesn't automatically terrify Teffy. In fact, it *excites* her. "We hope you'll sing along to this next one, and I need to bring out some friends to help us."

Liam, Taylor, TS, and Gemma come rushing out onstage in their T-shirts. Liam comes over to Teffy, beaming. Taylor struts onstage, loving the attention while TS and Gemma hold hands.

Kai starts "Cruel Summer" with the drums and then the guitar kicks in. The place goes wild and starts singing along with Tay.

Teffy feels comfortable, playing with a smile, as she watches her friends onstage. She knows this moment is going to live in Taylors infamy.

TS didn't think there was a better feeling than winning a game. But as she dances onstage with her friends and her hand entwined with Gemma's, she realizes that this love between her and Gemma is better than a fairy tale, since this love is real.

Taylor has always been strong. But everything she's been through with Hunter this summer has made her stronger. Being onstage surrounded by her best friends, she feels unstoppable. She spies Caleb in the back, and Taylor can't help but think that maybe she's ready to begin again.

Tay holds the microphone out and lets the crowd sing along to the bridge. This band, this moment, is better than anything in Tay's wildest dreams.

How on earth did Teffy ever think she wouldn't want to do this? Maybe it's the adrenaline. Maybe it's Liam dancing next to her. But this feeling right now is something Teffy isn't going to run away from. She knows she can truly do anything with the loves of her life who are by her side. She can't wait to see what's next. For her. For the Taylors.

Because what the Taylors have is truly timeless.

ACKNOWLEDGMENTS

Welcome to The Tortured Writers Department, where I attempt to convey how much gratitude I have for every single person that is responsible for this book. But also, like, make it funny. And try not to forget that anybody existed. (Hence the torture.)

First, to Jen Calonita, my Swiftie Sister and coconspirator on the Taylors. Love this story of us: first as publicist and author, then friends, and now working on this series together.

Look what you made me do, David Levithan! Thank you so much for thinking of me when you came up with this idea. Because you know there'd be some serious bad blood if you hadn't!

My amazing editor, Maya Marlette, who has the electric touch when it comes to my manuscripts. I can't wait to begin again!

Having a publisher who supports you and shows nothing but enthusiasm for a project is every author's end game. Because these books aren't done by just ME! To my Scholastic A-Team: Aleah Gornbein, Lizette Serrano, Maisha Johnson, Stephanie Yang, Brooke Shearouse, Seale Ballenger, Amanda Book, Rachel Feld, Mary Kate Garmire, Lara Kennedy, Madeline Newquist, Lori Lewis, AnnMarie Anderson, Jennifer Powell, Rachel Weinert, Kara Pauley, and Aurélie Goncalves.

You also know I love the London team: Julia Sanderson, Tina Mories, Kiran Khanom, and Alice Wain.

Liz Parkes, when I saw your illustrations, I screamed for whatever it's worth, "I LOVE THIS COVER AIN'T THAT THE BEST THING YOU'VE EVER HEARD!" Thank you!

I'll always have room in my getaway car for my agent, Kate Testerman.

Being the youngest kid means that in a way, I never grow up. Or maybe I'm just immature. Whatever. Thank you to my family: Mom, Dad, Eileen, Meg, and WJ. As well as my in-laws, Mark, James, Jill; and my nephews, Zach and Jacob—I hope this gives you some cool points.

I have loved writing these books and these characters. Plus, any excuse to listen to Taylor Swift on repeat and watch videos and call it "research." None of this would obviously be possible without the brilliance of the legendary Taylor Swift. There were teardrops on my keyboard analyzing your amazing lyrics and seeing the happiness you bring to so many people. I'm not kidding when I say, if you want to see me sob, pull up a video of any of the hat moments during "22." The love, the sheer *joy* you give so many of us is such a gift. It's something I rely on whenever people gotta be so mean.

The way I love every reader, bookseller, librarian, educator, and influencer who has given the Taylors and any of my books a chance. I couldn't do what I do without you.

ABOUT THE AUTHOR

Elizabeth Eulberg is the internationally bestselling author of dozens of books for young readers, including *The Lonely Hearts Club*, *Better Off Friends*, and *Take a Chance on Me*. But let's be real, you want to know her Swiftie credentials. She was gifted Debut ON CD, so she's a real one. Elizabeth first saw Taylor Swift perform in New Jersey (where Elizabeth used to live) in 2015 during the 1989 World Tour. Then, on August 19, 2024, she saw the Eras Tour at Wembley Stadium in London (where she now lives). Her surprise songs were "Long Live" x "Change" on guitar (SHE KNOWS!!) and "The Archer" x "You're On Your Own, Kid" on piano. She has still not fully recovered.

CAN'T GET ENOUGH OF THE TAYLORS? FLASH BACK TO SEE HOW IT ALL BEGAN!

A MIDDLE GRADE NOVEL BY JEN CALONITA

Taylor (aka Teffy to her family) is terrified to start middle school, that is until she makes friends with three other girls named Taylor and things start looking up! But then a surprise betrayal changes everything. How can their new friendship survive?

RELIVE *CRUEL SUMMER* WITH THIS CHAPTER TITLE PLAYLIST OF TAYLOR SWIFT SONGS!

. . . Ready For It?

End Game

I Did Something Bad

Out of the Woods

All Too Well

But Daddy I Love Him

Question . . . ?

We Are Never Ever Getting Back Together

Should've Said No

Better Than Revenge

I Can Fix Him (No Really I Can)

loml

The Lucky One

Wonderland

The Alchemy

right where you left me

the lakes

Superstar

I Can See You

Today Was A Fairytale

Is It Over Now?

Timeless

WHICH TAYLOR ARE YOU?

The Taylors are four best friends named after the greatest artist on the planet! After you've read about Teffy, Tay, TS, and Taylor, you'll want to decide: Which Taylor do you most resemble? Ready? One, two, three . . . let's go!

1) THE BELL RINGS ON THE LAST PERIOD OF THE DAY AND YOU GRAB YOUR BACKPACK. WHERE ARE YOU HEADED?

A. To a field of some kind. Nothing makes me happier than playing a sport as part of a team.

B. Why do I have to tell you where I'm headed? I like to take each day as it comes. I don't like being told what to do.

C. Lights, camera, smile! Show me where the crowd is, and I'll be sure to show up and put on a great show whether it's at cheer practice or dance, or maybe even gymnastics. The possibilities are endless!

D. Give me a quiet corner at a coffee shop any day. There you'll find me writing in my notebook. Maybe someday my scribbles will turn into a hit song.

2) YOUR FRIEND GROUP GETS INTO AN ARGUMENT. (HEY, IT HAPPENS!) HOW DO YOU HANDLE THE SITUATION?

A. We sit down and everyone gets to speak their truth. It's the best way to diffuse a situation.

B. I probably get mad at first and storm off, but inside, I'm miserable. I'll probably call everyone later to talk about what happened.

C. The best way to end a fight? Provide comic relief! I'll do anything to diffuse a difficult situation, even if it means standing on my head in the middle of a movie theater.

D. I hate fighting with my friends. It makes me feel ill. I'll do anything to make sure the fight ends quickly, even if it means dragging everyone together.

3) THE FUTURE IS FAR OFF, BUT IF YOU ASKED ME TODAY WHAT I SEE MYSELF BEING WHEN I GROW UP, MY ANSWER WOULD BE:

A. Hoisting a trophy over my head with my teammates.

B. Need someone to organize a fundraiser? Raise money for a worthy cause? Put together a team? I'm your person!

C. I need a job where my personality can be on full display. Is there an opening for late-night TV host?

D. Something creative for sure. I'd love to cowrite songs for Taylor Swift someday!

4) IT'S FRIDAY NIGHT: ARE YOU:

A. Going for a long run.

B. Organizing the most epic night.

C. Finding a microphone and spotlight!

D. Curled up with a good book.

5) YOUR SELF-CARE ROUTINE CONSISTS OF:

A. Who has time for products? I wash up and go.

B. I just borrow whatever my sister has and use it.

C. If you want to be noticed, you need to put in the time. Give me all the products to test and shoot videos with.

D. Keep it simple. A swipe of a good moisturizer and lip gloss and I'm good to go.

6) WHAT'S YOUR FAVORITE SUBJECT IN SCHOOL?

A. Phys Ed **C.** Speech

B. Debate **D.** English

7) IF YOU COULD ONLY USE ONE WORD TO DESCRIBE YOU, WHAT WOULD IT BE?

A. Competitive **C.** Exuberant

B. Loyal **D.** Shy

8) IF YOU COULD STAR IN A MOVIE, WHAT TYPE WOULD IT BE?

A. Action, for sure!

B. A courtroom drama where my love of speech could really shine.

C. A comedy and I'd be the star!

D. A sweet romance!

9) IF YOU LIVE ANYWHERE IN THE WORLD, WHERE WOULD IT BE?

A. Somewhere warm where I could be outside year-round.

B. Wherever my friends and family go, I'll be there, too.

C. Give me a city where there are lots of people to interact with. I love meeting new people!

D. Someplace where there is lots of live music that will serve as inspiration in my life.

10) WHAT TAYLOR SWING SONG FITS YOUR MOOD BEST?

A. ". . . Ready for it?" **B.** "Long Live" **C.** "Shake It Off" **D.** "Love Story"

ANSWER KEY:

Mostly A's: You're TS! You live for being outside and playing on a team. You're driven and focused. While you can sometimes be a bit too competitive, you're a team player forever and always.

Mostly B's: You're Taylor! If there's one thing you know . . . wait, you know a lot! You're so good, you can do it all: organize, prioritize, and strategize! You love to take the lead, but you're loyal and will never leave a friend behind.

Mostly C's: You're Tay! Are you excitable? Love the spotlight? Well then, it's you. Hi. You're like Tay! You're silly, energetic, and a people person. People love to have you around and you love nothing more than being surrounded by friends and family.

Mostly D's: You're Teffy! You love cozying up in a comfy cardigan with a swoony book or writing in your journal. While you may shy away from the spotlight, you're a creative spirit with a big heart . . . and some wild dreams.

DON'T MISS ANOTHER LOVE STORY FROM ELIZABETH EULBERG!

Evie is heartbroken and betrayed when a video of her confronting her cheating ex-boyfriend goes viral, but as she explores London for the summer she finds herself repeatedly running into a charming and beautiful British busker named Aiden. Could he be worth taking a chance on?